MURDER BY MUDPACK

A HONEY DRIVER MYSTERY

Murder by Mudpack

A Honey Driver Mystery

Jean G Goodhind

Murder by Mudpack

A Honey Driver Mystery

Published by Accent Press Ltd – 2014

ISBN 9781909520318

Printed and bound in the UK

Cover design by Joelle Brindley

Chapter One

Honey Driver eyed Steve Doherty suspiciously. 'I've got bad vibes about this.'

'Trust me. I'm a police officer. Just lay back and think of England. You'll probably enjoy it.'

'I'm not sure about somebody else doing things to my body – even if they are pleasurable.'

'You might find you could get used to it.'

'I don't like getting dirty – well, not that dirty anyway.'

Steve Doherty was on the floor, crunching his abdominals like nobody's business. He paused in mid-crunch, grinned, and winked at her. 'That's not been my experience.'

She pretended she hadn't heard and continued to study the brochure he'd given her for the health and beauty spa he wanted her to stay at that specialised in mud baths. She was to nose around while getting the full treatment from the very upmarket establishment. She wasn't into a strict health and beauty routine, mostly because she didn't have time. He kept stressing that this was in the line of duty.

'So you're one hundred per cent sure this wasn't an accident.'

Steve grunted an answer between crunches. 'It's as possible to drown in mud as it is in water. Her face was plastered in mud then a piece of polythene was placed on top of that with holes to breathe through.'

'To keep the heat in,' Honey explained.

'Is that right?' Steve looked stoical. He was at that age when the things women did to keep young and beautiful – and other things – failed to surprise him.

Honey assured him that it was right.

He nodded. 'Right. So, as I was saying, somebody adjusted the polythene face mask so that her nose and mouth were covered and then she was pushed and held under in the bath of mud.'

'Some way to die,' remarked Honey.

Doherty frowned. 'What is it with women and mud?'

'Anything that gives us a chance of maintaining our youth. Women continually strive for perfection. Men wouldn't understand. They're content with what they've got.'

'Gee. Thanks!'

'No offence.'

'None taken.'

'So what's happening on the suspect front?'

'Not a lot, though someone did see a scruffy character hanging around, but I don't really buy that. Why would a down-and-out go sneaking around a beauty clinic?'

There were other alternatives of course. Honey voiced one of them. 'She could have fallen asleep and slipped under.'

'Wouldn't you notice if you were chewing on mud? Nobody, but nobody could mistake it for chocolate pudding.'

Honey grunted back at him. The brochure she was thumbing through was glossy. The Beauty Spot (Health and Beauty Clinic) promised natural therapies to enhance just about every body part. The building it was housed in was beautiful too. But then, she remonstrated, what woman in need of a makeover was going to book into a shambles?

'Looks as though the murder victim outstayed her welcome,' Honey murmured.

Lady Carlotta Macrottie, a woman who'd made a career out of staying beautiful and spending her husband's money – not necessarily in that order – had been found drowned in a bath of tepid mud at the luxury health spa. The mud used for the face pack and full body immersion was advertised as being full of sodium, iron compounds, and various other minerals that were supposedly good for the skin.

The blurb was outrageous.

She read it aloud. 'You too could be drop-dead gorgeous. Our mud is special; sourced from volcanic deposits from Pacific islands where locals have long claimed the mud to have youth-giving properties.'

Steve was lying flat on the floor, all crunched out. 'It didn't do Lady Macrottie any good.'

After noting that Steve's abs were little different than they were before – and just as attractive – Honey turned thoughtful. 'Wasn't there another case of somebody dying as a result of treatment at the clinic?'

Steve shrugged. 'Not that I know of.'

Honey wasn't so sure. Closing one eye was a wonderful aid to concentration for some obscure reason that she couldn't quite account for. A front-page headline flashed into her mind. Some time ago she'd seen something in the *Bath Chronicle* and on local television about a woman who'd broken out in skin lesions after some kind of beauty treatment. She wasn't sure exactly what kind; it could have been a mud treatment or it could have been more than that. She couldn't remember. Needless to say, having turned out plug ugly instead of drop dead beautiful, said recipient of treatment was suing The Beauty Spot for a small fortune.

Steve looked only vaguely interested when she told him.

'Did she win the case?'

Honey shook her head. 'No. She died. A fire broke out in the bread shop below the flat she lived in. Charred remains. No body. No real evidence against the beauty clinic that the bad publicity had sent them running rampant with a firelighter. All

3

they did was bring her out in lesions. Seems that drop dead gorgeous could mean just that.'

'So?'

There was a hell of a lot of meaning in that solitary word and the single lifted eyebrow. She knew what he wanted her to do. Wriggling out of it was a definite option before he said the magic words that weakened her.

'A period of excessive pampering away from it all. No guests bending your ear about noisy bed springs. No chef threatening to slice the sous chef in two. And then there's your mother ...' The proposition was looking more and more attractive by the minute. Honey allowed herself to be swayed.

'We-e-e-ll ...' She made the effort to sound less than convinced.

'All expenses paid,' he added, recognizing one of her weak moments when he saw it. 'Courtesy of the city council and the tourist board. I think Casper had a go at them both. Beautiful city, beautiful body – you know what I mean?'

Honey's eyebrows shot skyward. Casper St John Gervais was chairman of the Bath Hotels Association and a personal friend. He was obsessed in protecting 'God's Little Acre' from serious crime, which was why he'd decided that the Association had to have a Crime Liaison Officer. Honey was it. Which was how come she'd got involved with Steve Doherty. There'd been a couple of dangerous moments in her part-time career. Doherty had asked her to do a number of interesting things, some of which had had nothing to do with solving crime. However, she'd never been asked to go undercover before.

'This place is out of town,' she remarked after studying the address.

'Not really. It's just up the road from Castle Combe and forty minutes tops into town. You'll be able to sneak out now and again. Grab the odd chocolate bar at the village shop.'

4

Up until this point she'd thought the plan was to attend this place perhaps once or twice a week. It turned out otherwise.

'You'd have to stay for a four-day break at least.'

'Steve, this may have escaped your notice, but the Green River Hotel does not run itself.'

'It's well staffed. Stop thinking things will grind to a halt just because you're not there. Delegate, that's the secret – so I've heard.'

He eyed her as though he really knew what it was all about. She sensed someone had been informing the uninformed.

'So you've heard!' She nodded her head slowly while fixing him with a hard stare. To add gravitas she posed one hand on her ample hip.

'It's not a one man and his dog outfit,' Doherty went on. 'You're the boss. You give the orders. You really should remember that.'

He turned over and did press-ups.

For a moment Honey got distracted. His back and bum muscles were equally as attractive as those at the front.

'According to Smudger the place virtually runs itself. It doesn't really need you. Besides, Lindsey will be there.'

He'd hardly puffed between press-ups.

'Is that so?'

The temptation was too inviting. Placing one foot on the small of his back flattened him. A big 'oomph!' of breath escaped.

'So you've been having words with my chef, have you? Well let me put you straight, Steve Doherty, my chef does not run things. He doesn't get to face the guests or my bank manager. Just because he's in control of the kitchen doesn't mean that the rest of the place runs itself.'

'Lindsey! Remember? I distinctly mentioned Lindsey.'

Doherty was stating an absolute truth. Lindsey Driver could run anything. She had a knack for taking charge, a fluent mind,

5

and more chutzpah than you could shake a stick at.

She decided Doherty needed needling and there was no better way to needle him than mention of her mother, Gloria Cross – four times married and on the lookout for number five.

'My mother frequents beauty parlours more than I do. She might be better at being your eyes and ears.'

Was it her imagination, or did Steve Doherty shiver?

'Your mother is not the Hotels Association's Crime Liaison Officer. Besides, I might think of committing murder myself if your mother gets involved.'

'Only joking.'

Good strategy, Honey decided, well aware that her mother, she of the immaculate fingernails, superbly made-up face, and designer fashion wardrobe, turned her lover into a nervous wreck. Thinking about it, he wasn't the only one. Her mother made her nervous too.

Once she'd removed her foot, Doherty turned over, proceeding to work his front.

Drawn by the sight of his naked abs, she went down on all fours on the floor beside him and peered into his face. Her hair was loose so it fell either side of both their faces as she went in closer.

'What do I get if I agree to do this?'

The nervous tic beneath his right eye, brought on by mention of her mother, shuddered to a halt as he smiled.

'Before or after the case is solved?'

'Both.'

He grinned. 'I have a few bonus moves in mind. A little on account beforehand. A little more after.'

She didn't need to ask what he would give her. One finger was already exploring her cleavage and his pants were getting too tight for his body.

6

Chapter Two

Serena Sarabande had a porcelain-white complexion and chilly blue eyes. Her cheekbones were high and her pale blonde eyebrows were plucked to arched perfection. She was tall with angular shoulders, long limbs, and the presence of a supermodel. Her slicked-back hair was short and blonde; not a single strand was allowed to flutter around her bone-hard features.

The principal of The Beauty Spot wore a white doctor's coat and looked every inch the seasoned professional in her field. Steve Doherty guessed that the professional look was in order to put her clients at ease; they were in safe hands. OK, there was a hint of glam medical TV soap about her, but it worked for a lot of people and was what they expected. He felt inclined to ask her if she'd ever played doctors and nurses as a child, but this was hardly the time and place. Besides, if Honey should find out she would cut off his credentials – or put them on the restricted use register.

Yep, Serena Sarabande cut quite an imposing image. Someone who looked like they could handle a scalpel was bound to be a wow with a pair of eyebrow tweezers and a pot of warm wax – weren't they?

'You've already questioned me once,' she said, her eyes unblinking above a classical nose, sculpted lips, and a blemish-free complexion.

'That's right. I did.' He rubbed at his brow, furrowing it

Columbo style; that goofy detective from the seventies – or was it eighties? He found himself warming to the part, even down to flicking at his thumb as though he were holding a smouldering cigar.

'But there are a few things that I haven't quite got a handle on. Sorry to bother you, but do you mind going over one or two things again?'

She sat down behind a black glass desk set in a chrome frame. 'I suppose not. What can I do for you?'

Not much, he decided, not on the sexual front anyway. Although worth the once over, a few minutes with her and he wasn't so keen. Too coldly professional for his taste.

He pulled up a chair though she hadn't invited him to sit down. When he did he realized she was still sitting higher than him; still looking down her nostrils. This babe liked her clients to be in no doubt who was in charge.

'I'm terribly sorry to trouble you, Ms Sarabande,' he said, feigning humility – just like Peter Falk used to do. 'There's just a few more points I'd like clarified – if you don't mind.'

Serena's features remained on deep freeze though one eyebrow rose quizzically.

Doherty noticed. 'Sorry. That was my Columbo. You know? The one-eyed guy from that American cop show.'

'No.'

Her voice was cutting and as ice-cold as her looks. Serena Sarabande expected professional people to be as coldly clinical as she was. Christ, he thought. I'd go mad if I didn't goof around now and again – a little innuendo here, a little leg pulling there – mostly with Honey, he reminded himself. She could take it.

Feeling like a first-class idiot, Doherty cleared his throat. 'OK. So let's go over a few things.' He got out his notebook and pen, flipping the cover and pages over beyond doodles and scribbled phone numbers to a clean, open page.

He asked a few general things he'd asked before. Number one, who had found the drowned body of Lady Macrottie, at what time, and how long had her ladyship been left submerged in mud before anyone checked on her.

He recalled that an assistant by the name of Magda Church had been attending to her. Each client had her own personal attendant catering to her every need. The attendant had left her immersed and was supposed to check on her every fifteen to twenty minutes. As far as he could ascertain Magda Church had done exactly as she was supposed to do.

'So, this Magda Church who found the body. Had she been working for you for long?'

'Two years and three months.'

He made a note to question Ms Church again. 'That's very accurate.'

'I am always very accurate. I always get my facts straight.'

'That's good for me.'

'I'm glad you think so.'

Verbally it was like exchanging gunfire with a seasoned sniper. Shoot at Serena Sarabande and she shot straight back; definitely the sort who'd want the last word.

'A place like this must take some running,' he said, switching to Mr User-Friendly Policeman mode. 'I suppose you have to be pretty well qualified too. Would that be right?'

'Yes.'

'So tell me,' he said, casually crossing one leg over the other. 'Where do you learn stuff like this?'

'Stuff?'

Her eyes glittered and her plush pink lips twisted in disdain. Stuff had not been the right word. What had he been thinking of?

Taking in a deep breath sent her bosoms thrusting against the buttoned-up white coat.

Doherty did his best to make amends. 'All these different

9

beauty treatments. They seem to come from all over the world. How do you get to qualify in them all? It must take some study. Some time too.'

He didn't really believe that; after all, how difficult must it be to plaster mud over a woman's face then immerse her in mud? The bath had a lid. He'd been shown it; just enough room for the shoulders to pop up. Never mind. He'd ruffled her feathers. A little compromise didn't come amiss.

Some element of his question must have flattered. She loosened up and told him that she'd learned her craft in Venezuela.

'Seems a long way.'

'And also in Poland,' she added. 'I started in Poland. I have also worked in Italy and Spain before I went to Venezuela.'

'You sound as though you favour Venezuela.'

'It is very vibrant,' she responded, in a voice that was about as far from vibrant as a frost-bitten bottom.

Overall Serena Sarabande was an iceberg in human form; cold and best avoided if you didn't want to get sunk before you got anywhere.

After he'd gone, Serena Sarabande phoned Dr Roger Dexter, the resident consultant.

'The police have been again.'

'And you told them nothing, of course.'

'Of course not.' Her breath caught in her throat. 'Of course not,' she said again, her voice far softer, far more affectionate than the one she'd used for Doherty.

Chapter Three

Steve had not moved in with Honey. She had her place and he had his. Every so often they stayed together, depending on shift patterns and whether the dishwasher at the Green River Hotel hadn't broken down. If it had and Clint (né Rodney) Eastwood wasn't available, then she was it; an evening spent wearing a pair of pink rubber gloves – or yellow – scrubbing pots and pans. Waitress shifts also intervened on occasion. On Doherty's part so did police work, though Steve had been lucky of late.

They were lying in his bed in his flat on Camden Crescent. They were on their second bottle of wine when he told her about his interview with Serena Sarabande.

'Cold fish,' he said.

Honey looked up at him from the crook of his arm.

'I bet you're just saying that. I bet she's absolutely gorgeous. People who work in those places usually are.'

'Depends what you mean by gorgeous. I mean, an iceberg is gorgeous. A snow-topped mountain peak is gorgeous. So's Baked Alaska …'

'Hold it right there!' Honey's hand slapped on his chest. 'Every word you've used to describe her is pretty cold, so I get the picture. She's gorgeous but not cute.'

Steve sighed. 'I think you'll be safe enough.'

'Why shouldn't I be? I'm only going there for treatment, not to ask questions.'

'But you will snoop? You won't just lie around and enjoy it?'

Honey gave him a withering look through narrowed eyes. 'Are you having me on?'

'What do you mean?'

'Are you expecting me to wander around covered in mud and surviving on a diet of carrot juice and vitamins in the faint hope of finding something useful without adequate victuals?'

'I didn't say they'd only feed you carrot juice.'

'Will my bag get searched on the way in?'

He eyed her with suspicious misgivings.

'Are you telling me that you're going to smuggle in forbidden supplies?'

'Smoked salmon and feta cheese would be good, followed by a whole box of Battenberg fancies from that cut-price German supermarket chain.'

'I know the way to your heart, Hannah Driver.'

'Marzipan R Us – with chocolate edging. Those Battenberg fancies are orgasmic!'

'Really? More so than me?'

He looked crestfallen when she took her time thinking about it.

'It's a close run thing,' she finally said.

'You'll be fine. It's only for a short time. You won't starve.'

She sighed. 'The things I do for love.'

'Sweetie! How can I ever replay you?'

'Don't you mean repay?'

'No. Replay. Let's play with each other again.'

Honey stroked his bristly chin. 'There you are. I need to keep up my energy levels. You wouldn't want me to lose my concentration through lack of suitable sustenance, would you? You'd be terribly disappointed.'

'Very likely,' he murmured, his head between her breasts.

Honey sighed, closed her eyes, and enjoyed. 'Nothing nasty

12

can happen in such a short time. And they won't kill me for supplementing their meagre rations now, will they?'

'Only if you don't share and share alike with the other inmates – sorry – clients.' He looked up at her from between her breasts. His look had turned serious. 'Be careful and keep your eyes open.'

'I will.'

'So,' he said, resuming where he'd left off. 'When are you telling your mother and daughter that we're sleeping together?'

'Lindsey isn't stupid.'

'And your mother?'

'I'm building up to it.'

Chapter Four

'I think the rest will do me good,' Honey declared as she sifted through her top drawer, trying to decide what sort of underwear might be appropriate. 'Besides, it's only for a few days. Do you think you can manage?'

Honey and her daughter, Lindsey, shared the converted coach house at the end of the garden. The front of the coach house faced the back of the hotel – an easy distance between home and work.

Lindsey appeared to be searching out her badminton racquet. She was quite a girl for exercise and fitness; Honey was at a loss to guess where she'd got *that* from.

'I'll come fetch you if anything comes unstuck – like Gran poking her nose into the kitchen,' said Lindsey.

Honey spun round. 'Whatever you do, you are not – NOT – to let my mother into the kitchen. Not under any circumstances. Is that clear?'

Lindsey grinned. 'Only joking.'

Gloria Cross had difficulty accepting that chefs can be dangerous if you stray into their territory. Honey had warned her that chefs had sharp knives and meat mallets. It wasn't wise to upset them.

The fact that only the head chef oversaw the hotel kitchen took some time sinking in. On one or two occasions she'd strayed in there, poking at a pudding, stirring a simmering sauce, oblivious to the fact that Smudger the chef had picked up his meat cleaver and was sharpening it with a Freddy Krueger craziness in his eyes.

'There,' said Honey as she patted a pair of towelling mules into the top of her bag. 'I think that should do it.

'What?' she said in response to her daughter's questioning expression. 'Have I forgotten something?'

Lindsey narrowed her eyes. 'Yes. You've forgotten that you and healthy living don't mix.'

'I'm going for the beauty treatments.'

'When was the last time you bought a facial mask or waxed your legs?'

'Quite recently.'

'You're lying.'

She hid her expression, looking busy by stuffing a pair of antique stays into her bag.

'My legs are fine. As smooth as a baby's bum.'

'You're wearing jeans.'

'I like wearing jeans.'

'And you won't need these.'

Lindsey took out the pair of antique stays. They were stiff with whalebone, starched linen, and lace.

On reflection it wouldn't have hurt to wax her legs. OK, she could get it done at The Beauty Spot, but shouldn't she have made the effort? With hindsight perhaps it was a good idea to give the impression that she kept a strict beauty treatment regime. The hotel trade meant long hours spent pampering guests, not herself. Staff needed pampering too. Staff were by nature demanding. When it came to pampering she was bottom of the list. When it came to hours to spare for any kind of rest and relaxation, sharing a bath tub with Steve Doherty won every time. The mudpack and the deep skin cleansing could go to hell in a bucket!

'It's just a little time to myself.'

She'd agreed with Doherty not to divulge where she was

going. The bush drums of Bath could blow her cover. Secrecy was paramount.

Lindsey's expression was unchanged. 'You're up to something.'

'Just because I want some time to myself?'

'It's something to do with Steve Doherty. I can smell it.'

'No. That's my deodorant. See you in a few days,' she said, grabbing the bag and bowling out of the coach house on comfortably attired feet. Trainers today. It added to the aura of a seeker after health and fitness.

On the other hand she felt like James Bond – without the licence to kill, of course.

Lindsey was curious but despite her youth she was up for the responsibility of running the Green River Hotel. According to her mother, Lindsey had been born efficient. Administration, paperwork, accounts – she took the lot in her stride. She could even cope with difficult guests.

She had more difficulty coping with guests who considered England was some kind of Disney set-up – a place where everything was green, fairies still lived at the bottom of the garden, and nicely spoken people were as honest as the day was long.

Mr and Mrs Okinara had been stuffed. That was the first thing to strike Lindsey as they proudly showed her an item they'd bought at an antiques market.

'It is very interesting, don't you think?'

Mr Okinara shone with enthusiasm as he showed her the contents of a long wooden box. Inside was a contraption of rubber hose and a few other sundry gadgets that she had no trouble in recognizing. Mr Okinara had bought himself a Victorian enema kit.

'Yes. Very interesting,' she responded, unsure what else to say. Did Mr Okinara know what it was, or had some heavyweight salesman told him it was for watering his bonsai or something?

This was one of those times when she would have to tread carefully, she decided. On occasions like this it was wise not to confirm the identity of the object.

'We collect such objects as well as more decorative items which we sell on to our corporate clients. Corporate clients pay very well for unusual things,' said Mrs Okinara, a smartly dressed little woman with a blue-black bob and impeccable taste in clothes.

To Lindsey's ears it sounded as though they knew what they were about, but she had no chance to talk further. One half of the double reception doors swung open. Accompanied by the smell of Chanel perfume and the fluttering of a long shot-silk coat in a fetching shade of fuchsia, her grandmother sailed into Reception.

'I was just passing,' she said, nodding at the two Japanese people who were closing their wooden box before going to lunch.

'Can you put it behind your desk for now?' asked Mrs Okinara. 'It will save us going up to our room.'

Lindsey said that she would. Mr and Mrs Okinara thanked her and said they would see her after lunch.

'What is it?' asked Gloria Cross, wrinkling her well powdered nose at the grubby, ancient casing.

'Something you don't want to know about. Now, Gloria, what can I do for you?'

Her grandmother swelled with satisfaction. She loved it when her granddaughter talked to her as an equal – calling her by her given name. She hated being reminded that she was a grandmother. It didn't suit her image of herself.

'Is your mother here?'

'No,' Lindsey said slowly and frowned. 'She's gone away for a few days to a health and beauty spa.'

Gloria raised her eyebrows. '*Your* mother – *my* daughter – has gone to a health and beauty spa?' The eyebrows fell back into a frown. 'I don't believe it. What's she up to?'

Lindsey chewed the inside of her mouth. Like her grandmother she had the gut feeling that something was going on that her mother didn't want her to know about.

'I don't know, but I do think she's up to something. She wouldn't even tell me which health spa she was going to.'

Gloria's eyebrows rose higher. 'Which makes you think what?'

Lindsey shrugged. 'She's up to something that she doesn't want us to know about. Perhaps it's very personal – you know – something to do with a man.'

'A man? She doesn't know any men,' her grandmother exclaimed.

'How about Doherty?'

Her grandmother's jaw dropped. 'But he's a policeman. What in this whole starry universe does he have to offer her?'

'They hang around a lot together.'

Gloria didn't believe in frowning or narrowing her eyes too much. To her mind it was the main cause of wrinkles.

'Do you think she's considering getting married?'

Lindsey prided herself on her patience, but her grandmother really was the limit at times. She slammed both hands on the highly polished reception desk, palms down. 'Of course not. She'd tell us if she was.'

Gloria looked at her in disbelief. 'I hope there's nothing going on there. I hope that it's purely a professional arrangement.'

'No it isn't. They've been sleeping together for a while – mostly at Doherty's, I think. But they did sleep in the coach house when I had that week in Malaga the week before last. And when I had those days at Wimbledon. Then she's been having the odd night away. Best of luck to her I say.' She said the last words under her breath.

'She told me she was staying with Mary – and sometimes with Dee. It avoids drinking and driving, though Mary Jane did offer to pick her up after a night out.'

'I don't think having Mary Jane pick her up was an acceptable option – though on second thoughts it would sober her up pretty damned quick.'

Mary Jane was their resident professor of the paranormal who had landed some time earlier from California and had made the Green River her home. She'd stated she was destined to live there, seeing as some long-dead relative haunted the room she lived in.

Lindsey went on putting forward her opinion.

'I reckon that when he's not been sleeping here, she's been sleeping at his place.'

'But they're not married!'

Her grandmother – not coy when it came to interesting liaisons and a well-primed sex life – sounded appalled.

'I know. But do you think they're going to be?'

Gloria tapped the reception counter with red-painted fingernails. Diamonds flashed from her fingers.

'I'm going to find out where she is and ask her.'

'She won't be pleased.'

'I don't care. I'm her mother. I've got a right to know what's going on.'

Now it was Lindsey who raised an eyebrow. Her mother was on the wrong side of forty and old enough to make up her own mind. But Gloria Cross was a doting mother. She couldn't help but interfere.

Lindsey thought on her feet. Sidetrack her, otherwise her grandmother would be running on the same rails at Christmas.

'When's Enid getting married?'

It was definitely the right thing to say. Her grandmother beamed.

'Three weeks' time. I'm so looking forward to it,' she said, hands clasped, eyes shining. 'It's so romantic. Cuthbert swept her off her feet, you know. He cuts such a dash. Of course, being a celebrity helps with his attraction.'

'A celebrity? I didn't know he was on television.'

'He's not. Not all celebrities are on television. He's a columnist for *Mature Times*. We all read it and we all had a crush on him at some stage.'

Hope springs eternal, thought Lindsey. Her grandmother sounded like a seventeen-year-old groupie.

The ringing of the phone and the appearance of Mary Jane cut the conversation dead. Gloria Cross was off to take tea and natter with Mary Jane.

Relieved and still feeling that she was in charge, Lindsey picked up the phone.

'Hello? Is that you, Lindsey? It's me,' hissed the voice on the other end.

Despite it being just above a whisper, Lindsey recognized Clint's voice. Their casual washer-up, paid in cash, was relatively reliable but had a rather shadowy lifestyle.

'It's me.'

'Look, Lindz. Sorry, mate, but I'm in a spot of bother. I won't be able to make it tonight.'

'Sore throat?'

'What?'

She was referring to the hissing tone. She could barely hear him.

'Do you have a sore throat?'

'No. No. Wish I did. I've got a problem. A fucking big problem.'

'Oh really. How big?'

'Somebody's out to kill me.'

'That's pretty big.'

'Shit.'

The connection was cut.

'Well,' she said, emphatically replacing the receiver. 'Here endeth the first day – and aren't I doing well!'

Chapter Five

The Beauty Spot Health and Beauty Clinic was housed in an elegant pile built by a sugar merchant back in the eighteenth century. At one time it had been surrounded by green grass and approached through an avenue of elm trees. Thanks to Dutch elm disease back in the seventies there were no longer any elms. The building was now approached through an avenue of houses. Like the slavery the owner's wealth had been built on, the park surrounding the house was no more. The grassland had been divided up into convenient plots on which 'executive-style' four-bedroom homes had been built. Kids' scooters and tricycles now skidded where red and fallow deer had once grazed, while Land Cruisers and BMWs had replaced a coach and four. Phases one and two of the development were completed and occupied. Phase three was still being constructed.

Like a dowager duchess, the grand old house remained, its presence dominating and aloof from the square boxes with their plastic windows and manicured lawns. The Old Manor House had survived over two centuries and looked good for its age. The soft Bath stone glowed like clotted cream, the windows were big and brave and neat little mulberry trees sat in square green pots on either side of the door. In short it suited its present purpose. Like the clientele it catered for, the old house was refurbished anew every now and again, the ravages of time treated to an in-depth makeover.

Gathering up her trusty bag in which she'd secreted a few necessities required to sustain her energy levels – her favourite cakes, half a pound of Cheddar cheese, and sundry nibbles – Honey headed for the door.

'Here goes,' she muttered, patting the spot in her bag where the smuggled goodies lay hidden, wrapped tightly in two new pairs of Marks and Spencer plus-size pants.

She couldn't quite get to grips with why she was so nervous; yes, she was here to snoop a little. As Steve had said to her, 'Women talking facials and fat busting can go more places here than my enquiries are ever likely to.'

The fat-busting quip had gained him a quick slap, but basically she'd known what he was getting at. Woman to woman gossip could go further than coppers sticking their noses in.

Soft music was playing in a reception area that smelled of the sea, or at least the manufactured version of what the sea *could* smell like, irrespective of sewage outlets or the detritus of ice cream cornets and cardboard packaging. There were soft colours on the walls and floors. The carpet was thick. Never mind that the old house might have boasted shiny marble floors in its sparkling past, the carpet was there to aid the air of peace and tranquillity.

The receptionist looked as though she should have been named Miss Perfect. Her name badge said otherwise. Karen Pinker.

The smile was wide and welcoming.

'Mrs Driver? My name is Karen. Welcome to The Beauty Spot Health and Beauty Clinic.'

Honey immediately gave Karen Pinker the name of Karen Perfect. Women who didn't regard themselves as ugly or a bit shabby around the edges would certainly do so after being faced on arrival with such perfection. Honey had an inkling this was done for a purpose. Designer psychiatry – be what you

24

see before you – at a given price of course. If you didn't feel a need for improvement before arrival, you certainly did after meeting Karen.

'Thank you.' It was hard to smile and be courteous to someone who made you feel like a toad, but Honey was pretty certain she'd made a good job of it.

Karen's pearly whites flashed like diamonds at the bottom of a fifty-foot well. 'If you'd like to sign in, then I'll take you to your room. Lovely!'

The exclamation was delivered with an air of breathless wonder. The flawless complexion of the girl in the white coat shone with the confidence of youth. Not a wrinkle creased the creamy soft skin. Her lips were like two little velvet cushions pouting from her face. They looked so soft, so beautifully formed. Honey briefly wondered if designer lips were readily available; if they were then this chick had them.

Honey found herself sucking her lips in. Despite having adorned them with a nice apricot shade that morning, compared to the luscious lips on this babe they were as becoming as a couple of stale cream crackers.

Still, that's what you're here for, she reminded herself. You'll be a new woman when you leave.

Karen handed her a folder which she insisted held everything Honey needed to know. A few taps of the keyboard and she was signed in.

'Your itinerary and general information on your stay here, but do ask if you need clarification. We are here to assist you become the woman you wish to be. This way please,' said a smiling Karen.

Karen Pinker from the rear was as perfect as Karen Pinker from the front. A tight bum and slim hips filled out the white coat of the girl in front of her. Karen looked pristine as well as pretty, all lightness and brightness; stark contrast to Honey's dark jeans and black sweater, – uniform for someone who knows they're overweight but does their best to hide the fact – which basically is treating the symptoms not the cause, she said to herself. She knew this off by heart because her mother had told her so. Her mother was always telling her so.

The room allotted as hers oozed the same ambience and sense of calm as the rest of the place. The bed looked comfortable, the colours were cool, and the north-facing window sparkled with pure white light. Artists favoured pure white *northern* light. An artist had told her that once when she was maybe nineteen or twenty. He'd been trying to get her to strip off so he could paint her in the nude. Sensing her hesitation he'd breezily begun gathering easel and charcoal, at the same time expounding on the benefits of clear northern light on her youthfully firm flesh. 'It'll make it look like satin,' he'd said. 'I can strip off too if that puts you at ease.'

Was she kidding?

Judging from her beaming smile, no, she was not. This was surreal. No. Worse. Sincere. The girl really meant it.

In retrospect the artist being in the nude would have had some definite advantages. His clothes perpetually smelled of linseed oil and turpentine; pretty unappealing stuff on the how-to-smell-seductive front. So she'd never given in to his sexual overtures. His true intentions had been obvious from the tightness of his trousers, but it was no good. She couldn't fancy the man and swiftly bid him adieu.

The last sight she had of him was standing with his jeans undone and primed for fallout. Because his hands were on his zip, he was reduced to holding two paint brushes in his mouth.

She'd slammed the door, swearing to God that she'd never get even remotely involved with someone artistic ever again. The thing about the northern light had stayed with her though.

'Here's the closet.'

Karen swung open the door of a slim closet neatly set into an alcove. It was very narrow, hardly enough to take the few items and the bag Honey had brought with her.

'And here's your robe and slippers. Our mantra is that by supplying simple but luxurious items for you to lounge in, everything of the outside world will be left outside the door. We espouse that inner calm is the natural basis of external calm and therefore beauty.'

Honey didn't argue, but watched intrigued.

A terry towelling robe, as neatly presented as everything else in the spa, hung on a beechwood hanger. No grotty plastic or wire hanger salvaged from a dry-cleaning article here!

Karen took the robe and slippers out of the closet. The slippers were placed on the floor in front of a chair. With dextrous ease she arranged the robe on the bed, one arm of it stretched out and the other neatly tucked into the belt. It looked almost human – as though it were about to run away or whip open in an act of devilish ecstasy, exposing whatever lay within.

'You're scheduled for the mud therapy at three. It should take about fifty minutes. Tomorrow morning you're scheduled for your first treatment. First a seaweed cocoon wrap followed by immersion in an anti-aging Hawaiian pumice bath and collagen-infused mudpack.'

'I am?'

Honey stalled her imagination with regard to the robe.

Karen smiled her sugar-sweet smile, holding her head pertly and prettily to one side like an inquisitive pigeon.

'We always make an effort to match our clients to the most suitable treatments. That's why our inquiry form asks for so much personal information. Of course, if anything does not suit your requirements, we can always discuss suitable alternatives. But that really should not be necessary. We pride ourselves on being very accurate and I'm sure you will agree that we've chosen wisely. Certain criteria match certain clients.'

All the time she was speaking, Karen Pinker maintained her

sugar-sweet smile but still pouted, the Botox keeping things in shape, Honey supposed.

'Oh really,' said Honey. 'So how do you do that?'

'Mostly it depends on your age. Some treatments are more suited to younger complexions. The seaweed cocoon, the collagen-infused mudpack, and the Hawaiian volcanic pumice bath are particularly beneficial to the older woman.'

She sounded as though she'd learned the mantra off by heart by the same method – and with as much enthusiasm – as Honey had once learned her two times table. Once learned, never forgotten.

Honey studied the programme she'd been given. Yep. There was no mistake. She was down for everything Karen had told her. They'd taken note of the year of her birth – round about the time juke boxes still had places in public bars.

'Now if you'd like to take off your clothes and put on your robe.'

She was instantly reminded of turpentine and an artist's list of excuses to get in her pants. Not that Karen had any ulterior motive of course. It was just a bit unnerving, what with the white northern light and now getting stripped off.

The last thing she wanted was for this so-perfect young woman to see her own less-than-perfect bits. A sense of panic broke in.

'Can you just give me a minute?'

Karen smiled sweetly. 'It's no bother. I'll help you. There's no need to be embarrassed.'

'Everything?' *The lumpy bits! The fat pants! She'd see it all!*

Little Miss Perfect carried on, oblivious to the fallout of a long-ago liaison – or rather near-miss liaison.

She was reciting again. 'You'll find that everything you need is provided for you. From personal hygiene items to paper underwear and cleansing cream. No make-up, of course – after all, you're here to be cleansed and beautified.'

Honey opened her mouth to protest, but really, was there anything to be worried about? Everything was provided. Karen the beautiful had said so.

Obediently, in a manner she hadn't assumed since she was seven years old and had been caught wearing her mother's pure silk underwear as a pair of pirate trousers, she meekly disrobed.

'No need,' said Karen, as Honey reached for the hanger on which the towelling robe had been hanging – the only hanger in the closet? How odd was that?

'I'll put everything in here,' she said, neatly folding and putting things into Honey's bag. 'I'll put it in storage until you need it.'

Disaster! Karen was already unzipping Honey's bag in which she had everything she needed – including food.

'What about my purse? My phone?'

She yelped those words with as much fervour as the radio operator on the *Titanic* had tapped out an SOS on seeing an iceberg.

Honey looked on with silent alarm as Karen pushed everything into the bag.

'You won't need any of this,' she said. 'It's a rule here. We are quite stringent in our rule-making as opposed to lesser establishments, but we do guarantee to do wonders for tired bodies and faces. As I've already explained to you, the aim is to leave the world and your belongings outside. In effect we require that you put yourself entirely in our hands and come to us, let's say, as naked as a newborn babe.'

The naked bit hit her bad. The smell of turpentine resurrected itself in her memory. But there were worse things. On the one hand she wanted to say that her face and body weren't that tired-looking and Doherty seemed quite taken with them. Her social life was good and she could get by without looking like an escapee from a heavily airbrushed makeover picture, thank you very much. On the other hand she was here professionally. Snooping, not sniping, was the job in hand, so she held her tongue.

Did she really want to jeopardize everything for a box of Thorntons chocolates, two baguettes with cheese and chutney, and two packets of salt and vinegar Hula Hoops? All that besides the half a pound of Cheddar, et cetera …

The truth was difficult to ignore, but she had to be strong.

Mouth-watering desperately, she watched as her hidden feasts were taken out of her sight. She had no choice but to bow to the inevitable.

'You won't be sorry,' Karen said breezily.

'No,' said Honey in a small voice. The girl didn't even know she was doling out torture.

It's only for three days, she told herself after Karen had left her to meditate, calm her inner being, and study this evening's menu.

Velouté of plaice with simply cooked vegetables and herbal tea. Her stomach rumbled in rebellion.

She closed her eyes and tried not to think of food. Despite everything visions of Aberdeen Angus fillet covered in Diane sauce and washed down with a glass or two of Cabernet Sauvignon persisted. Her stomach groaned. The evening meal seemed like aeons away. Her stomach was desperate, her mouth was dry. She had to chew something. Her desperately searching fingers grabbed something softly attractive; her brain not really questioning what it was as long as it was something.

She began to chew. Whatever it was, it was tasteless, but she couldn't stop herself.

When she opened her eyes the end of her towelling bathrobe belt was a soggy mess.

Chapter Six

Honey tossed and turned. In her dreams she was eating sausages. The dreams were so lucid that she could almost smell them, their cholesterol-inducing presence sizzling and spitting, filling the air with a delicious aroma.

Waking was almost disappointing.

'Well, it makes a difference from flying through the air naked,' she muttered.

First port of call was breakfast. Blueberries, a handful of nuts, and a cup of acorn coffee.

The other women – who Honey couldn't stop thinking of as inmates – swapped stories of past health and beauty treatments. Between talk they chewed like hamsters.

Honey was the only one eating with her eyes closed.

Someone noticed, commenting that she'd read about how meditation aided the absorption of carotene into the system.

In the process of swallowing the dreadful stuff, Honey jerked her head in an unintended nod.

The others took this as confirmation that meditation did indeed do that. She opened one eye. Should she tell them that she was pretending to eat sausages? No. Why burst their bubble?

No doubt the nutty breakfast should make her feel like shinning up a tree. Instead she reached for the end of the belt holding her robe together. One end was already soggy so she started on the other.

Ten o'clock and it was assessment time.

'Ms Serena Sarabande is the resident consultant,' Karen explained in hushed tones.

Honey tucked the belt ends in her pocket and entered the oh-so-white consulting room. 'I can't wait.'

The main relief to the pristine whiteness was down to a fat black Buddha sitting on a low glass table in front of the window.

Serena Sarabande was as white as her room. She shone and, standing in front of the window as she was, it seemed like a bright white halo had formed around her.

'Mrs Driver. Welcome.'

Her chin was held high. Her eyes scrutinized.

Honey cringed inside her towelling robe. She didn't want her body open to criticism. Criticism didn't sit well on her shoulders; or her hips; or her thighs.

She began the usual rigmarole. Getting weighed came first. The lectures would come next, along with the two most dreaded words in the English language – dreaded by her that is. Diet and exercise.

'You're overweight.'

Really.

'You need to exercise. Do you have gym membership?'

Honey shook her head dumbly.

'Never mind. We can do a quick fix if you wish it.'

Honey's ears pricked up. What was that? She didn't need to exercise?

'Oh!'

There was a lot of meaning in that little word and Serena Sarabande was right on it.

'Let me measure you and see where things go. Undo your robe please.'

Being careful to hide the chewed belt ends, Honey opened her robe.

Bust, waist, upper arms, lower arms, hips, thighs and calves; nothing escaped Serena Sarabande's measuring and jotting down of figures.

Ms Sarabande's attention lingered on Honey's breasts. 'These could be firmer. Have you thought about surgery?'

Honey looked down to see that Serena was cupping her breasts in her palms as though they were two dollops of cold custard.

'I don't really … I mean … I thought … I mean …'

Good God, listen to me stammering, she said to herself. She hadn't done that since Carl, her deceased husband, had asked her to marry him – something she'd lived to regret.

'It would work wonders for your uplift,' Serena pointed out. 'And an opulent bosom is *so* unfashionable!'

Intrigued, she rose to the occasion. There was no harm in finding out and anyway, this stay was partly about research after all.

'What does that entail?' asked Honey.

Serena took a green marker pen from her desk and began to draw lines over Honey's breasts, at the same time explaining the procedure. 'This is where we will make the cuts, take out the fat, and reform your breasts into a more pleasing style.'

There was a style in breasts? Well how about that!

Serena stood with one hand on her hip, thoughtfully eyeing the lines she'd drawn.

Honey looked at them too. She looked like the beginning of a crossword puzzle.

'The surgeon would have to reposition the nipples, of course.'

Honey gulped. 'Of course. And just how would that be done?'

'Simple,' said Serena with a nonchalant wave of her hand. 'The surgeon would cut it out from where it isn't wanted and sew it on where it is. Of course, the sensitivity can be affected.'

'I see.'

And she didn't like it. What was the point of something looking pretty if its function was impaired?

She had to play along. 'And you do that here?'

Serena let loose with a superior smile.

'No. Of course not. We just advise our most valued clients where they can get it done. There are various options. You can opt to have it done in this country, but the cost ...'

She paused, her whole body sighing as though disgusted at the outrageous demands of the nip and tuck brigade.

'I'm not a millionaire.'

Serena nodded as though she understood. 'We favour Venezuela. Very good clinics, very good surgeons, and a very, *very* good price. Would you like to discuss the options with Dr Dexter?'

'I would have to think about that.'

'It's a very good price,' Serena repeated.

Honey thought of her bank balance. It would *have* to be good. Play along, play along, she told herself.

'It's not the money. I'm just a bit nervous about having an operation. It would be awful if something went wrong. Do things often go wrong?'

She fancied a faint pinkness flushed Serena's cheeks before dissipating.

'No. Of course not. You'll be perfectly safe with us.'

'I'm sure I will. Somebody doesn't get murdered here every day of the week. That must have been difficult for you.'

Serena's ice cool features went Arctic before a minimum thaw set in. 'A random incident and beyond our control. Very unfortunate.'

'Yes. Very. Especially for Carlotta Macrottie.'

Chapter Seven

Steve Doherty stared longingly at the state of his desk, silently wishing that he had a fairy godmother who would whisk everything away. There were papers everywhere. Some needed filling in with details he wasn't sure he knew; the necessary red tape that seemed to cover everything nowadays from arresting a felon to getting a cup of coffee from the machine at the end of the corridor.

He sighed. Paperwork never had been his strongest point, but he needed the desk space. There was nothing else for it but to act swiftly and confidently. Placing one pile on top of another in no specific order, he opened a drawer and shoved the lot in, slamming it shut with an air of finality.

'That's that,' he said, brushing his hands together before sitting himself down and booting the computer into life.

Before clocking in, he sent a third text message to Honey, not having received any response to the first two. Not that he was worried; Honey had probably thrown herself into her work and into the varied beauty treatments on offer. She was probably enjoying herself while taking the job seriously.

He answered 'Come in' to the knock at the door. The office door cracked open just as he was about to type in his computer authorization code.

'Black coffee, no sugar,' he said without looking up.

Christine Palmer, his new aide in all things administrative, knew what time he expected coffee and had appeared as if by magic. She was learning fast. The kid was keen to please and even if constantly fetching him cups of coffee might be viewed as sexist by some, Christine didn't seem to mind as long as it gained her brownie points on her record. Doherty was obliged to write a report on her ability at the end of her placement. She was doing all in her power to ensure it glowed with praise.

Today, however, she didn't scurry off like a racing hare to do his bidding.

'Sir, there's someone to see you.'

She always called him 'sir'. Other lesser officers called him 'guv', 'governor', or even 'Steve' if they'd known him for ages. Some names he got called were unmentionable but on the whole not from his colleagues. Basically he was a popular guy.

He glanced up from the screen where he'd called up the details of the 'mudpack murder'. The pathologist insisted that it could not have been an accident judging by the way the mud had been inhaled. Nobody would purposely suck it in as though they were guzzling a choc ice. There'd been no sign of a struggle. No bruises. And nobody there had been around at her death, so it seemed.

Something Honey had told him resurfaced. There had been a report in the *Bath Chronicle* about a woman suing the clinic for lesions suffered after surgery. The claim had got nowhere as the woman had died in a fire. Was there any link between the two?

The woman's flat above a bread and cake shop in the old Southgate shopping centre had been gutted by the fire. The shop itself, famous for its unusual cakes and traditional Christmas puddings, was gone now, part of the redevelopment of that area of the city. So there was no chance of sifting through the rubble.

What he did know was that bread shops and bakeries could be highly combustible. Wasn't that how the Great Fire of London had started? He smiled at the fact that the baker's shop had been named The Pudding Club and the Great Fire of London had been started in Pudding Lane.

Stick to the facts, he said to himself, re-examining the paperwork. Strange facts though. The partner of the woman in that instance had insisted that she'd stayed at the clinic for two whole weeks. Two weeks! Why the hell would anyone want to immerse themselves in mud for fourteen days? It didn't make sense to him.

Christine was still lingering at the door and there was no sign of impending coffee. She was giving off nervous vibes. He assumed the visitor wore a top brass uniform. Top brass always made people nervous – including him.

'So who is it?' he asked nonchalantly, his eyes still fixed on the screen.

There was something of a pregnant pause on Christine's part, like she'd just taken a big intake of breath and was holding on to it.

'Your daughter.'

Steve's head jerked up. He stared.

Suddenly aware that he was not alone, he looked up. Christine stared right back, though hers was forthright whereas his was outright surprise. He sat back from the screen, speechless, slumped in his chair.

The trusty sound of his desk phone jerked him back from the brink. If it had been his mobile phone he might have ignored it. He couldn't ignore the landline. The landline phone always had to be answered. Most likely it would be the Chief Constable; high-ranking officers were more partial to land line phones than they were to hand-held mobiles. If high-tech crime prevention by robotic means ever came in, it wouldn't be until the present hierarchy was long retired.

'The coffee for now,' he said to Christine before reaching for the phone, his hand clammy with nervous sweat.

'Is that Stephen?'

The accent was refined.

'Casper.'

Casper St John Gervais was chairman of Bath Hotels Association. Casper was the reason Hannah – Honey Driver – had landed the job of Crime Liaison Officer. She hadn't wanted the job at first, but Casper had pointed out to her that she too had a vested interest in keeping a lid on crime. 'Besides, you used to be an officer in the probation service,' Casper had pointed out to her.

She'd pointed out in return that she'd merely been a clerical officer, typing and filing the details of everyday crime. She'd been persuaded to accept on the grounds that it would improve her room lettings – in other words she would get preferential treatment when it came to package-deal room bookings. It wasn't important in the height of summer, but in the depths of winter it helped keep the bank manager – a wolf in sheep's clothing if ever there was – from the door.

'How did you get this number?'

'I have ways, dear boy. I'm looking for Hannah.'

The way he said Hannah instead of Honey, as was his usual term of address, sent alarm bells ringing.

'Is there some problem?'

'The tasting. She promised to lend me that exquisite epergne she showed me a while back.' He sounded quite put out.

A line of question marks floated like high-kicking showgirls before Doherty's eyes. The word meant nothing to him.

'She promised to lend you a what?'

Casper breathed an impatient sigh. 'An epergne, my boy. An epergne! She has a cut crystal Victorian one – quite unique. Quite beautiful. We both agreed it would make a most worthy central decoration for the tasting.'

Although no connoisseur of antiques, Steve Doherty had a pretty good grasp of language – though mostly bad in his job, not the kind of vocabulary you'd use in front of your mother.

'So it's an antique that you want her to bring along to some tasting. I take it it's a wine tasting?'

'On this occasion, yes. Australian wines. I'm not a connoisseur of vintages produced by our Antipodean cousins, but vintners are vintners after all is said and done. With regard to the epergne, I would wish to have it in my possession before the actual event.'

'Shall I get one of her staff to arrange it?'

'She's not there?' He sounded put out more than surprised.

'The Beauty Spot. Remember?'

'Ah! Yes. I hope she does not over-indulge herself in too many treatments. She is there for a purpose after all.'

'We wouldn't want her to forget that, would we, Casper?'

'Certainly not. Under the circumstances I do not think it sensible for me to call round and pick up the epergne myself. I do so hate having to lie to people.'

'I quite understand. We wouldn't want anyone guessing where she is. Gossip whips around Bath like a champion greyhound. Her family have not been informed of the truth and that's for the best.'

'My staff tell me that everyone at the Green River seems to think she's with you.'

Doherty sensed the amusement in Casper's voice.

'They won't think that when I call round for this *epergne*,' he said, stressing the last word in an effort to spike the amusement in Casper's voice.

Sometimes spiking Casper's conversation worked. On this occasion it did not. He was positively bubbling.

'The rumour below stairs – if you'll pardon such an old-fashioned expression – is that she's gone away to lose a few pounds and beautify herself with regard to imminent nuptials!'

'Nuptials?'

'Marriage. To you, my dear Detective Inspector. Isn't that

terribly amusing?'

The bubbling evolved into a full-scale chuckle.

'Well, you know what staff are like,' returned Doherty, his jaw aching with tension. 'They thrive on rumours.'

'Her mother is not amused, of course.'

Doherty threw back his head. 'Christ,' he exclaimed out of range of the mouthpiece. He went back to the job in hand.

'The thing – the epergne – I'll see that it gets to you. I'll see that someone gets the message. When is the tasting, by the way?'

'Friday. The Assembly Rooms. Hoteliers and guests only.'

'Great. I make a good guest.'

The phone snapped back into place. In his head it sounded sharp, like a bone breaking. Normally he wouldn't be feeling that edgy about this. Honey working undercover was really no big deal. She could take care of herself. But the arrival of his daughter was something else.

When Christine came back with the coffee he asked her to show the girl in.

'She's gone,' said Christine.

Doherty blinked. 'Oh.'

Few people knew he had a daughter. Honey wasn't one of them. Somehow he'd just never got round to telling her. He couldn't explain why. He'd have to soon. If Rachel was still in Bath she was bound to turn up again. She always did.

Get it off your chest, he said to himself, picked up his cell phone and punched in Honey's number. The message service kicked in immediately. Her phone was switched off.

His second option was to phone his wife. Cheryl answered almost immediately in that breathless, always-in-a-hurry way of hers.

'Oh it's you! I might have known.'

'Of course you do. Cheryl always knows best.' He hadn't meant to sound sarcastic, but Cheryl brought out the worst in him. Her tone of voice made him feel like a worm – one that was about to be chopped in half.

'Now listen here right now! You're to put Rachel on the next train back. Phone me immediately you've done that. Hugh and I will be at Paddington waiting for her.'

'Hugh? I thought it was Ralph you were shacked up with.'

'It's none of your bloody business. At least he comes home at night.'

'Hugh or Ralph?'

'You won't wind me up, Steve. Just get Rachel on that bloody train. My God, you never were around when I wanted you to do something.'

'I used to work at nights, Cheryl. It comes with the job.'

'Just get Rachel on that train.'

'I don't know where she is.'

Cheryl hit the buffers, though not for long. 'Then do what I did. Check her credit card statement. She booked a ticket with it.'

'I haven't seen her yet.'

'Then go and find her. You're a policeman. That's what you're supposed to do.'

Doherty rolled his eyes. Listening to Cheryl ripping him off a strip took him back to the two-bedroom flat, the crying baby, and the constant demands on him for more money to get them out of there, more money that had come from extra shifts – night shifts. That had been the trouble with Cheryl; she'd wanted the extra money but she'd also wanted him home at night.

'I'll see what I can do.'

'You'd better!'

The sound of the phone slamming down echoed around his skull. As if he didn't have enough problems to contend with. A woman murdered after being force-fed a mudpack. Honey undercover, a missing daughter, and not forgetting a cut-glass epergne. On top of that he had to choose the right time for telling Honey about Rachel. That, he decided, was the hardest thing to do.

Chapter Eight

True to form, Lindsey was on top of things at the Green River Hotel. The staff were either supportive or totally oblivious to the fact that the boss was away.

The guests got their meals, their fresh towels, and their morning calls on time, there were no professional moaners, and the hot water was staying hot.

Most were staying no more than two nights. The exception was the Japanese couple who were staying for ten days. They were serious travellers; also serious collectors.

'I have bought two dragons,' said the Japanese gentleman.

'You do like a bargain, Mr Okinara.'

'And interesting items,' he puffed. He was presently manhandling one of the aforesaid cast-iron beasts into the reception area with the help of a cab driver. Both men were soaked through by virtue of the slow process of heaving the beast from the taxi to the front door.

The guests' storage facility beneath the stairs already held the Victorian enema kit that he'd purchased, plus an ancient atlas, its paper map bright pink with old British Empire territories.

And now dragons! She only hoped they weren't too large.

'Please. Take a look,' Mr Okinara invited cheerily while he paused for breath.

Lindsey peered over the top of the reception desk in the manner of a slow cuckoo coming out of her clock. History was her lifeblood. She knew lots about history. Lots about mythical beasts too.

'Mind if I make a comment?' she asked.

He nodded, which sent the sweat dripping off his chin.

'That's not a dragon,' she declared. 'It's a wyvern. See? They've only got two legs. A proper dragon has four.' She came out from behind her desk and peered more closely. 'They're boot scrapers.'

Mrs Okinara clapped her hands. 'Wonderful!'

Lindsey was in her element. Medieval history was her favourite.

'Mythical medieval beasts. Saxon rather than Celtic and a symbol of Alfred the Great rather than Arthur.'

'Can I put them with my other purchases until I can arrange for freight home?'

Lindsey reached for the key to the closet beneath the stairs. 'Come this way.'

Once the first of the cast-iron boot scrapers was safely incarcerated, Mr Okinara and the taxi driver went back for the other one.

'As I believe I have already told you, we are antique dealers,' said Mrs Okinara. 'These will look very good at the entrance to a corporate building, don't you think?'

Lindsey agreed that they probably would look very nice. She was too polite to ask how much mud littered the streets of Tokyo or any other centre of corporate business to warrant the purchase of two very heavy and quite large boot scrapers. She also wondered about the cost with regard to excess baggage, but decided that the end might indeed suit the means. Corporate businesses had plenty of money, didn't they?

Mrs Okinara patted the threatening combs of each cast-iron biped. 'I think they look like velociraptors – you know – those dinosaurs in *Jurassic Park*.'

Lindsey agreed with her that they did. 'Except that wyverns were said to run on the tips of their wings while using the talons on their toes to claw your heart out. I think velociraptors had forearms, though you're right, they did kill with the big claw on their rear limbs.'

'Well, they do have only two legs, so I suppose they would find it very hard to walk and claw at the same time.'

'That's the idea.'

Mr and Mrs Okinara sorted themselves out and went up to their room. A group of people from Poland were having a picnic in the conservatory, the rain having scuppered their plans to eat outdoors.

Apart from them, all was peace and quiet.

Lindsey didn't mind at all being left alone to run Reception. If things got too hot she could always buzz for Anna, one of the chambermaids, to give her a hand. So far she hadn't needed to, but when Steve Doherty came through the door bringing the smell of the outside inside, she went with it.

'I want to speak to you,' she said to Doherty.

'Ditto. Tea on the terrace?'

He said it dead chipper; Lindsey burst his bubble. 'Shall we settle for my mother's office?'

While she set up two mugs and began pouring coffee from a constantly refreshed percolator he looked out of the window. Rods of rain were hitting the flagstones of the courtyard that separated the hotel from the coach house where Honey lived with her daughter. Looking at the coach house and remembering the last time he'd stayed there overnight made him feel warmer.

She set a mug before him and settled her hands around a steaming mug for herself. Before sipping she inhaled the fumes.

'I'm needing this,' she said to him.

'So am I.' She wanted to ask him what the big deal was with her mother staying at a spa. She didn't hold with her grandmother's assumption that it was a prelude to getting married. Gran was a romantic. Her mother was not – well, not that much anyway.

'I'm wining and dining your mother on Friday. She'll be home then.'

She suddenly had second thoughts.

'On Friday?'

'After she gets back from the full engine overhaul and gearbox service.'

Lindsey pursed her lips.

'She isn't a car.'

'Oh, I don't know. We're all a bit like cars. Every so often we need our bits tweaked and tidied. Just like cars. I should think your mother was enjoying her time away. She doesn't get much time off.'

Lindsey eyed him thoughtfully. Gran's idea about them marrying was difficult to get out of her head.

She asked herself, would she mind Steve Doherty becoming her stepfather? Possibly not. This was basically about wanting to be in on the secret – if there was one.

'It's not like her to go off to a health spa – if that's really where she's gone.'

'At least the phone won't ring in the middle of an Indian head massage,' he pointed out after blowing on his coffee. 'Anyway, you didn't seem to mind before she went.'

Lindsey raised her eyebrows. 'She told you that, did she?'

'Sure. So why the sudden interrogation?'

The truth was that she didn't like not knowing the full picture. She liked to think that she and her mother were close. They *were* close.

So why the sudden suspicion? It wouldn't do to mention that her grandmother had phoned demanding to know all the details. 'What's she getting herself spruced up for?' her grandmother had queried, then paused as she answered her own question. 'She's getting married again! That's it. Why else

46

would I act out of character and go in for a spot of rejuvenation if it wasn't for that?'

The seed of suspicion had festered and sprouted a green shoot.

'She told me she was having a few days away but wouldn't tell me where. She's never done that before.'

'And you don't like not being in the loop.'

'I suppose not.'

Steve put his coffee mug down on the table. 'You have to agree that she deserves some time away. She'll come back like a new woman.'

'I like her as she is. Don't you?'

The question caught him off balance. He didn't really want to disclose the true reason for Honey's days away. They'd agreed not to say anything until she'd actually gone. Questions were easier to deflect that way. They weren't going to know where she was and she didn't have to lie because she was no good at it.

Doherty was all smiles. 'Of course I do, but seeing as we're looking forward to a special occasion ...'

'Special?' Lindsey cocked an eyebrow. She was all attention.

'On Friday. That's why I'm here. I've come to ask you something ...'

She held her breath. 'So this is it. You're going to ask me something that I may not be able to answer until Mum's here.'

He frowned. 'I'm not sure about that. It depends whether you can put your hands on it without her around. Casper was adamant that your mother knew all about having it.'

Lindsey frowned. 'Pardon me?'

'He was rabbiting on about a table decoration for this wine tasting that's going down. An epergne I think he called it.'

'Oh!'

Lindsey felt embarrassed. There she was, thinking that she

was about to be informed that her mother was getting married again and hey presto! Casper and his demand for a Victorian table decoration had filled its place.

Her face must have reflected her consternation.

Doherty frowned. 'What were you expecting me to say?'

Lindsey knew how to fluster. Her mother flustered. Her grandma rarely did, purely because she considered she was always right and therefore had no need to fluster.

'Um. Purely a misunderstanding.'

'Aha!'

Lindsey had a knack of getting out of scrapes before she actually fell in them. The marriage thing was put to bed – and then Gran arrived.

Gloria Cross wafted into the room looking a dream in an oyster-coloured suit with black accessories including knee-high boots. She was also wearing a nose stud.

Lindsey did a double take. The nose stud was new, daringly hip for a woman who wouldn't see seventy-one again. She heard Doherty swear beneath his breath.

Gloria sallied forth. 'I want a word with you, Stephen!'

Doherty was already making small backward steps towards the door. 'You do?'

Lindsey found her voice. 'No you don't, Gran.' She shook her head in warning.

Gloria Cross ignored the warning, skewering her with a pair of chill blue eyes surrounded with harmonized eye make-up.

'Of course I do. If it concerns my daughter's future, then it concerns me. And don't call me Gran. It's aging.'

Lindsey muttered an apology. There was no sense whatsoever in pointing out that her grandmother – a glamorous puss if ever there was – was over seventy years old. Calling her 'Gran' was therefore no big deal.

Doherty was looking confused, his head jerking from one side to the other like a spectator on the centre court at

Wimbledon.

'Would someone mind telling me what's going down here?'

Gloria Cross was nothing if not blunt. He stiffened when she fixed him with a full-frontal assault. Her eyes were that powerful.

'I'm not sure that I approve of you marrying my daughter.'

'You don't?'

'I do not.'

'I'll bear that in mind if I should ever get round to asking her.'

Honey's mother frowned. 'You mean you haven't asked her? Then why has she gone off to have beauty treatment?'

Doherty smirked. 'She's taking the benefit of the very good advice that you've given her over the years.'

Gloria made snake eyes at him. 'I'm not sure that I trust you, young man. Are you taking me for a fool?'

He shook his head vehemently. 'I wouldn't dare.'

'Then what have you come round here for?'

'An epergne. Casper wants it,' Lindsey swiftly interjected.

Gloria addressed Doherty. 'So why the big secret to going away?'

Doherty sighed. 'She wanted a break. That's all.'

'Do you know where she's gone?'

'She swore me to secrecy.'

'OK. So tell me.'

Doherty threw back his head and inwardly groaned. Gloria Cross was one of those people who didn't think rules applied to her, certainly not ones concerning her family.

'I've just told you. It's a secret.'

'How dare you! I'm her mother.'

'Don't I just know that,' he muttered.

'What?'

Doherty winced. There was something about Gloria Cross that brought out the wimp in him. Perhaps it was the shrill

49

voice. Or it might be the piercing look that could emasculate a bull elephant.

'Sorry,' he said, delving fiercely into his pocket while increasing the length of his backward steps. 'That's my pager. Got to go.'

Pager? The last time he'd used a pager was in 1988! But lying was in order under the circumstances. Gloria Cross scared him.

'Steve!'

Lindsey grabbed his arm. Lindsey he could cope with. Her brown eyes looked up at him.

'Don't worry about the epergne. I'll get it over to Casper.'

'Oh yes.' He'd almost forgotten the reason for popping in.

Lindsey's eyes narrowed at the same time as her fingers tightened their grip on his arm.

'I don't believe you, Steve Doherty. You and my mother are up to something.'

'It's perfectly legal,' he said, sounding as innocent as he was ever likely to sound.

'And probably official,' Lindsey added knowingly, dropping her voice. 'She's off on a case for you, isn't she?'

He gave a light laugh. 'Fancy you thinking we were going to get married.'

'Hmm,' she said. 'Just fancy.'

Chapter Nine

Mrs Evelyn Van Rocher had been a beauty queen in her youth. The bone structure was still obvious, though the jowls had gone south a bit. Her hair was neon white, fluffed up at the crown, and wispy around her face. So far she didn't have a double chin but the jowls had to go; that's why she was here. The clinic offered a plastic surgery consultation service to regular clients or those referred by them.

Dr Dexter had given her the once over, his cool fingers gently prodding the offending areas that she was keen to get rid of.

'I see no reason why we cannot dispose of the excess flesh. Do you have any particular time scale for pursuing this course of action, Mrs Van Rocher?'

His voice was smooth, like oil on troubled waters.

Evelyn Van Rocher flushed like a young girl. 'I'm getting married again.'

'How romantic! And who is the lucky fellow? Anyone I know?' The doctor scribbled in the margin of her notes – a question mark. He paused, waiting for the clarification he wanted to hear, the one that would sway his decision on where Mrs Van Rocher – who was good for the cash – would get her facelift done. It would also make him a lot of money.

She flushed a little more.

'I don't think so. He's foreign and quite a bit younger than me. But we are soul mates, Dr Dexter. We knew it from the moment we met, when I saw him waiting on tables at the hotel I was staying at,' she gushed, eyes approaching fifty glistening like a girl's of twenty.

Dr Dexter congratulated her on her good fortune. 'How very wonderful. Well, you certainly have to do your best for your new man. You want to be beautiful for him.'

'Oh yes,' she sighed in swoon mode ecstasy. 'I have to look my best for the big day.'

Dr Dexter smiled his professional smile. Inside he was counting the bank notes. This stupid woman had gone on holiday abroad – probably North Africa – and nabbed herself a nubile young local desperate to escape hard work and poverty. Pretending to be in love with her, he'd allowed her to stand the air fares and now they were headed for a civil wedding with all the trimmings – provided by her of course. Well, she wasn't the first to be blinded by love and she wouldn't be the last. It wasn't for him to be judgemental – just helpful.

'So when are you tying the knot, Mrs Van Rocher?'

'Six weeks' time. I know it's short notice, but he can only spare so much time over here until the paperwork is finalized ...' An anxious tongue licked at her lips as she paused to ask him what he knew she would ask him. 'I'll pay extra if you can fit me in.'

She wore an earnest look on her face; her eyes were pleading like a spaniel who wanted to go for a walk.

Dexter knew all the signs. Now came the play acting. Doctor Roger Dexter was good at that too.

'Ah! There could be a problem with that ...'

'Oh dear!' Evelyn Van Rocher's fat fingers gripped tightly at the clasp of her Christian Dior handbag. It looked to be a genuine designer handbag, but then, he concluded, you couldn't really tell nowadays.

Dr Dexter moved behind the plate glass desk in his sumptuous office.

'Perhaps there is something I can do …'

He saw her lean forward slightly, all ears to what he was about to propose. He likened it to reeling in a large fish; dangle the right bait on the line and they couldn't resist.

'Would you be averse to travelling abroad?'

She looked apprehensive, one fat hand travelling to her mouth, finger posed on chin. 'Well … I don't know. Will it cost very much more?'

He shook his head. 'About the same when you consider that flights and accommodation are included. But going abroad makes sense if you want something done quickly for an important occasion. Would you like to think about it for a few days?'

Just as he'd expected, her decision came swiftly.

'If it costs the same, then what have I got to lose?'

Chapter Ten

Dr Dexter had closed his file by the time Serena Sarabande entered his consulting room.

'Mrs Van Rocher has paid the fifteen thousand in full. She's leaving tomorrow. I'd already booked her in at the clinic, though I have to say you were chancing your luck. How did you know she'd decide that quickly?'

His smile was slow and considered. 'She's a woman in love – another May and September holiday romance. And you know the old saying about love being blind.'

Her smile slid across her face, not warming it, but purely altering the contours into something more catlike, more calculating. 'It goes along with the saying that there's no fool like an old fool. Anyway, by this time tomorrow she'll be on her way to Venezuela.'

'She'll love it at the Francesca Del Rio Clinic …'

He stopped, catching the look on her face. 'You did book her in there, didn't you?' The smooth voice was now hard edged.

'It was full. You know how it is. First come, first served. And the American referrals always manage to get in first. I had to send them to the Agrippina Delicata.'

'For Christ's sake!'

'Don't worry. It was a one-off slip-up. It won't happen this time. It'll be OK. Trust me.'

'Lucky for us that she was burned to death. We might not

55

be so lucky a second time.'

He looked at her, edgy at the prospect of a patient undergoing surgery somewhere there'd been problems. Miss Porter and her lawsuit would have ruined them. Miss Porter had been a mudpack regular and had then gone on to have surgery. Firstly she'd reacted to the mud. That should have told them something about her sensitivity. Then she'd had surgery in a less-than-first-class clinic. Neither should have happened.

'Don't worry, Roger. Everything will be fine.'

Her voice was like silk. So was her skin, of which he had intimate knowledge.

He thought of the clinic, thought of that bloody woman with lesions, then thought of the money Mrs Van Rocher was paying for her treatment. The money made him feel better. It all added up to a very nice arrangement and a very nice profit.

'Let's hope so.'

Dr Dexter stretched his arms, rotating them in order to free the stiffness in his back muscles. 'We aim to please. Now, my dear,' he said, his demeanour changing from professional to suggestive. 'Is there anything I can do for you?'

Her perfectly pink lips swept into a smile. Reaching up behind her with both hands, she let loose her pale blonde hair.

A low moan rumbled in the doctor's throat.

The tip of Serena's delectable tongue flicked along her lower lip. At the same time her hips undulated; sexily seductive.

'I have this ache, doctor.' She was fingering the buttons of her white coat as though she couldn't find them and certainly couldn't unfasten them without his help.

Dr Dexter got the message and unbuttoned his own white coat. 'Perhaps you need to lie down and show me where you feel the pain.'

Chapter Eleven

Karen plastered the mudpack on Honey's face. It didn't feel
bad. It didn't smell bad either. After that she helped her into the
bath of warm mud. She felt like a profiterole being slowly
dunked in chocolate.

The vessel holding the mud could vaguely be described as a
bath; a horse trough would be nearer the mark, though its
likeness to a coffin couldn't be entirely ignored. This particular
trough had a lid that fastened on either side of her. The lid
covered her full length up to her chin. She figured she must
look a right fright, her eyes like blobs of cream, twin centres of
a chocolate base.

She'd been immersed in here for two hours and figured that
was long enough. The problem was that the attendant had told
her that four hours was best if she were to receive the full
benefit of the treatment.

'It'll make you look years younger,' the perfectly formed
Karen told her.

'I'm scared.'

Karen laughed. 'Whatever for?'

'That woman that got murdered ...'

'Don't be silly.'

Karen Pinker bustled around her, picking up her towelling
robe and throwing a towel over her arm.

The sudden ringing of a phone seemed to make the girl
start.

'I won't be long.'

She rushed off without a backward glance. A door close by slammed shut, reopened and slammed again.

She'll be back, Honey told herself and didn't mind at all.

Warm mud and that pampered feeling combined to great effect; she dozed. When she woke up the mud had turned cold. She couldn't tell for sure how long she'd been in here, but surely she was only supposed to be in here for half an hour?

Where was Karen?

Where was anyone for that matter?

She began to wriggle. OK, the siren voice of vanity had urged her to stick with it. It wouldn't hurt at all to look years younger.

The problem was that the mud was making her itch and it was getting quite worrying. What if it wasn't just plain old itchiness she was experiencing but some odd allergy to sticky mud – Hawaiian pumice mud in particular? Did she have an inbuilt aversion to the stuff?

She tried to remember other incidents when she'd come into close contact with mud. Had she broken out in a rash at any time? Thinking about mud took her back to her childhood. Mud had played a big part in her life as a child, mud pies first and foremost. Had she itched then? She didn't think so.

On the other hand this was allegedly Hawaiian pumice mud, which was a totally different thing from good old British mud. It had to be. Pumice was the stuff that came out of volcanoes as lava, then cooled down into mud and bits of stone that was good for scraping rough skin from the feet.

The nearest volcano to Bath was either in Iceland or Italy, so it was pretty definite that she'd never had the pleasure of playing or laying in it before. Hawaiian pumice mud had to be totally different to the sort she was used to, which got deposited on the banks of the River Avon and swirled up and down the Bristol Channel.

An irritating itchiness had erupted in her left buttock. It was difficult to get to.

She swore and wriggled a bit more but to no effect. The itch was still there. It was no good. She just had to get out of there.

She called out. 'Hello! Is anybody there?'

Scratching itchy bits while immersed in mud was not entirely successful. The problem was that the mud was still there being irritating, slopping along the length of her body. Her fingers scratched but the cause remained.

It suddenly occurred to her that nasty things lived in mud – like worms and crabs. Fleas too.

Panic set in. 'Hey, I'm being eaten by mud worms. They're carnivorous. I swear they are.'

Despite her unsubstantiated claims that she was being eaten by flesh-eating worms, nobody came.

Breathing in until she could squeeze out beneath the board – they must have got that idea from a medieval torture chamber – she prised herself up into a semi-sitting position, her shoulders pushing against the edge of the lid. Bringing her fists up, she punched against the lid. Being a fairly loose fitting, the little clasps holding it in place were shaken free. One of them sprang. One side of the lid lifted. One side was enough. She was out of here!

Raising one hand, she pushed on the rim of the trough, brought up her knees and slid out from beneath the lid. It wasn't easy. The gap was pretty narrow, but with a bit of manoeuvring she popped out like a cork from a bottle accompanied by a loud slurp.

She looked down at herself. 'God, I look like the Creature from the Black Lagoon!'

Frightening memories of watching a flick on late night TV came back to her. The babysitter had been asleep. Honey had had total control of the situation. A curious kid and a mud-dripping monster. She'd loved it – but that was back then, – not now. And she was looking like the monster.

Guiltily, she eyed the mud splats on the floor. Each step she took left a muddy footprint. She needed a shower. Now where were they?

There was another consideration to be borne in mind in her hunt for the showers – all she was wearing was mud. Mud from top to toe.

Karen Perfect had trotted off out of the glossy white door and back along the white-painted passage. Honey recalled passing a bathroom out there, half way between the treatment room and the changing room. It was bound to have a shower.

Squelching and leaving distorted footprints, she made her way carefully, arms held out from her sides in case she slipped.

Bliss! She found a bathroom.

Half a minute later she was standing under a power shower. Mud-coloured water swirled around her feet. She watched fascinated as the white flesh she remembered began to show through. First her upper torso appeared, then her lower torso and then her limbs. The mud around her ankles and feet was proving the worst to get off, mainly because what didn't get washed away in the water was gathering there. She looked like she was wearing a pair of clay galoshes.

Taking a firm grip of the shower attachment she trained it on her feet. 'Get gone!'

The clay boots obligingly disintegrated. Finally she was clean, every trace gone down the drain, to the sea and in time, possibly back to Hawaii.

Smoothing back her hair she let out a deep sigh. At last she was clean.

A quick glance in the full-length mirror showed no sign of injury but a few red marks in the itchy areas. It was hard not to scratch but she didn't go there. It would all clear up in time – she hoped.

Now all she had to do was towel dry and go back to her

room for a lie down. Though on second thoughts perhaps she shouldn't. Lying down meant dreaming. She'd dream of food. Her stomach rumbled at the thought of it. Carrot juice and vitamin supplements were no substitute for a sirloin of prime Aberdeen Angus. With chips. And garlic mushrooms, and all liberally sprinkled with Worcester sauce.

Just the thought of decent food made her almost faint away. And this after one night?

'Drat,' she muttered. 'Now where are those towels?'

She eyed the single glass shelf. Nothing there. She looked inside a glass locker of chrome frame and smoked glass. Nothing. What was even more surprising was that there was nobody around. It made her wonder about the day Lady Macrottie died. Was there nobody around on that day too?

The prospect that she might end up as another mud-caked casualty of neglect made her put a spurt on. She had to get dressed. Sleuthing was a big no-no when you were naked.

Another locker beneath the sink looked promising. That's where they would have to be. Whoever heard of a bathroom without towels?

Yippee! There was – not a very big one, granted, but a towel all the same. Just one. No doubt Karen Perfect had gone off to get a fresh batch.

Honey held the towel up to the light. She had a decision to make here: wipe herself dry with it or cover her rude bits and make her way to her room where she knew a big terry towel sat waiting for her.

It had to be the latter and even though she wasn't likely to meet a man on her way back to her room, who knows if it was window-cleaning day, and window cleaners were always male. It was also rumoured they saw a lot of action and bare flesh on their rounds. The point was that she didn't want them to see HER bare flesh.

The towel was causing a problem. If she pulled it up over

her bosoms her bottom was exposed. If she pulled it down to cover her bum her boobs popped up over the top of the towel.

She reminded herself that she was on a case here and investigating agents lacked gravitas if they hung around semi-naked.

She spotted a roll of black plastic bin liners and pulled one free. A few adjustments and she'd be OK. With a hole ripped in the bottom and one more on either side it did the job. Her bosoms were covered and the tiny towel was now tied round her waist and doing the job over her bum.

Looking like a refugee from a punk rock festival, she cracked open the door and took a look outside. All was peaceful. The doors to other treatment rooms were firmly shut, a red 'no entry' light switched on outside each one. Corridors went off corridors.

Why is it, she asked herself, that old buildings designed as houses and converted into something different always have inexplicable corridors? If anyone was going to take a wrong turning it was her.

Padding over the pale cream carpet she came to a 'T' junction. The sign on the wall said Consulting Rooms, Reception and Rooms One to Six. Room Four was hers. The other direction pointed to Reception only. Confusing, but that was the way it was in old houses. All roads lead to Rome – or in this case Reception.

'Oh! Oh! *Ohhhhhh*!'

The sound stopped her dead. The sign on the door said Special Treatments.

'You're not kidding,' she murmured.

She listened. That was it as far as the loud noises were concerned. The rest were kind of muffled.

Reminding herself what she was here for, she pressed her ear closer.

Subdued sounds were all she could hear but she didn't need

a diagram. What caused that sound was nothing to do with seaweed wraps, aromatherapy or reflexology – though the latter did have a part to play.

Best not to butt in, she decided. Not in this getup.

All would have been well; she would have gone without anyone being the wiser, specifically the two people on the other side of the door.

Unfortunately the tail end of one of her black bin bags caught on the door handle. If the bag had been of the cheaper kind it would have ripped and she would have sidled off, the room's occupants unaware that she was even there. But The Beauty Spot was a top-notch establishment; no economy lines for this place! The bag was a strong one.

Her first reaction was to jerk away. The bag held. She bounced back then forwards again, still attached to the handle.

The door flew open.

A George Clooney lookalike with grey hair and velvet brown eyes was frowning at her. Serena Sarabande looked livid, an uncharacteristic pinkness suffusing her cheeks.

'I'm sorry …' Honey blurted.

The pair of them might have said something right away if their eyes hadn't been fixed on her outfit.

An explanation was in order.

Honey managed a sickly smile. 'You would never believe just how itchy that mud can be. Must be hard bits of pumice still in it,' she said with a light laugh. 'I just had to get out. Oh, and by the way, you could do with putting a few more towels in that bathroom. This one …'

Seeing their eyes open wider as they swooped downwards, and feeling a sudden draught, she looked down too. The towel was around her ankles.

'Ohmigod!'

Turning pink all over she swooped down to retrieve the tiny towel. Then she was off, taking her towel, her blushes and her semi-naked form off to her room.

If she'd had chocolate she would have consoled herself. She briefly wondered if the toilet paper was made from rice paper. Rice was edible – even in processed form.

Instead she consoled herself with a hot bath and the fact that these people were used to seeing plenty of naked women. No problem.

Following Honey's swift spring along the corridor and out of sight, Dr Dexter and Serena closed the door behind them.

Serena eyed Dexter nervously. 'How long do you think she was there?'

'I always said you make too much noise.'

'Never mind that,' barked Serena. 'I meant we were talking about the clinic and the money our latest old bitch is paying us. Do you think she heard that?'

His eyes were heavily hooded and looked almost closed as he thought about it, his chin cupped in his hand.

'Who knows? But we can't take any chances. We're too close to the end of this. You'll have to keep a closer eye on her. We have her address. I'll get Mandril to make enquiries.'

Chapter Twelve

'Room nineteen, sir. Here's your key.'

The man Lindsey was checking in studied the key in the palm of his hand with interest.

'A real key. Well there's a novelty.'

Lindsey knew what he was getting at. Modern hotels didn't use old iron keys. The Tower of London had old iron keys, useful for locking up traitors and people past monarchs hadn't taken kindly to. Old keys equalled old buildings.

'We're a listed building,' Lindsey informed him. 'There are rules as to how modern you can go.'

She conveyed the information in her usual courteous way, though something about Mr David Carpenter unnerved her. It might have been the way he was taking everything in, though furtively, as though he didn't want her to notice.

Working in a hotel had made her observant and very sensitive to people. He was looking around as though searching for someone. Everything about him advertised brute force and ignorance. It was his shape that did it. Those outside the hospitality trade wouldn't know that people could be split into shapes. Her mother for instance was an oval. Her grandmother was a very thin rectangle. Mr Carpenter was definitely a square.

He had a square-ish face; the bristly haircut didn't help. His eyes were little chinks of blue above square-ish cheeks. His chin was square. His body was square. Although he wasn't that tall – possibly five-eight – he looked powerful. She could imagine him in a kilt tossing a caber, though she didn't think he was into that. If his name had been MacDonald perhaps he would be.

He patted the key into the pocket of his navy blue blazer, bent down, and picked up his bag – just one bag – a navy blue holdall that might have contained clothes though it could just as easily have contained sports equipment, a musical instrument, or an assault rifle.

She gave him directions to his room, accompanying them with the requisite friendly smile as though she felt comfortable in his presence – which she did not.

He made a disparaging noise. 'I've stayed in better.'

'So why stay here? There are plenty of hotels in Bath. You don't have to stay.'

Something in her tone seemed to pull him up short.

'No need to be defensive.'

'Isn't there?'

Business was business but she wanted him gone.

He seemed to sense it. 'Your employer is lucky. You're very loyal. Have you worked here long?'

'Long enough.' She made no excuses for being brusque. She didn't like him.

'Do you enjoy it?'

She reminded herself that he was paying the bill. 'Yes I do. It's a very nice hotel.'

Lindsey felt an unexpected sense of pride as the man scrutinized the elegant reception area. The walls were a chill blue and the mirrors, chandeliers, and paintings were very Louis Quatorze in style. It hadn't long been done – a bit haphazardly after the interior designer had snuffed it and a kindly German had got stuck in to the job.

'We'll see.'

The comment was seemingly made to himself.

Lindsey heard. Suspicion was like an unidentifiable smell beneath her nose. David Carpenter had looked around Reception as though he were giving it marks out of ten. On top of everything else he was a single man with little luggage and a searching look to his eyes. And he'd come now when her mother was away, the worst time to choose.

The terrible truth hit her. The hotel inspector! It had to be him!

First priority – tell the chef. Then the chambermaids. Then Dumpy Doris, who was pushing the vacuum cleaner around the restaurant.

Luckily she was wearing trainers. Speed mattered.

'Anna! Take over! And get the polish out.'

Anna looked perplexed. 'You want me to polish? I polished this morning.'

'It doesn't smell strong enough,' Lindsey hissed. 'Spray it around a bit too. On the carpet will do. Make the place smell nice.'

'OK.' Anna nodded slowly while looking at Lindsey as though she had suddenly lost her mind.

Lindsey dashed to the kitchen, being careful to knock before she entered. 'Damn. Damn. Damn,' she muttered as she went in.

Smudger was using a wooden tenderizer on a batch of veal escalopes. The mallet paused in mid-air as his eyes met hers.

'You're going to tell me we have a problem,' he said solemnly. He didn't look at her as though he was mad. He looked at her as though he might get mad if he didn't like her answer.

Lindsey took a deep breath. Her heart danced on, the quickstep slowed to a fast waltz.

'I think we have a special guest staying in room nineteen.' Even to her own ears she sounded almost awestruck.

'I don't suppose the Queen's graced us with her presence.'

'I know you'd like it to be, but it's not.'

'Shame. Rumour has it she's been shopping up in Milsom Street again. You'd think she might pop in for one of my curries or a home-made baguette with goat's cheese and cranberry sauce.'

'I heard that rumour too and it's a shame that she doesn't, but I'm afraid I have to disappoint you. Perhaps she's waiting for the January sales. Everyone's on a budget these days.'

'Shame. So who is it?'

'Think worst case scenario.'

Still with his mallet in salutary pose, Smudger raised his gaze to the ceiling.

'Now let me think.' His gaze transferred to her face. 'Give us a clue!'

Another deep breath. Lindsey's heart was almost back to normal.

'OK. If I tell you he'll be examining the plug hole upstairs, checking on the booze measures in the bar, eating table d'hôte this evening, and ordering everything at breakfast, will that help?'

Smudger's mallet gradually came to land on the table with a loud bang. 'Shit! The hotel inspector!'

Up in his room David Carpenter was blissfully unaware that the hotel's head chef would like to bring a mallet down on his head. He was doing what all hotel guests do: testing the bed springs, seeking out the kettle, and examining the view out of the window.

He liked the view. The window looked out over the street. The pavement was wide. There wasn't too much traffic, just enough to remind you that you were in the middle of the city.

The green hills surrounding the city of Bath were dotted with multi-storied houses. Most had been built in the nineteenth and eighteenth centuries to be a coach drive away from all that Bath had to offer.

It had offered a lot. It still did.

He'd wandered the city centre before coming here. The street performers were particularly interesting. Some pretended to be statues, keeping so still that pigeons roosted on their shoulders.

Some were quite talented. He'd watched a girl standing beneath the colonnade by Bath Abbey. She'd been singing an operatic aria and singing it well. Passers-by had thought the same, an unusual number throwing money into the open bag in front of her.

He hadn't of course. He didn't believe in charity. He only believed in himself and the job in hand.

The road outside was wide enough to complement the pavements. There was plenty enough space for cars to park, leaving room for two-way traffic.

He spotted a traffic warden coming from the direction of Laura Place. Like ninety-five per cent of the population, he didn't have much time for traffic wardens. He'd shoot them all if he had his way.

He watched as she walked slowly past his car, one heavily shoed foot following the other. Not elegant; not the shoes and not the traffic warden. Wide in the beam and broad in the shoulders, she waddled as she walked. Damn it. He didn't like fat people. They were eating because they were sick of life. Stuff the views of the politically correct; it was his opinion and he was sticking to it.

His eyes narrowed with vicious intent as a thought occurred to him. Turning back into the room he went to the bed, unzipped his soft grey holdall, and brought out a towel-wrapped bundle.

He went back to the window and placed the bundle on the sill. Carefully he unfolded the towel, exposing the item within.

The small-bore Magnum was basically designed for a

woman; it fitted into a purse, a handbag, or even a large pocket. Added to that it was light and although it didn't have a great range, it was good as a defensive weapon. Not that it wasn't lethal.

Raising his left arm in front of his face at chin level, he brought the gun up in his right hand, while resting it on his left forearm. Closing one eye he aimed the muzzle at the loitering traffic warden. The bitch! Her pen was poised in one hand; her pad of parking tickets in the other. She deserved to die, he thought to himself. What civilized person would do a job like that?

The gun was aimed at the dead centre of her forehead. If he let off a round now, she'd be dead. He squeezed the trigger. If the gun had been loaded the traffic warden would be dead by now. But it wasn't. Nothing happened except that David Carpenter was satisfied that the old magic was not dead. He could still kill if he had to. But that wasn't what he was here for – not yet anyway.

Chapter Thirteen

Day Two. The pampering! Massage with beautifully smelling oils.

Honey was lying face down with just a towel covering her behind. Karen Pinker – Miss Perfect – was giving her a massage. The aroma of the oils being rubbed into her back was calming. The rubbing itself was relaxing. Dozing off was more than likely if she didn't keep focused; she was here to investigate – her eyelids weren't quite on board with this.

Now where to start her questioning?

Sugar and spice – a little bit of sympathy hiding a teeny weeny question …

'Uh … Sorry about yesterday. Hope I didn't get you into any trouble, but that mud – you'd be amazed where it gets and how it itches when it gets there. And I couldn't find my robe.'

'My fault,' said Karen. 'I shouldn't have left you alone that long. Patricia was sick but had a client booked in. I had to cover. The robe was in the bathroom though. I'm surprised you didn't see it.'

Miss Karen Pinker sounded embarrassed at what had happened. Honey was sure the girl's cheeks were turning pink. Miss Pinker was getting pinker!

The robe had *not* been in the bathroom. She guessed that must have been the excuse she'd given Serena Sarabande.

Honey recalled hearing a phone ringing. That was when Karen had rushed off. Now what would cause a young woman to abandon her job and rush off like that? Easy peasy. A boyfriend.

'Do you have a boyfriend?'

There didn't seem much point in not coming right out with it.

Karen coloured up even more.

'Yes.'

'A serious boyfriend?'

'I don't know. He's gorgeous though. No boy has ever treated me like he does.'

'Wow! Lucky you!'

Karen was beaming.

'What's his name?'

She simpered a bit and blushed some more. 'Dec.'

As in Declan, Honey presumed. The phone call had to be from him.

'I understood from Ms Sarabande that treatment is usually on a one to one basis. Obviously problems can arise if someone is off ill. Does it often happen that you have to cover for a colleague?'

She detected a thoughtful pause before Karen Pinker answered. 'She couldn't help being ill. I couldn't blame her for it. You have to help out when someone's ill.'

'… *if you want to keep your job* …'

Honey didn't voice what she was thinking but considered it likely that Karen could be out of a job if she refused to cover for absent colleagues.

'I'm sorry if I got you into any trouble.'

'You didn't – not really, but I would have been along shortly.'

Honey wasn't fooled. The second half of the sentence sounded like a reprimand.

'I'm sorry I broke the catch on the mud bath, but I couldn't stand it any longer. See?' She shifted the towel so Karen could

72

see the remainder of the red marks where she'd been scratching herself.

Karen kept massaging but slowed enough to take in the red whip-like marks.

'Oh yes. The lid is designed to keep in the warmth. The mud is a natural product, but even so, it does affect some people like that. Not generally though.'

Something in Honey's brain clicked. The woman who had died in a fire above a bakery shop had complained of lesions. Honey herself had broken out in red marks. Doherty hadn't mentioned the deceased Lady Macrottie having any red marks or lesions, so she presumed she had not. No reason for killing there then.

Still, this line of questioning seemed to be going places. It was worth persisting.

Question two coming up!

'Is it an allergy?'

Karen's response was immediate.

'Oh no! I expect it was something you ate before coming here, or possibly it could just be that you're unusually sensitive to mud.'

Well it certainly wouldn't be a reaction to the food I'm getting here, Honey thought, her chin resting disconsolately on her folded arms. Today's lunch had been far from gourmet – or plentiful. Parsnip gratin – without the cheese – some kind of soy alternative. Apple and sultana terrine. Compote of carrot and grapefruit served with soured cream. The cream was the clincher. She'd licked that plate for all it was worth. Luckily it hadn't had a pattern. It wouldn't have been there after the licking she'd given it.

The other women had looked at her in amazement.

Pride was the first casualty of her hunger. 'Anyone not want theirs?'

No chance. They'd eaten theirs too.

'I was never allergic when I was making mud pies,' Honey said to Karen.

Karen laughed. She had a pretty, tinkling laugh. Honey found herself thinking that men must find Karen's prettiness and tinkling laughter attractive. She was a trophy waiting for a man aged over forty-five and currently going through a mid-life crisis. His other attributes were likely to be a villa in Marbella and a yacht in Monaco.

'I read something in the paper about someone suing the clinic when she broke out in lesions.'

There was a definite pause. 'Ah yes. Ms Porter.'

'You knew her?'

'She wasn't one of my ladies. She was one of Patricia's.'

'Did she get itchy in the mud?'

'I don't know. As I've just said, she wasn't one of my ladies.'

The girl's reply was brusquely delivered. In Honey's experience, if someone who had been pleasant began snapping they had something to hide. Wisdom such as hers was not present in ordinary human beings. You had to be involved in the catering and hospitality trade to acquire the nose of a sniffer dog for that kind of thing.

Such experience had been gained as a result of guests trying to check themselves out along with a few mementoes of their stay like toilet rolls, a linen tablecloth, or a pair of bedside lamps – the latter obtained by cutting through the live cables. The perpetrator had got away with his life and the hotel hadn't burned down, but he hadn't got away with the bedside lamps. A wire had been trailing from his suitcase and the conical glass shades had clanged against the reception desk when his wife bent down. She'd secreted them in her brassiere. She was an ample woman. In Honey's opinion it must have been a tight squeeze.

'Was Lady Macrottie one of yours?'

She felt Karen's hands stiffen on her back. 'Yes.' The sharp tone was gone. She sounded frightened or horrified. The tone could be interpreted either way. Big dollops of sympathy were needed.

'Oh, that's terrible, Karen. How awful for you to find someone dead like that.'

'I didn't discover her. Magda did.'

Ah, yes.

'Just as well you weren't here that day. Or were you on the phone?'

Honey sensed Karen's hands stiffen on her back. She'd hit a raw nerve. The phone again.

'Declan phoned you?'

'He …'

'Karen! Is anything wrong here?'

Honey recognized Serena's voice and decided to be forthright.

'Karen was telling me about the day of the murder. It must have been awful for you all.'

'Dr Dexter wants to go over the Botox list with you for the morning. You might as well do that now.'

There was no doubting that Serena was ordering Karen to clear off, and clear off she did.

'So, Mrs Driver. Shall we recommence where Karen left off?'

Serena's fingers were long and cold. They were also rock-hard, exerting more pressure than Karen had done.

The heels of Serena's hands kneaded Honey's shoulders and back. Her tension dissipated; it wouldn't dare do anything else.

The message was obvious. Serena Sarabande was not amused. Honey decided that there was nothing for it but to be honest.

'We were discussing the murder. It must have been terrible for Magda – discovering the body like that.'

The hands changed position. The fingers slid over between her neck and her shoulders, thumbs pressing against the nape of her neck.

Honey gulped. She'd read somewhere that professional assassins could kill people like that. She reminded herself that this was a health and beauty spa, not a killing field.

Still, she was nothing if not gutsy.

Serena more or less repeated what Doherty had already told her.

'We had an intruder. A tramp. We think he came in looking for food or drugs.'

Drugs, decided Honey. Not food. It wouldn't be worth his while.

'I take it they haven't found him.' Of course they hadn't. She knew better than Serena did.

'Not up till now.'

'I take it you've stepped up your security as a result of that.'

'Absolutely. Everything valuable is locked away and as an added precaution we have installed more security cameras.'

Honey mused on Serena's statement about everything valuable being locked away.

'I suppose that includes my phone and everything else in my bag.'

'It does indeed. For the duration of your stay personal items are locked firmly out of your reach. That includes your cell phone – and other non-essentials.'

Because she was lying on her front she couldn't see Serena's face, but she could imagine that face being crossed by a knowing smile. The smuggling of calorific goodies was nothing new to this babe. Still, she did have supper to look forward to – for what it was worth. Her stomach rumbled. It sounded quite vocal.

Get me out of here! Give me food!

Soon. Quite soon.

Serena Sarabande was not amused. Her perfectly shaped lips in her perfectly shaped face held no hint of a smile. It wasn't often she escorted clients to their rooms, but she made an exception for Hannah Driver. The client had looked at her and enquired the time for 'lights out'. She'd said it laughingly. Serena didn't find it funny.

Once she was sure that Mrs Driver was safely behind the door of her room, she made her way back along the corridor to Roger Dexter's consulting room.

The light above his door was glowing a steady green. He had no patients, so all she did was to give a terse knock before going in.

Her face flushed with anger at the sight that greeted her. Dr Roger Dexter was in a clinch with Karen Pinker. They were leaning against the desk for support, his leg wrapped around her thigh. A little more of an angle and Karen would be flat out on the desk with Dexter on top of her.

'Serena!'

Surprisingly for one caught out, Dr Roger Dexter looked almost amused.

He straightened. With one hand he smoothed back his sleek black hair, with the other he zipped up his fly.

Karen was buttoning up her blouse. Her cheeks were pink and the flush was swiftly travelling down her neck.

Dr Dexter smiled. 'I wasn't expecting you.'

'Obviously not!'

Serena glowered at him. Not that it did much good. Whatever Dr Dexter wanted, Dr Dexter got. He had an expensive lifestyle and a rampant libido. Both were well taken care of, mostly by her. Just lately she'd suspected his loins of travelling to pastures new. He'd denied it of course. But now she had proof.

She turned her blazing eyes on the very flustered Karen.

77

'Get out.'

'Take these,' Roger added. He handed her the client records she'd been sent to collect.

Head lowered, Karen didn't look at Serena as she scurried from the room.

Serena slammed the door after her.

Roger Dexter went behind his desk and began to take off his white coat.

Serena's eyes narrowed as she looked at the man she thought she loved.

'How much more do you want, Roger?'

He smirked at her, one side of his mouth lifting, one dark eyebrow raised above one brown velvet eye.

'I'd like to die a multi-millionaire.'

'That wasn't what I meant, but whilst we're on the subject, is there such a thing for you as too much money as well as too much sex? When do you intend to stop?'

He was slow answering. He fixed her with a triumphant look, a look that said 'I know that you want me.'

The bastard! He was right of course. He knew damned well that just one look from him and she was on fire. She would do anything for him. She *had* done anything he'd wanted, supported him in his business interests even though they were dicey and eventually there would be a price to pay.

'As long as stupid women pay me extra to pack them off to a third-rate plastic surgeon, I shall keep taking their money.'

When he smiled there was no charm like that he reserved for his patients. Instead his lips had a surly, cruel twist.

'Shame you're no good at surgery yourself.'

The comment was meant to hurt. Dr Dexter had a wonderful bedside manner. He was pretty good between the sheets too, but when it came to actually nipping at bags beneath the eyes and boob enhancement, he just didn't cut the mustard. He'd failed the exams. Understandably he hated being reminded of

78

the fact.

His anger hardened the velvet eyes. Recognizing his temper was rising, Serena curbed her desire to say more.

Slowly he emerged from behind the desk, his eyes not leaving her face, mesmerizing and frightening.

Serena felt herself go cold. He was going to strike her. It wouldn't be the first time. She had to divert him, greedy, egotistical pig that he was.

'She has to go! She's been talking to that woman. Mrs Driver. I think she's spying on us. I think she's from the insurance firm.'

He stopped, one set of fingers resting tripod style on the desk. He frowned.

'Mandril hasn't reported back yet. Her address is the Green River Hotel. He'll get back to us when he can.'

'Soon I hope.'

'What did Karen tell her?'

'I caught them talking about Lady Macrottie and about Pansy Porter. But that's not the only thing. The mud affected her. She was scratching.'

A deep sigh erupted from Roger's body as he threw back his head in exasperation.

'Another insurance claim! We can bloody well do without that, old fruit.'

The change in tone, erring towards affectionate, made her bold. Pressing herself against his side Serena fingered the nape of his neck, twirling the dark soft hairs growing there around her index finger.

'There are insurance claims and then there are insurance claims. See what I do for you, my sweet?'

He smiled, and if she had cared to analyse that smile she would have shivered at the selfishness within it. But she didn't go there. No matter what he did she would always be at his beck and call. She couldn't help it.

Chapter Fourteen

Andre Pietro considered himself a *maitre d'* of the highest order, even though he was only termed a head waiter.

His piercing eyes, small and furtive as a ferret's, noticed if a guest was without water on the table, or had been waiting too long for a course, or dared to open a packet of cigarettes in a public dining area.

He had the air of someone from a finer restaurant, a more upmarket hotel. He was here because it was convenient for his girlfriend and baby son. Being suave, svelte, and having a superior manner, he didn't give the impression of being married and a family man. But that was the way Andre was; professional at work, patriarch at home. He kept his two worlds strictly apart. So far, no problems.

Having been told that David Carpenter was very likely a hotel inspector sent by the Automobile Association, Andre had given him one of the tables by the windows. By virtue of the cellar below which itself had windows, there was a gap of some eight feet between the building and the road. From the window tables it was possible to look out at the passing world without the passing world being able to look in.

The hotel inspector had ordered the scallop starter and the steak main course. Andre had made it his task and his alone to collect the dirty plate from the main course. The head chef, Smudger Smith, was waiting for him in the kitchen.

'What did he say?'

Smudger's brow was damp with perspiration. The kitchen was hot, but Andre knew by the wild look in the chef's eyes that the sweaty brow was due to nerves more than heat.

Putting down the dishes, Andre rolled his eyes. 'He said it was OK.'

'OK? OK? The bastard! I sweated my bollocks off over that steak. It was perfect! Fucking perfect!'

'Pleeeease …' murmured Andre, closing his eyes in exasperation. 'There is no need for such bad language.'

Impervious to anything except the hotel inspector's response to his cooking, Smudger muttered further expletives. His eyes glazed over with what Andre could only interpret as temporary madness. He shuddered at the thought of past chefs he'd known. Some could easily have committed murder. There was no guarantee that Smudger couldn't rise to the occasion and commit murder too, given the right incentive.

Smudger tried again. 'He must have said something.'

'Yes,' snapped Andre. 'He said he'd have the raspberry crème brûlée.'

Smudger blinked. He seemed to let it sink in before he came to. 'Right. Raspberry crème brûlée it is. The best ever! The bloody best ever!'

Determined to elicit some comment from the hotel inspector – however painful – he was off like a greyhound, dashing around the kitchen, gathering ingredients, dishes, and pans – and all for one guest.

Andre watched in amazement with a tight expression on his finely chiselled face. Sucking in his cheeks and pursing his lips, he made one final observation.

'Hotel inspectors do not usually make comment until they check out.'

Smudger waved an egg whisk in his direction. 'Trust me. He's all that. Lindsey spotted the signs.'

Andre let sleeping dogs lie, concentrating on taking the

main courses out for two well-known local businessmen. Catching snatches of conversation, it appeared they were bidding for land on which to build a series of retirement apartments.

'Enjoy,' he said to them.

Noting that the hotel inspector's wine glass was drained, he went to his table next.

'A little more, sir?'

'Certainly. I wouldn't pay for a whole bottle unless I was going to drink it, now would I.'

The man's tone was surprisingly surly. Hotel inspectors were usually courteous, even in a hotel that might have been running alive with rats and cockroaches. If any of his staff had upset the man, they'd be for it. As he poured another measure into the glass, Andre's eyes flitted from one waiter and waitress to another. None of them looked flustered. None of them looked as though they'd refused him another bread roll or spilt gravy into his lap.

As he poured he sensed the man's eyes on him. Like the true professional that he was, Andre did not meet the look. Like all good staff and servants it was best to pretend that he hadn't noticed.

'Tell me,' said the man. 'Do you know a Mrs Hannah Driver?'

'Of course.'

'She lives here. Is that right?'

'Yes. She lives here.'

David Carpenter nodded thoughtfully. 'Has she lived here long?'

'About four years, sir.'

The man frowned. 'That's a long time to be a hotel resident.'

It was on the tip of Andre's tongue to say that far from being a hotel resident, Mrs Hannah Driver actually owned the

83

place. But something stopped him. He'd been in the restaurant trade long enough to be able to weigh people up. In his experience it was always wise not to give too much information. Answer the question. No more.

On going back into the kitchen to fetch the crème brûlée, he told Smudger about their conversation.

Smudger frowned as he thought about it. At last his frown departed.

'Perhaps he appreciates the personal touch. You can't get much more personal than an owner living on the premises.'

Andre wasn't so sure, but he didn't argue. The dessert was ready – and Smudger had gone overboard. The crème brûlée was presented in a porcelain dish served on a white porcelain plate with soft Virginia amaretti biscuits.

A look of surprised amusement crossed Andre's face. Chef was determined to get some kind of accolade.

'Thank you, chef.' He set off and found he was not alone.

A trio of kitchen staff – including Smudger the chef – followed him out and along the corridor that connected the kitchen with the restaurant.

Andre paused at the door and turned, eyeing them enquiringly.

'Well go on, man,' said Smudger, shooing him on with a floury hand. 'Let us know what he says. We'll wait here.'

As he crossed the restaurant floor, Andre pondered on chefs he'd known. Basically they were all like Smudger Smith; praise for their cooking meant more than money. Without praise they pined away.

He waited until the hotel inspector had taken three or four mouthfuls before approaching to ask if it was to his liking.

'Very nice,' he replied.

Very nice. Truthfully, Andre had wanted him to say more than that. The words 'very nice' troubled him all the way back across the restaurant. 'Very nice' was too generic to satisfy the kitchen staff.

Just as he'd expected, Smudger and the gang were still gathered there, waiting with goggle-eyed anticipation.

Andre took a deep breath.

'He said it was wonderful. The best he'd ever tasted in fact.'

Smudger punched the air. His crew were all smiles.

'Yes! Yes! Yes!'

But something was still niggling Andre.

'Are you absolutely sure that he's the hotel inspector?'

'Trust me, man. And he knows his onions! Know what I mean?'

Andre's reservations increased along with the hotel inspector's consumption of alcohol and further questions regarding Mrs Hannah Driver.

If the two businessmen on the next table hadn't lingered over their coffee and brandies, he would have mentioned his doubts to Lindsey, but it was late and he decided not to bother. His wife and youngster were expecting him home.

Leave it until tomorrow, he said to himself. By the time he came in the man would be gone and it wouldn't matter. Only the man wasn't gone in the morning, and it did matter, it mattered very much.

Chapter Fifteen

Dressed in a white towelling robe, a towel wound turban fashion around her head, Honey Driver was lying supposedly relaxed in a treatment room. This particular treatment room had an interconnecting door to Serena's office. Needles and plumping-up of lips had been mentioned, along with the eradication of facial wrinkles. The plumping-up seemed good. The needles not so good.

'The things I do in the interests of this city,' Honey muttered.

'Did you say something?'

Serena Sarabande was sorting out the items needed for her treatment.

'Just my teeth rattling. I hate needles.'

'Nonsense!'

The fact that Serena Sarabande was the one giving her the treatment and the treatment itself involved a hypodermic needle was unnerving.

'This won't hurt very much.'

'Don't you mean it won't hurt at all?' Honey queried in a high-pitched voice.

'There are no guarantees.'

Serena was her usual coldly proficient self and thus bereft of sympathy.

This wasn't good.

Honey's breath steadily increased like a nervous wreck on a

ghost walk. She followed the needle with her eyes. The fine point was heading for her chin, aiming to discharge a face-rejuvenating filler into the so-called 'marionette' lines running downwards from the corners of her mouth. Needles had always scared her. She just didn't want to go there, but how best to opt out?

Faint! That's what you have to do. Pick your time and faint away!

The needle was fast approaching. Now seemed as good a time as any.

Her sigh was long and heartfelt. – That's if Serena Sarabande should ever have a heart – which Honey doubted.

Her eyes closed. Serena would see she was out of it. And stop.

Nothing happened. She felt a slight prick, then another. Was the woman going on with the treatment? Damned right she was. Honey couldn't believe it. All the same, she'd decided on this course of action and she was damned well sticking to it.

She opened her eyes just a few seconds after feeling fresh air being fanned on to her face.

'Did I faint?' she asked weakly, her eyes fluttering open.

'You did. But I did it anyway. No point in wasting the occasion – or the Westalyn. It costs money.'

Yes, thought Honey, and the Hotels Association – in conjunction with a few other interested parties – were paying for it.

As Serena Sarabande entered details into the laptop computer sat on her desk, Honey felt the sides of her mouth where the needle had gone in.

'The effect will last for six months minimum, twelve months maximum.'

After a short rest Honey looked in the mirror, which was fixed on to a pedestal at the side of her recliner. The results were quite cheering. It wasn't all blood and baddies being a

Crime Liaison Officer.

It was perfectly true that she hated needles, but there was method in her madness. Serena Sarabande was keeping a close watch on her following her conversation with Karen Pinker, plus the fiasco outside Dr Dexter's door when she'd caught her bin-bag tunic on the door handle. She wanted to get at those client records. Appearing incapacitated might give her the opportunity.

'Are you able to get back to your room?' Serena asked.

Honey made a weak attempt to rise before falling back, her eyes fluttering.

'Not yet,' she whimpered.

Serena gave an impatient sigh. 'Well I suppose you'd better rest here for a while.' She glanced at her watch. 'I'll leave you for now. I'll send someone along to help you.'

Honey nodded weakly. 'Thank you.' She hoped it would be Karen who came along to help her. Another conversation with her could be useful.

Lying back, she closed her eyes and waited for Serena to leave the room.

Pretending to faint had been easy. The worrying thing about it was that Serena had carried on with the procedure of sticking the needles in. It didn't seem either ethical or safe. Would she have been in any great danger if she'd really fainted?

She wasn't sure. Medicine was hardly her forte, though she'd once dated a dishy doctor in the days when husband and hotel were all in the future.

Medicine hadn't come into it. Playing doctors and nurses had. The dishy young doctor had still been in training. He'd declared that nothing beat an intimate body examination. She'd had to agree. His hands-on procedure was second to none.

She listened before moving. Nobody was coming just yet. Wrapping her robe tightly around her, she made her way through the door into the office. It wasn't locked.

The computer was still on. She went behind the desk to take a closer look. The light from the screen lit up her face. She stared at it, trying to make something of what it was showing. She had to get in there somehow though she wasn't entirely sure what she was looking for.

'Abnormalities.'

She'd uttered the word herself, though she couldn't resist looking over her shoulder.

Yep! It was her that had said it. Abnormalities in record keeping – that's what she was after. There had to be something not quite right. She had a nose for these things.

The computer was still on; she could tell that much about it. Computers never had been quite her thing. They were a useful tool but she'd never got her head round the logic on which they functioned. It wasn't her logic. Still, now was a time for seeing what she did know.

Feeling apprehensive and out of her depth, she opened a few unlocked desk drawers just in case the computer files were backed up with good old-fashioned paper ones. They were not.

Perched on the edge of the black leather swivel chair, fingers poised above the keyboard, she stared at the screen.

And stared.

And stared.

'How the hell do I get into this thing?' she said out loud.

She didn't know. Not knowing loomed like a twenty-foot high fence at Aintree Racecourse. Even a horse would have trouble jumping as big a fence as that, so what chance did she have?

She didn't know. No matter how hard she stared at it, getting into the system was beyond her. The damned thing was asking her for a password. She didn't have one.

A brisk rummage through the desk drawers didn't unearth anything that might have contained one. In a situation like this there was only one thing she could do – contact an expert.

There was a phone on the desk. At last she had contact with the outside world!

'ET phone home,' she muttered and did just that.

Lindsey answered.

'Green River Hotel, good –'

'Lindsey! Listen carefully. I don't have long. I will say this only once …'

Now she was sounding like some old-time French resistance fighter. Was her mind going, isolated for only a few days from the outside world?

'Mum! I'm so glad you phoned –'

'Lindsey, I need to break into a computer system.'

Her voice rasped with the effort of keeping it low.

'I think you need to come home … Gran seems to think –'

'I can't. I have to do this.'

'OK, OK.' Lindsey sighed. 'You can't get into a system just like that. How long have you got?'

'Five minutes. Perhaps ten.'

'Forget it. It's not that easy.'

'I was afraid of that.'

'Why do you want to get into this system?'

'To check some records at a beauty clinic.'

'Got it! The clinic where the woman was drowned in a mud bath. Doherty put you up to it, I suppose.'

'She wasn't drowned in mud. It was the mudpack that did it. Anyway, this is all expenses paid. I've had these Botox injections in the lines at the side of my mouth. I pretended to faint, but they went ahead and injected anyway.'

'Yuck! That doesn't sound right.'

'So what do I do – about the computer?'

'Nothing. Not in five minutes.'

This was not good.

'That's a shame.'

While on the phone she had been going to ask how things

91

were at the Green River; the normal everyday things like had Smudger decapitated any grumbling diners or had Mary Jane, their resident professor of the paranormal, frightened away the guests as well as the ghosts with her garish outfits.

She only got the first few words out when the door opened. Serena Sarabande entered, and her stomach turned over.

'I have to go now, Lindsey. Somebody's just come in.' The phone clicked back into place. 'My daughter,' she said and chanced a smile.

Serena Sarabande's face looked as though it were set in cement. Her eyes were unblinking. If she attempted to smile her face would crack.

Serena opened the door wide, an obvious invitation that Honey should pass through it – and quick!

Seeing as Serena gave her the creeps, she went meekly, half expecting the woman, who was taller than her, to give her a clip around the ear as she passed. How scary was that?

She stopped suddenly. Why the hell am I feeling like a frightened school kid? This won't do for Bath Hotels Association's Crime Liaison Officer! I've an image to maintain, and a life. Number one priority is to get out of here!

Summoning all her courage – it took some to stand up to Serena Sarabande – she said what was in her mind.

'Much as I love it here, I'm afraid it's necessary that I check out early. My mother is old and not in the best of health. Unfortunately she's taken a turn for the worse. It's not good news, I'm afraid. She's very fragile. A little senile in fact.'

The thought of her mother ever finding out the damning description she'd just uttered was too scary for words. Far from being senile or decrepit, Gloria Cross was the Cindy Crawford of the Senior Citizens Club. Possessing the firmness and figure of a Barbie doll, she had a designer label wardrobe to die for. Referring to her as 'old' was bad enough; referring to her as 'senile' was downright dangerous. Normally Honey wouldn't

92

have dared, but she judged it was time to make a swift exit. Besides, her mother was out of earshot and would never find out. No problem!

Dr Dexter stood behind Serena Sarabande at the window that ran full length from floor to ceiling. Both of them watched Honey getting into her car and driving away. Both of them visibly relaxed once she was safely out of sight.

'As if we'd want her to stay,' murmured Serena.

Dr Dexter smiled. 'That was all rubbish about her mother being ill. I caught most of the conversation. The daughter certainly didn't mention anything about a sick and senile granny on the phone, which goes to prove that she was as keen to leave us as we were to see her go.'

'As long as neither of us was mentioned.'

Serena's voice was as seductive as the movement of her behind against his body.

Roger Dexter gripped her hips, pulling her more tightly against his groin. 'No. We were not.'

'Then we can consider the matter closed?'

'We can.'

Freeing herself from his hands, she turned round to face him. Her smile was just for him. Her eyes said it all. 'Now, Doctor. What can we find to do between now and the next appointment?'

He smiled back at her. 'Just a moment and I'll pop a pill. I'm sure we'll think of something.'

Chapter Sixteen

The moment she arrived back at the Green River Hotel, Honey knew that something was wrong.

Blue lights flashed from two emergency vehicles; one was a police car, the other an ambulance.

A crowd had gathered. Assumptions and observations were being made, word of what was going on passed from one onlooker to another.

'Someone's been found dead.'

'Murder?'

'No, natural – so somebody said. Perhaps they were old.'

Oh no! Honey pushed through the crowd with one thought in mind. Please God, I didn't mean to tempt fate. I just wanted to be out of that place.

There seemed to be more emergency service people than necessary for the body of one old lady.

At first Honey thought that the reception area seemed colder than usual until she realized it was her that was cold, chilled to the bone with the fear of what she had done.

Anna was manning the reception desk. Not that anything was going on there. Guests were hanging around. Usually they'd be out seeing the sights. Honey surmised that they liked the action here; after all, it wasn't every day you got to see a dead body.

Anna spotted her.

'Mrs Driver!'

'Where's Lindsey?'

'In the dining room.'

'Oh my God! She died in there?'

Holding her hand over her mouth she stifled a gasp. Her mother had died in the dining room?

The first sign she had that all was not doom and despair was when she saw Lindsey coming towards her from the direction of the dining room. A pair of medics was following on either end of a stretcher.

Lindsey looked concerned but not desolate. Professionalism. That's what it is, Honey told herself.

'Tell me what happened.'

'You're back.'

'What happened?' she asked again, grasping her daughter's upper arms, too worried to breathe, too guilty at first to notice that the stretcher was bearing a bulky form that must be at least twice her mother's weight.

Lindsey gently removed her mother's digging fingers from her arm. 'I'm not sure. That's why they've decided to have a post mortem. At first we thought that he'd drowned in his porridge, but the paramedics think he had a heart attack and *then* drowned in his porridge.'

Honey felt all the tension, the guilt, and the sheer stupidity fall down through her body and rush out of her toes.

'A man! A man died?'

'Yes.' A knowing smile crept across Lindsey's face. 'You thought it was Gran, didn't you.'

'Well …' This was awkward. This was embarrassing. 'We have to accept the fact …'

Lindsey's smile widened. 'It's OK. I won't tell her.'

Honey was still suffering the after effects of the shock.

'Phew! Well that's a relief!' she said, patting her chest with the flat of her hand in a bid to get her breathing back to normal.

Someone held open the double doors so they could more

easily get out.

'Not for him, Mother.'

The formal use of the word 'mother' did not go unnoticed. Honey reined in her sudden exuberance.

'Poor man. Still. These things happen.'

'Gran would be livid.'

Honey cleared her throat and looked to where the ambulance doors were being shut on the corpse. 'That's about it. So who was it?'

'The hotel inspector. Or at least we think he was.'

'What?'

The cold shivers returned with a vengeance along with a list of what ifs, chief among them being what if he hadn't died from a heart attack? What if it were food poisoning? How would that affect their three star rating?

It was hard not to throw back her head and moan, so she didn't try to stop it.

'Of all the people to have die on me!'

'Are you in charge here?'

The two occupants of the police car left parked outside had been whiling away their time in the dining room with cups of tea and buttered scones. The evidence – the butter from a toasted tea cake – had made their chins shiny.

'Yes.'

'Can we have a word?'

'Certainly. I'm Mrs Hannah Driver. I'm the owner.'

'Just a few details, Mrs Driver. Can you tell us what time the body was discovered?'

'No. I wasn't here.'

'I was.' Lindsey offered her services.

While Lindsey helped the police with their enquiries, Honey phoned Doherty, taking her phone into the restaurant where she proceeded to help herself to a buttered chocolate croissant, two slices of cold bacon, and a large cup of regular black coffee.

Detective Inspector Steve Doherty answered on the third ring.

'Steve? We've had a death at the hotel.'

'So I understand.'

He sounded casual, as though bodies found dead in hotels was happened all the time – which presumably they did, though not necessarily drowned in a bowl of porridge.

'Good job I left the clinic when I did. Not that I could have stood it there for much longer. They took away my phone. I've only just got it back. And my clothes.'

'And your cookie jar?'

'I didn't take a cookie jar. I took packets of cookies – and other things. The cheese was going a bit ripe.'

'Naughty girl. So. How did you get on?'

'The mud bath made me itch.' She scratched at the memory of it. 'You wouldn't believe the red mark I've still got on my derrière.'

'Leave it with me. I've got just the thing for itchy derrières.'

The lechery of his smile came full throttle down the phone.

'I know your game.'

'Good. Then you know it takes two to play it.'

The thought of playing at his place following drinks at the Zodiac Club was very appealing. However, although she'd sensed things weren't right at The Beauty Spot Clinic, she didn't really have anything concrete except that Serena Sarabande had walked straight out of a freezer. Although she'd seen Dr Dexter, she didn't really have anything on him except that he was balling Serena on a regular basis.

'One of the girls there is or was friendly with Magda Church, the girl who discovered the body. I know you've already interviewed her, but I thought she might be worth a visit. I got her name from Karen Pinker.' She frowned. 'Funny, I didn't see Karen before I left. It must have been her day off or something.'

But what was it Karen had said? She was working five or six days a week at the moment, seven if they could twist her arm. On the way out she'd asked the girl at Reception where she was. The girl had been offhand.

'I think she's left, but I wouldn't know for sure. I'm new here.'

Karen's departure from the clinic was too sudden to be taken as pure chance. She'd been sacked. Honey was sure of it, and suspected it might have been her fault.

Chapter Seventeen

Honey slipped off one shoe and rubbed her aching sole.

'Hey ho. Running a hotel is such a soothing pastime!'

'You love it really,' muttered Lindsey from the corner of her mouth.

Honey was thinking that she should have stayed resting up at the beauty clinic for a bit longer. But here she was, back into the nitty-gritty of hotel life, and she was run off her feet.

A group of accountants were busily spending their clients' money in the restaurant as part of their conference passage.

Following five courses they were now downing liqueurs. Drambuies, sambucas, tequilas, and B-52s were being ordered in quick succession.

Also in quick succession dirty crockery and glassware was piling up in the kitchen.

Smudger Smith, head chef and one time all-in wrestler, was getting red in the face, growling like an out-of-sorts Rottweiler as he paced from one end of the kitchen to the other.

He was waiting to clean down, close the door, and shove off to the pub. Unfortunately the dishes and glasses kept coming.

The hold-up was also due to the fact that Clint had done a runner halfway through scraping the residue of steak and kidney pie from an oven dish.

Apparently this sudden incident had occurred when someone had delivered a note to the barman. The barman had passed the note on to Clint, who had immediately vanished, muttering something about not wanting his assets cut off and made into a pudding.

Honey, flustered from doing what all hotel owners have to do at certain times – wait on tables, serve drinks, and keep one step ahead of drunken diners hoping to give her a grope rather than a gratuity – was told what had happened.

'Saturday night is music night in my books,' grumbled Smudger, whipping off the red bandana he wore around his head and looking as though he might strangle somebody with it – Clint at this moment in time.

The fact that chefs could expect to be at their busiest on a Saturday night cut no ice with Smudger. Getting to the pub to meet his mates was a ritual not even the Queen would dare to interrupt.

Rubbing her forehead with one hand and her pinched posterior with the other, Honey sighed.

'Run along and play. I'll finish off here.'

She regretted the words the minute they were out, but had no chance to retract them. Smudger was already unbuttoning his splattered chef's jacket.

'You couldn't just stay ...'

He stiffened, his eyes diminishing to pinpoints of inner angst. His look said it all.

She waved him off. 'No. Forget it.'

'Here we are again,' she said to herself as she tackled the clearing up while Smudger headed for the nearest pint of beer.

It was after midnight by the time she'd finished. Some of the accountants had stumbled up to bed. A few hardened conference delegates were balanced on bar stools, treating each other and the long-suffering barman to clichéd jokes and anecdotes from other accountancy conferences they'd attended.

The kitchen was preferable before one of them began their 'my wife doesn't understand me' routine.

She did what she had to do until the kitchen was pristine.

After that she went out for some air in the back yard.

The air was chilly, the sky was bright, and the shadows thrown by bushes and rambling roses were sooty black.

The sound of the city hummed like an idling lawnmower on the other side of the wall. A bush on this side of the wall rustled.

'Psst! Psst!'

To an untrained ear it sounded like a gas leak, but Honey Driver knew better.

'Oh for goodness sake ... Clint! Cut the impersonation of Hissing Sid and come out here. Do you realize you dropped me in it tonight? Look at me. Hotel owner covered in sweat when I should be floating around playing at being hostess with the mostest.'

Clint's expression was unflustered. 'Your flattery is formally accepted. Now, what is it you want in return?'

She fancied she saw him grin but it was too dark to be sure.

He stepped out into the light, his eyes flickering nervously towards the kitchen door.

Clint's neck was covered in tattoos, mostly of spiders' webs. Centred on his skull was something resembling a large black tarantula.

Striking and somewhat frightening as his tattoos were, Clint was something of a pussycat. He was also almost always available when it came to being short of someone to wash the dishes. He would do anything asked of him, the original Jack of all trades. Nothing he was asked to do required great skill, but he was willing, which counted for a lot in the hospitality trade. He led a flexible working life. At the last count he had four different jobs, one as bouncer on the door of the Zodiac Club, the smoky, open late hours haunt of pub landlords and off-duty hotel owners and managers ...

'It's like this,' he began. 'I need a favour. A really big favour.'

103

Honey eyed him sceptically. She was under no illusion. Clint was a shadowy character and some of what he did wasn't entirely legal.

'If it's illegal, don't ask me.'

'No! No! It's nothing like that.' He swallowed hard, his eyes still flickering towards the kitchen door. 'I was wondering if I could stay with you tonight.'

'Is that a proposition?'

He chuckled. 'No, of course not!'

She folded her arms, hands still slightly damp from a surfeit of washing up. He read her look, stammering something that was almost an apology.

'I wasn't meaning that you're too old to go to bed with. I mean a few years ago you must really have been …'

'Thanks, Clint. You really know how to flatter a woman, you know that?'

'Christ!' he said, hiding his face with his hands. 'I'm that bloody wound up and I rattle off insults as though they're bloody bullets. That ain't what I meant,' he said, dropping his hands from his face. 'The point is I'm in a bit of bother. And it ain't illegal,' he added quickly on seeing the look on her face. 'Fact is that I've been a bit of a prat. There was this Italian piece you see. Well, Sicilian really. Her name's Gabriella. I met her at college –'

'You've been going to college?'

He nodded. He looked a bit bashful. 'I fancy meself as an artist. Always have been good with a pencil and a few paints. And I'm not bad at it. The teacher said that I was pretty good in fact, especially at life drawing – you know – people and portraits. That's where I met Gabriella. She was the model and she was …'

'Naked?'

'Well … yes … but it was a life class. I mean it's not as though it was top shelf stuff. It was art. Proper art.'

Honey nodded and muttered a soft 'Of course,' at the same time thinking how funny it was that a paint brush altered the emphasis of nudity.

'Anyway, we got friendly and one thing led to another.'

'Not in the middle of the class, I hope!'

He laughed. 'Nah! Course not!'

'So? What's the problem?'

'We-e-e-ll … besides the fact that she's pregnant …'

Honey closed her eyes. 'Bad, but not insurmountable.'

'There's more. There's worse.'

She groaned. 'Go on.'

'Her husband.'

'Ah!'

'He's Italian.'

'Dodgy.'

'Sicilian in fact.'

'Worse still.'

He shook his head. 'It's not funny. Luigi isn't just the owner of the best Italian restaurant in Bath. He's more than that. A lot more than that.'

Honey blinked. Rumours abounded in the fair city of Bath about who was or might be a bit of a crook. Some were true. Some were not. The one about Luigi Benici being Sicilian and therefore a Mafioso had been going the rounds for years. The point was that if what they said was true and Clint had been messing with his wife, the proof of the pudding, as they say, was about to be tested.

'So your relationship was abruptly cut off.'

Clint balked. 'It could be more than my relationship being cut off if he catches me. That was what the note was about. They're out to get me. They're watching me out front and following me, waiting for the right moment. That's why I ran out here. I figured that if you could hide me for tonight and smuggle me out tomorrow in your car, I should stand a good chance. Once I've gathered up a few things, I'm on the road. I don't know where I'm going but I sure as hell know it's time to go.'

Honey found herself analysing whether her life would become more complicated as she got older.

'My car's in the garage.'

'We can get round that. Well? Can I stay with you?'

He looked pretty dejected, so dejected in fact that she could forgive him for not wanting to go to bed with her. In fact it was something of a relief. Doherty was quite enough, thank you!

'OK. But there are rules. Tidiness at all times.'

He visibly brightened. 'Right!'

'And pyjamas. I insist you wear pyjamas.'

He blinked, not quite working out that much as she liked him, she had no wish to see any more of his many tattoos than she was used to. However, there was one query.

'Just as a matter of interest,' she began slowly, tilting her head to one side. 'Is it true about the fox and the hounds?'

She was referring to rumours that he had a famous tattoo – the fox seemingly disappearing between his buttocks, the hounds following on behind.

His hands dived to his waistband. 'Do you want to see it?'

She shook her head. 'A simple yes or no will suffice.'

He grinned. 'That's for me to know and for you to find out.'

Chapter Eighteen

The next day Clint asked if he could stay a bit longer. Honey looked at him. She liked her place to herself, but couldn't see him out.

'If you have to.'

An employee of Luigi Benici came calling at noon.

Mother and daughter had helped themselves to salad. Honey had followed hers with a freshly prepared rum baba and Lindsey had gone for a quick jog around the block.

Reception was fairly quiet, though cutlery clinked reassuringly from the restaurant. Twenty people. Not bad for a lunch time.

Honey got on with the things she had to do, including entering the calorific value of a rum baba in her diet diary. Some of the women at the clinic kept a diet diary and swore it aided their eating habits and therefore weight loss.

Even the words 'rum baba' sat lumpy under the simple word 'salad'. She'd promised herself that she wouldn't sin, which in dietary terms was eating anything that a rabbit wouldn't eat.

Her decision to cross it off and forget it was interrupted by the opening of the double doors leading out on to the street.

A man entered. For a moment he held both doors wide open, his dark eyes raking the place as though checking it was safe to enter.

Honey sized him up. He had to be something to do with

Luigi Benici. He had the strutting, confident look of somebody who demands answers or promises blood on the carpet.

He gazed round for a second time, head high, nostrils dilated. He looked as though he expected to see Al Capone sitting there reading a newspaper.

The Japanese couple looked up, voicing a lilting good afternoon.

He nodded and responded while heading for Reception.

Honey exchanged greetings with him.

He got to the point quickly.

'My name's Carlo Pratt. I work for Luigi Benici.'

She guessed his mother was Italian, his father British. He had the look.

Clint was in the coach house, well out of reach. For that she was thankful.

However, there was no doubt in her mind that anything to do with Luigi Benici meant trouble. Wasn't it Luigi Benici who'd threatened Casper with the rough end of a pineapple at a charity event?

It had been all to do with seating arrangements. Luigi didn't like the table he'd been given. Unnerved by Luigi's colourful threats – and the sure knowledge that he was likely to carry it through – Casper had caved in. Luigi had got the seating arrangements he wanted.

There was no doubt in Honey's mind that he would want the same level of compliance from her.

Still, she reckoned she could hold out for a while. Until mention of torture or torching the premises.

A beaming smile might help.

Grinning like a Cheshire Cat she asked, 'So what can I do for you and Mr Benici?' As if she didn't know!

His smile was seductive. His teeth were white against the olive tint of his skin. He ogled her like the Big Bad Wolf. She felt like Little Red Riding Hood, or worse still Grandma.

What big teeth you have, grandmother.

'Let me explain, dear lady.'

He attempted to cover her hand with his. She snatched it back, at the same time giving him a sour look.

Unfazed, still smiling, Carlo Pratt (now what sort of a name was that?) explained his business and lied as though he were telling the truth.

'The young man is a friend of my employer,' said Pratt, his teeth flashing and smile fixed on his face. 'There is a query about a job he did for my employer. There are items outstanding that need immediate attention. We would very much like to locate him as quickly as possible. I hear that he sometimes works for you.'

'He sometimes works for a lot of people. I believe I'm one of many.'

'Quite so. Quite so.' His teeth gleamed. His hair glistened.

Honey eyed him warily, not able to make up her mind about his provenance. Was he really half Italian or Sicilian as his first name suggested, or had he taken it on to diminish the plainness of his surname?

She decided on the former. His classic good looks and confident style evinced the Italian stallion type. Women usually dropped at his feet because he insisted they did. Well she wasn't one of them, even though his clothes shouted money. The cashmere sweater, matching powder-blue trousers, and white leather loafers, didn't look as though they'd come from a Sunday market.

'Well if you'd like to leave me a phone number, I'll give you a ring the minute I hear from him. In the meantime, do you happen to know anyone skilled at scrubbing pans?'

There was no kidding this guy. The smile went on hold for a split second before resetting into something halfway between sincere and sadistic. Powder blue might be his colour of choice, but he was no pastel on the pushy front.

In a flash he'd grabbed her hand, and none too gently. His fingers were like a vice and her hand was being crushed.

'Don't treat me like a fool. You treat me like a fool, you treat Mr Benici like a fool. He will not like that. Now. Where is he?'

'You're hurting me.' She struggled to throw him off. It didn't work.

'Where is he?'

'I don't know. Why should I be party to what he does? He only washes dishes here. It's not as though he's irreplaceable!'

His action did not go unnoticed. The Japanese couple had fallen silent. Mr Okinara was rising slowly from his seat. His wife placed a restraining hand on his arm. He dislodged it gently, rose to his full height, and padded towards the reception desk.

'Is there a problem?'

The eyes behind the glasses Mr Okinara wore were dark and quick. He was also light on his feet. She hadn't heard one single footstep. It crossed her mind that he might be proficient in unarmed combat. She certainly hoped so. A karate chop to Carlo Pratt's neck would be most welcome – though not by Mr Pratt of course.

Defiance flashed from the eyes of Luigi Benici's messenger. There was no sign in the chiselled face of backing down. This was not good.

Perhaps things might have got ugly if Lindsey hadn't come back from lunch and Mary Jane hadn't come tramping down the stairs like a herd of African elephants.

'There's a psychic fair going down at the sports hall today. I'm off there to give readings. Can't wait,' she said, barging into the small gap Mr Pratt had left between him and the reception desk. 'This is my big break. It might even lead to writing a book or at least a regular newspaper column. How great would that be?' She suddenly seemed to notice Mr Pratt and Mr Okinara. 'Sorry, you guys. Am I interrupting something?'

She looked from one to the other. Both men were shorter than her. Most people were shorter than Mary Jane.

Mr Okinara was like a coiled spring or a high jumper psyching himself up to leap into the air. His black-eyed gaze never left Mr Pratt's face – not that Mr Pratt was a man to be intimidated. However, it was pretty obvious from the look on his face that he knew a lost situation when he saw one. This scene was at an end. He could do nothing more. The smile transmuted into a lop-sided snarl.

'I'll be keeping an eye on you,' he murmured.

He threw Mr Okinara a menacing look before leaving. Mr Okinara's stance remained solid, legs slightly parted, arms akimbo, and fists clenched.

'You have a very bad aura,' Mary Jane called after him.

Mr Okinara was joined by his wife. 'You are all right, Mrs Driver?'

Honey took a deep breath. 'I am now.' She thanked Mr Okinara.

He shook his head. 'Think nothing of it.'

Mary Jane was enthralled. 'My, I bet you can do a deadly karate chop.'

He laughed. 'No, but I do like a pork chop.' Husband and wife looked at each other and giggled.

Honey couldn't help giggling too, and soon Lindsey and Mary Jane were doing the same.

'What are we all laughing at?' Honey asked.

'The joke,' said Mr Okinara. His wife covered her face with her hands, tears of laughter streaming down her face.

'It's like this,' said Mr Okinara. 'We are Japanese. All I have to do is adopt the right stance and the minds of Western people run riot. I'm no Ninja, Mrs Driver, but all I have to do is look like one. People's imagination does the rest. I blame

Bruce Lee and the Ninja Turtles.'

It was only fair to stand the Okinaras a meal that night. They'd saved the day. So had Mary Jane to some extent, but she was off out. The psychic fair beckoned and nothing could prise her away from the world of spirits and things that go bump in the night.

However, there was still the problem of Luigi Benici and their washer-up.

Honey and her daughter regarded each other with the same thought in mind. Honey voiced it first.

'I think it's time Clint was leaving us.'

'So do I. Why is it men always leave the lavatory seat up?'

'No idea. It could be a control thing.'

Honey had had the good sense to stay at Doherty's place overnight. Lindsey was not so lucky. She'd managed bravely, but good housekeeping went out of the window once a man moved in – even for one night.

'I'll have a word with him.'

Leaving Lindsey covering Reception, Honey crossed the courtyard to the coach house she usually shared with her daughter. Clint had slept in her bed the night before and would have done so tonight. But this was serious. She was under threat and so, to some extent, was Lindsey.

The sound of singing accompanied by the strong smell of jasmine greeted her as she entered. She followed her nose and knocked on the bathroom door.

'Clint. I want a word with you.'

'Come in. It's OK. I'm covered with bubbles.'

Just as she'd suspected, he was lounging in the bath, his legs spread wide and his feet resting on the roll-top lip.

It was a heart-stopping moment, but luckily he was telling the truth about the bubbles. He'd gone overboard with half a bottle of Molton Brown shower and bath gel. The bubbles were piled up like small replicas of the Alps in winter.

He was also wearing a pile of bubbles on his head. He beamed at her as though he hadn't a care in the world. Well, she was about to burst his bubble.

'A man named Carlo Pratt paid me a visit just now and he wasn't collecting for charity. He was looking for you.'

The smile vanished. 'Shit!'

Suddenly his eyes were looking her up and down. It made her feel uncomfortable. Could he possibly be thinking lustful thoughts at a time like this?

'What are you looking at?'

'Your arms and legs are OK?'

Sitting down on the lavatory seat – once she'd put it down – she wiggled her legs and waved her arms.

'They're fine.'

'I thought they might be broken.'

'I'm unhurt – thanks to Mr Okinara.'

'The Japanese who's been buying all that junk – sorry – antiques?'

'The very one.'

'Is he a samurai or something?' he asked, his eyes shining with admiration.

'No. He's an antiques collector. Mary Jane was there too. She dwarfed our friend Mr Pratt.'

Clint's earlier good humour had totally disappeared. He looked worried. 'I've got to get out of this bath and then out of Bath.'

'Do you have somewhere to go?'

He nodded. 'An old girlfriend of mine runs a smallholding in the Forest of Dean.'

It crossed Honey's mind that Clint had quite a lot of old girlfriends. For the most part they seemed on amiable terms, willing to take him in and protect him like they would a stray dog.

'Somewhere isolated sounds right up your street.'

He frowned. 'They'll be watching this place.'

'I thought they might.'

His eyes were round and scared when he looked at her. 'You've got to help me, Mrs Driver. If Luigi Benici gets hold of me, I'm for the chop – literally.'

Honey folded her arms and looked at him accusingly. 'It's your own fault. You should practise some self-control.'

His grin had only half the intensity it usually did, but Clint wasn't the sort to be down for long.

'I prefer to practise my seduction techniques.'

She got up from sitting on the lavatory seat. 'Clint, I do not want your blood all over my carpet or your private bits blocking up my drains. I've only just had them cleared out. You've got no alternative but to give your friend a ring. Tell her to get the bed aired. You're making arrangements to leave Bath tonight.'

'I am? Entire or in easily managed packages?'

'Don't look so scared. You're going in disguise, which is a pretty tall order for a guy covered in pictures. But you're lucky, Clint. I've got a really creative daughter and a resident with a ghastly taste in clothes. You don't mind dressing up as a woman – more precisely as a friend of Mary Jane?'

He frowned but shook his head. 'Whatever it takes.'

'Right. Get out of the bath, phone your friend, and leave the rest to me.'

Chapter Nineteen

Mary Jane kept a pretty frightening wardrobe. The colours were a little garish but the size was right. Her stuff would fit Clint and if she were willing, she was the one who could get him to his destination unharmed. Who could possibly suspect a very tall Californian driving a pale pink Cadillac? She was so noticeable she was bound to be ignored by Luigi Benici's men.

Prior to her doing the job, she insisted on knowing every detail.

'Why aren't you taking him to this ex-girlfriend's place?' She was bug-eyed about it and speaking in a hushed voice. 'I gotta know the background to this caper – in case I'm interrogated.'

Mary Jane was a keen James Bond fan and into big secrets. Honey put it in simple terms.

'Because Pratt said he'd be watching here and that means he'll be watching me – Lindsey too possibly. He knows we're Clint's friends and will put a tail on us. He won't follow you.'

Explaining everything to Mary Jane had gone smoothly enough. In fact Mary Jane was very excited about it.

'It's a long time since I had a wild adventure,' she said wistfully, hands slapped together in front of her face. 'The last time it was down in Tijuana. I hadn't taken the trolley like other folks. I wanted a bit of excitement and what the hell kind of excitement do you get riding the trolley? I went down in my car and took a friend with me. She was as wild as me, but her

115

husband went ballistic. "Who the hell goes to Tijuana in a pink Cadillac?" he asked. I told him that I did. That car is kind of my trademark, you know, and you may have noticed that I try to coordinate my outfits with the colour of the car. We kind of go together.'

'I wouldn't argue with that,' murmured Honey. 'Now. This does mean that you have to take Clint along with you to your psychic fair. You don't mind that, do you? Only they need to see you leave, and we need to check that they don't follow you, though I doubt it. After all it's me and Lindsey they're more likely to be watching, not you.'

'Someone's got us in the picture.' During the conversation between her mother and Mary Jane, Lindsey had been watching what was happening outside. 'There's someone hanging around on the other side of the road. And there's a car going around the one-way system. It keeps coming back, slips into a parking space, then goes again.'

'Shall I bring the car around to the front door?' asked Mary Jane.

Honey shook her head. 'No. Clint has to appear relaxed like any other American tourist heading out for the evening.'

'In these shoes?' Clint had made his entrance.

'I did the best I could with the material I was given,' smirked Lindsey.

Two elderly gentlemen who'd asked to have their coffees in Reception – with brandy chasers – gave the new arrival the eye.

Clint was a belter in a turquoise trouser suit, a white wig, and enough make-up to open a shop.

Honey looked him up and down. 'You'll go down a treat at the over-sixties' club.'

Clint snarled.

'Clint, you've only got yourself to blame. We've done our best for you.'

'Yeah, yeah. I know you have, but these shoes …'

'Men have a bigger foot width than women. You're lucky we found anything to fit you. Luckily for you a transvestite cage fighter left a pair behind when they had a convention here.'

'You should have sent them on,' grumbled Clint.

'We couldn't,' Lindsey interjected. 'His wife thought he was at a convention for model railway makers.'

Mary Jane sighed with satisfaction. 'It's such a long time since I had a night out with a girlfriend.'

Clint rolled his eyes as Honey tried to tie a chiffon scarf over his silky white wig.

'Do I really have to wear that as well?'

'Yes. In case your wig falls off.'

'Are we driving with the hood down?'

Honey shook her head and lowered her voice. 'It hasn't got a hood. It's just got Mary Jane driving it.'

Despite the make-up she fancied he turned paler. Well, there it was. She'd done her best.

One of the old men came over, brushing close by where Clint was standing.

'You fancy a tipple later?' he said, his chin almost resting on Clint's shoulder.

Clint was speechless.

'He's from out of town,' Mary Jane interrupted.

The old guy's face dropped. 'Shame. Never mind,' he said, brightening suddenly. 'Next time. Right?'

Clint visibly jumped as the old guy patted him on the rump, and exclaimed, 'What a liberty …'

Honey calmed him. 'Now, now, Abigail. You mustn't take offence.'

'But he just …'

'And how many times have you …'

Honey eyed him accusingly. Clint got the message. He'd

117

patted a few rumps in his time – pinched a few too. She found herself wondering if he'd ever go there again after being on the receiving end. Possibly. A man was a man for all that.

'Hey,' said Clint, being careful to keep his voice down. 'I'm not sure I'd like to be called Abigail. Why can't I choose my own name?'

Honey zipped up the large shoulder bag in which she'd stuffed all of Clint's clothes.

'I asked Mary Jane to choose the name. It had to be a name that would pop into her head before your real one had chance to. Hence, Abigail.'

'My dearest friend,' said Mary Jane, wiping a tear from her eye. 'My, but I miss her. So you're kind of her spiritual replacement,' she said tearfully before noisily blowing her nose into a man-size tissue.

This seemed to please Clint. 'Hey! That's kind of nice. Am I as pretty as she was?'

'No.'

'Oh!' Clint sounded hurt.

Mary Jane pressed her fingers against her forehead and closed her eyes.

'Are you all right?' Honey asked.

'Just tuning in to Abigail's vibes, asking her to be with us tonight,' Mary Jane replied. Her eyes flicked open. 'I do hope she comes through tonight, though you can never tell. Few psychics do animal crossings.'

On hearing this, Clint looked for clarity from Honey and Honey obliged.

'Abigail was Mary Jane's cat.'

'The best friend I ever had,' Mary Jane stated.

Lindsey was taking another peek through one of the huge Georgian windows. 'Careful,' her mother warned her. 'They might be able to see in.'

Lindsey pointed out that they'd need binoculars.

Smudger chose that moment to come marching through the door on time to do his evening shift. Without his chef's whites on he was a cool dude in baggy-bummed jeans and designer trainers. His hair was fired upright with enough gel to stick bricks together.

'Hey! Did you know there's a guy across the road eyeing this place through a pair of binoculars?'

Honey nodded. 'It had entered my mind.'

'Oh. Right.' Smudger's voice trailed off at the same time as he took in the vision in the turquoise trouser suit, red high heels, and matching shoulder bag. Mary Jane had embellished the outfit with a bright red chiffon scarf festooned with the Stars and Stripes, explaining that it used to be Abigail's.

Clint began to scratch.

Smudger looked Clint up and down.

'Hi, Clint. Love the getup. Got a hot date tonight?'

'Kind of,' Clint replied.

All of them stared after her head chef as he disappeared through the door that led to the corridor that in turn led into the kitchen.

Honey broke into the stunned silence. 'Take no notice. He's a chef. Chefs don't think like normal people.'

Chapter Twenty

Mary Jane reported back that Clint had got away OK. The only problem had occurred at the psychic fair.

Clint had become quite taken with all that was going on, so he paid his money and had a few readings done.

Some psychics looked a little confused at the readings they were getting. Another put it quite bluntly and suggested Clint go for the operation if dressing in girls' clothes was really up his street. The psychic also suggested it might happen anyway if he stuck about in Bath.

'Staying in Bath may endanger your health.'

Well, that much was true.

It was while Honey was shopping in Waitrose, replenishing her stock of comfort food, that she spotted a face she knew.

Karen Pinker was wearing civvies: a navy blue tracksuit, white trainers, and headband, her hair tied back in a ponytail.

She was in the company of another girl with coffee-coloured skin and dark red hair. The girl moved with catlike grace and she was wearing dark glasses. The sunlight outside didn't warrant it; the sky was grey and the sunbeams were fighting a losing battle.

With a wince of envy, Honey noted Karen's flawless complexion. At the sight of it she checked her own in the glass doors of the freezer cabinets.

Although glass doors enclosing bags of frozen peas and sausages couldn't complete with a proper mirror, she didn't think she looked too bad. The treatment might have helped of course. Either that or the sticky finger marks on the glass helped smudge the true picture.

Karen Pinker was handling a packet of reduced-fat turkey rashers. Honey made a mental note of the brand and resolved to purchase the same. Acquiring a svelte figure and flawless complexion had to be worked at.

Honey looked into her own shopping basket. The chocolate truffles looked guiltily back. Too late to put them back without Karen seeing her sin, she grabbed a large packet of rice cakes. They'd go back as soon as she'd completed her mission. Until then they totally obscured her chocolate temptation.

'Hi,' she said breezily. 'Fancy meeting you here.'

Caught off guard, Karen's face drained of colour. Either the pallor was due to sudden fear or she wasn't wearing any make-up. She exchanged a quick glance with her tall, elegant companion who was also dressed as though she'd just come from the gym.

Honey's eyes swept enviously over each trim frame. How many times had she promised her body that she would take it to the gym? Too many. Her body had always protested at her intentions. She took it from that that her body knew better than she did. Who was she to force the issue?

Karen Pinker was hesitant at first. Then her face kind of broke – like from reserved into acknowledgement.

'Mrs Driver, isn't it?'

'Honey. My real name's Hannah but everyone calls me Honey.'

Her husband Carl had called her Honey all the time as a term of endearment. The name had stuck. Carl hadn't. A sailing yacht, an all-girl crew, and an Atlantic storm had seen to that. Even without the storm they'd still have ended up on the rocks.

'Right,' said Karen.

Karen might have wanted their meeting to end there, but Honey couldn't allow that.

'I didn't see you before I left. I was going to ask you where my stuff was so I could hightail it out of there. The Botox was OK, but me and the mud didn't mix.'

'Sensible woman.'

The comment came from Karen's companion.

Karen looked at her disapprovingly. 'Magda, I don't think you should say any more. We did sign a confidentiality clause …'

'Stuff it. Stuff Serena Sarabande too. She must be sick in the head pandering to Dexter. Creeps, the pair of them.'

Magda?

Honey made a guess.

'You're the girl who discovered the body of Carlotta Macrottie?'

She looked surprised.

'Karen mentioned that you were the one who found the murdered woman. That must have been dreadful for you.'

The girl slid her sunglasses up on to her head amid the dark red hair. She had liquid brown eyes. Like Karen Pinker she was stunning, but with attitude. One long-fingered hand snaked on to her slender hip.

'So what?'

The old hotelier's built-in radar checked in. Magda was being defensive about something or someone.

Honey shrugged into her cool cotton blouse.

'It must have been a pretty grim experience.'

There was wickedness in Magda's seductive smile.

'Bad enough. Poor cow. All I could see was the top of her head.'

'So how come you left?'

'I got sacked. I told her I was fed up of being left alone to deal with six clients at a time. I told her it wasn't right and that

I would report her. She said, "Well you won't be doing it any more anyway. Get out." So I got out. Bitch!'

Honey commiserated. 'Poor you. I can't say I exactly warmed to that woman. Can't say the same about the doctor because I didn't meet him.'

'Just as well!' Magda exclaimed. 'He's a money-grabbing shit! Best steer clear, especially if you're middle-aged.'

Magda had all the mannerisms of an actress. It was possible that she was merely acting a part now. She might not hate Dr Dexter. It was difficult to tell.

Recognizing that this was the time to turn into an agony aunt, Honey shook her head. 'I picked up on the atmosphere. Bad vibes. Not surprising I suppose, seeing as someone was murdered there.'

Magda Church folded her arms. 'You bet there were bad vibes. Imagine how I felt when I found her.'

She jerked a thumb at her chest to emphasize the point.

Honey oozed sympathy. 'How terrible for you. Did you see the man who did it?'

'Magda …' Karen Pinker sounded nervous. She looked it too. A little wrinkle lifted her brows above her nose.

Magda Church was far from nervous. The defiance Honey had detected earlier remained. If Doherty was here he'd take full advantage and press home the advantage, thought Honey.

Doherty wasn't here to question Magda and Karen, but she was. It was all down to her.

'I'm telling you now,' said Magda, pointing her painted fingernail at the bony bit between Honey's breasts. 'No one else saw any scruffy tramp hanging around. Nobody except for Serena Sarabande.'

'That's strange.'

'You bet it is.'

'But the police believed her.'

'Ha!' Magda exclaimed. 'Get the picture, sister. When

124

Serena Sarabande flutters her eyelashes, the guys come running. She gives it like a bitch on heat.'

'Really? You think the officer handling the case fell for that?'

She knew damn well that Doherty had handled the case. He'd said nothing about any statuesque ice queen flashing her lashes at him – but then what red-blooded man would own up to it?

The cogs in her brain clanked over.

He didn't fall for it. He couldn't prove anything so he got you on the job!

That was why she was here, but she'd ask him anyway.

She hadn't liked Serena, true, but ice-cold types with perfect figures and cool demeanour got her that way. Stupid to be sidetracked but there it was. And what about this Dr Dexter? She'd only glimpsed him – thanks to a black bin liner that was doubling up as a quick-cut Honey Driver creation.

Magda's comment about him and middle-aged women itched something chronic – worse than the damned mud bath.

'Can you tell me what you meant about the doctor being dangerous to middle-aged women?'

Magda was nothing if not obliging. She really had it in for her ex-employers.

'Simple. Without middle-aged women worrying about their crows' feet and their sagging tits, there wouldn't be a clinic. It's them that need the most help.'

Honey sighed and rolled her eyes. She should have seen that coming.

'Point taken.'

Chapter Twenty-one

Doherty lived in a very nice apartment in Camden Crescent, the largest crescent in Bath, with a superior view of the city. Estate agents' particulars pontificated about the view in the vain hope that nobody registered that the Georgian builders had failed to provide garage space. Parking was roadside and at the peril of the car owner. Flexible wing mirrors that sprang back into place after being hit were far more than a matter of desirable design. In Camden Crescent they were a necessity if you didn't want to be sued for decapitation. Cars passing too close to those parked there meant that flying wing mirrors were a definite health hazard.

The estate agents were right about the views though; they were breathtaking.

On arrival at Camden Crescent, Honey scanned the road for a parking space. Car after car after car lined the kerb; it didn't look promising, but driving slowly with eyes peeled brought a result.

The sudden departure of a dark maroon Volvo left a decent space into which to manoeuvre her Citroen C3. Manoeuvring into any parking space took nerves of skill and reflexes only seen on centre court at Wimbledon. You had room to shunt backwards and forwards into the space left by a Volvo; not so if it had been a Honda Civic or a Ford Fiesta.

Aware that the driver of a car coming from the other direction looked as though he were scanning for space, she made a quick move. She braked hard. Too hard. As a consequence her large brown shoulder bag, her constant companion in her waking hours, fell off the front seat, its contents spilling on to the floor.

'Damn, damn, damn.'

Each individual utterance accompanied the throwing of tampons, a fold-up umbrella, a Greek dictionary, and other emergency supplies back into the bag. She was the epitome of a boy scout; be prepared. And she was.

A bit red in the face, she took a deep breath, carefully avoiding eye contact with the other driver. She knew his lips were moving. Whatever he was saying was silently cocooned within his own car. He drove off.

Once she was sure he was gone, she got out of the car, took a big breath of air, and stood looking at the view. Night time. Cool and dark and humming with sound.

The lights of the city below looked like stars that had fallen into a black pool – if you had the right imagination that is. Anyway, the lights were all she was going to get. No stars tonight. No moon either. Rain was forecast. The lack of stars and moon seconded that opinion.

The view from up here never failed to please. Glued to the grandeur of it all, she backed slowly on to the black and white tiled apron in front of the entrance to the building that housed Doherty's flat.

'Lovely,' she breathed.

Light flooded out as the door behind her opened. Doherty slung an arm around her shoulders and guided her backwards.

'Are you going to come in or are you camping out?'

He could be so domineering at times; enticingly so, though he knew his limitations of course.

'I could be camping out permanently if that hotel inspector is found to have died from food poisoning. It's not good for business.'

128

'He didn't and he wasn't,' said Doherty as he manfully manoeuvred into his flat, closing the door firmly behind them with a sound kick. 'He died of natural causes.'

'Great.' Her spirits soared. Shoulder bag was whipped off her shoulder and mouths met.

'Not for him,' murmured Doherty, his lips on her mouth, one arm around her, and his fingers unbuttoning her shirt.

'No. I mean.' She took a breath, mouthing each statement between kisses. 'The poor man.' Another kiss. 'Fancy going about your job ...' Another kiss. Hotter this time. Tongues were touching. Nerve ends were tingling. 'Off to bed for a good night's ...' Her eyes closed.

'He wasn't a hotel inspector.'

'Great.'

The bedroom was looming up over Doherty's shoulder and although it did interfere with her concentration, she was hearing what Doherty was saying.

'David Carpenter wasn't his real name.'

'Is that so?'

It wouldn't be the first time someone had booked in under an assumed name.

'It is.' Doherty had the same problem with talking. At the same time his fingers were beneath the thin straps of her bra, easing them off her shoulders. She was doing better, pulling his T-shirt up from his waistband – but there, it was accepted as scientific fact that men were useless at multitasking.

He carried on anyway. It amused her and she loved him for it. The shivers went straight to where he'd shortly be going.

'At least,' – they kissed – 'we know how he died.' Another kiss, or more accurately taking on from where the one before had left off. 'His name wasn't David Carpenter and he wasn't a hotel inspector.' He said it quickly so the kissing and unbuttoning could recommence.

'If he wasn't a hotel inspector, who was he?'

129

'I've just told you. He wasn't even David Carpenter.'

Doherty was doing some very delicious things between each sentence. Licking her ear lobe was one of them, but she knew he wouldn't linger there. She had more interesting areas to offer. Never mind her toes curling up, someone could have used her nipples as coat hooks!

'Ummm,' she moaned. 'You certainly know your stuff.'

'I'm a good cop.'

'That wasn't what I was referring to.'

At the same time as all this was happening, Doherty was guiding her swiftly backwards in the general direction of the bedroom.

She managed a question at the same time as shrugging her shirt off her shoulders.

'So who was he – this hotel inspector who wasn't a hotel inspector?'

'A man named Mandril. A private investigator.'

Honey leaned back against Doherty's arms, which were presently entwined around her.

'I get the feeling there's more.'

'He's of dubious reputation.'

'More?' She purposely kept him at arm's length while still leaning against his enclosed arms, the only thing that kept her from falling backwards.

'He's dangerous.'

There was no way she was going to hold out against Doherty's superior strength – and her own inclinations – for too long.

'What does that mean?'

She lisped her question out of necessity by virtue of the fact that Doherty's tongue was laying heavy on hers.

'It means he's been known to use physical violence.'

Doherty didn't elucidate, by virtue of the fact that he was determined to find out if absence did make the heart grow

130

fonder – and the erogenous zones hyperactive.

She was wrapped in his arms and she liked his arms. They were only hairy on the forearms. His chest had a smattering of hair; just enough to remind her that he was a man, but not enough to believe she was being smothered by a grizzly bear.

When it was all over, she eventually got round to staring at the ceiling, a pastime incredibly beneficial to the solving of everyday crime.

Evidence and clues from all over the place seemed to come together when you were staring at the ceiling. Little titbits of information also came to the fore – like who the hell was Mandril and what the hell had he been doing at her hotel.

'You haven't told me,' she exclaimed.

Doherty, who had been snoring gently, came half way to full wakefulness.

'What? Oh, it was great. Have I ever told you that you've got the cutest rear and the best handful of breast that –'

'That's not what I mean. I mean this bloke Mandril. What was he doing at my hotel?'

Doherty snuggled his face against her shoulder and groaned. 'Can we forget work for two seconds?'

She elbowed him away. 'You've had your two seconds.'

He pulled a little-boy-hurt face. 'That's insulting.'

She cupped his jaw with one hand and gave him a peck on the mouth. 'That wasn't what I meant and you know it. I just wondered what he was doing at my place.'

'Well he wasn't inspecting the toilet bowls. And he didn't say he was a hotel inspector, did he?'

Honey frowned and returned to lying on her back staring at the ceiling. 'No, but then they never do. They book a room like normal folk, sign in, eat in the restaurant in the evening, and take a full English breakfast in the morning.'

'Sounds good.'

'They're very particular about sausages and whether the

131

eggs are free range or battery farmed. They like the bacon to be prime back; none of that rubbishy streaky stuff.'

'Sounds even better.'

Honey puffed out her cheeks. 'I should have been there.'

'You had a job to do, Honey. And much appreciated it was.'

He smoothed her hair over where he'd kissed her on the top of her head.

'Thanks. Lindsey thought he was the hotel inspector because his eyes seemed to be everywhere and he wanted to know how long she'd been employed there. He asked her if she liked working there. So if he wasn't a hotel inspector, what was he doing there? What did he want to know?'

Though it pained him to do so, Doherty stopped trying to re-arouse her passions. Folding his arms beneath his head, he too turned on to his back and stared at the ceiling.

'We don't know what he was doing there.'

She breathed in the smell of him, wondering if armpits were the main storage area of testosterone; just the right amount to turn her on.

She was just contemplating the possibility of responding to further approaches on his part when her mobile phone chose that moment to belt out 'Bohemian Rhapsody'.

She swung her legs over the side of the bed. 'Damn. I forgot to turn it off.'

He reached out. She felt his fingers brush down the curve of her spine. 'You don't have to answer it.'

'It might be important.'

'It might not be.'

'That depends on your point of view.'

There was a slight pause. 'I like the view I'm getting from here.'

She knew very well that he was regarding her posterior as she bent over her bag, got out her phone, and checked the number.

She mouthed the words 'my mother' over her shoulder.

Doherty grimaced and pulled the bedclothes over his head.

'Mother! How are you?'

'Where are you?'

Fired back at machine-gun speed, the question was laced with suspicion.

'At Sandy's.'

She crossed her fingers behind her back. Lying was preferable to the third degree. Her mother might just believe her. Sandy was an old friend whose shoulder she'd cried on in the aftermath of Carl's demise.

'Don't lie to me, Hannah.'

Her mother's voice brought to mind a snapping turtle she'd once seen in a zoo. Its mouth had opened and closed at breakneck speed – for a turtle.

Honey made eye contact with Doherty. His eyes were the only thing she could see above the bedclothes.

'I think my mother's psychic,' she offered, her hand pressed firmly over the mouthpiece.

'She's a witch,' muttered Doherty.

Both observations might just be right.

There was nothing for it but to come clean about her relationship and the current state of play.

'OK. I'm with Doherty. I'm staying here tonight. I stay here quite often. I need the rest.'

'You're resting?'

The tone of her voice said it all. Rest didn't come into it. A certain amount of exertion did; it certainly beat the gym.

'It's nice here. There's a great view.'

The response was growled. 'What of?'

'The city. Of course.'

'Hannah! You are entangled with a policeman. Do I really need to tell you that he's got little to offer you?'

Honey chewed her lips around. Her mother was talking of

133

material things, i.e. great pad, great car, great money. Her priorities were somewhat different. Did Doherty measure up to those priorities? You bet he did!

'We're fine,' Honey offered, but her mother was having none of it. Even though Honey was the wrong side of forty, her mother couldn't help wanting to shoehorn her into the life she thought she should fit. Her next move would be predictable; Honey prepared herself for what she knew was coming.

'Well I think you can do better. There's someone I want you to meet. Be at my place for tea tomorrow at four. Without fail!'

Honey was wise enough to know that her mother was demanding she come alone. Doherty wasn't invited, that much was for sure. He never would be. Steve and her mother didn't like each other and neither made a secret of the fact.

Doherty came out from beneath the bedclothes, which he pushed down to his waist. His chest looked inviting; somewhere to cushion her head.

'I take it she didn't care much for your sleeping arrangements.'

Honey managed a smile. 'I like them.'

'But she doesn't.'

'She's invited me round tomorrow for tea. I think she intends giving me a good talking to about sharing a bed with unsuitable men.'

She couldn't help the smile as she bent down to put the phone back into her bag, her backside turned towards him.

When she turned round, Doherty's grin was laced with something more than humour.

'So! Will you be Mummy's best little girl and take on board all that she says?'

Honey climbed back into bed, crawling up over his body which was still hidden beneath the bedclothes.

Her hair fell over their faces as she kissed him.

'I think I've grown out of being Mummy's good little girl. I kind of like being Steve Doherty's naughty little girl.'

He beamed. 'You do. Well, Honey Driver, that suits me very well. Very well indeed.'

Chapter Twenty-two

Her mother had a very nice apartment in the centre of town, which meant she could swan around to her heart's content without having to drive. She preferred to be chauffeured around and when there wasn't anyone to chauffeur her, she took a taxi. Simple.

Honey walked there. Mary Jane had offered to give her a lift and although it would have been interesting to hear more about her night at the psychic fair with Clint in high heels, she resisted. Having to cope with her mother's matchmaking and Mary Jane's driving was just too much to handle in one day.

Matchmaking was definitely what her mother was up to. She'd said four o'clock and it was now six. Honey had deliberately come late. Whoever her mother thought to fix her up with had probably got tired of waiting and gone home by now. But nothing was definite. She needed to be on her toes.

She could tell the moment she walked into her mother's living room with its French chateau curtains and silk cushions that her ruse appeared to have worked.

'Hannah! You will always miss the best opportunities. You disappoint me.'

Mumbling her apologies did nothing to alleviate her mother's tight jawline. All was explained through gnashing teeth. The would-be suitor had left – not for home but for a game of golf with his friends from work. Apparently he was a civil servant and had been for over twenty years, working at the same desk in the same office.

'So rare nowadays for a man to have a job for life,' her mother exclaimed.

Behind her mother's back, Honey raised her eyes to heaven and thanked whoever happened to be her guardian angel. It had been a close-run thing. Tea time would have been torture, having to make conversation with someone whose life batted between a desk and a golf course.

Gloria Cross wore a lipstick that matched her outfit. Her hair was beautifully shiny and her make-up was impeccable. Her jewellery was Christian Dior and very collectable. For a seventy-odd-year-old she shone; even if she'd been younger she would still have outclassed her daughter. But Honey was used to it, just as she was used to the petulant pink lips and the anger in her mother's eyes.

'I laid this on specially.'

Honey resigned herself to the fact that her mother would take days to get over this. Everything in the room was so perfect. Even the air seemed quite refined. The furniture was polished, the silk cushions arranged on the diagonal so that each point faced in the same direction as the cushion next to it. The best china had been laid out and Gloria Cross looked a dream in pale green chiffon with a cropped silk jacket.

Just in case said man had still been there, Honey had gone out of her way to look unappealing. She'd stuck to a pair of scuffed jeans, a black sweater, and a pop art waistcoat with 'Don't you think I'm sexy' printed across the back and embellished in sequins. High fashion it was not. She'd also scraped her hair back into an elastic band at the nape of her neck. Elastic band and printed slogan contradicted each other in that elastic bands had never been sexy. She supposed it depended on what you did with them, but she wasn't kinky like that.

'You're looking wonderful, Mother. It's a wonder he didn't

ask you out, never mind your dull, dowdy daughter.'

Her mother didn't rise to the flattery. She was in severe sulking mode. The crockery and tray of clotted cream and strawberry jam were being bundled on to a tray heading for the kitchen.

Her mother's mouth was screwed up into a mean little moue and her narrowed eyes glittered with fury.

'Sorry. I got held up,' said Honey.

The guilt caught up with her. She made an attempt to make amends. 'Don't I even get a cup of tea and a cream scone?'

Slamming the tray down in the kitchen, Gloria Cross turned to face her.

'Hannah! I do my best for you. I only do what I feel is in your best interests. Malcolm Piper would have been the ideal man for you, a kind, honest, hardworking man who would have looked after you. If you'd played your cards right you could have been wife number four ...'

'He's had three already?'

Her mother was dismissive. 'Unfortunate circumstances.'

'They died?'

'Drowned.'

Honey gulped. 'All of them?'

'It was unfortunate, but yes. All of them drowned.'

'It wouldn't have been in a bath by any chance?'

Her mother looked at her as though she'd taken leave of her senses. 'Of course not. One had dizzy spells. She fell into a puddle. The other got cramps while swimming in the sea. I think the third fell into a canal.'

'Great. If I get involved with him I'll remember to stay away from water.'

'You're being facetious.'

'No. I have a strong survival instinct.' She frowned. 'Were the police involved in any of the deaths?'

'Of course not! He was just unfortunate.'

139

The afternoon had soured so there was no point lingering. Throwing her bag over her shoulder and stripping the elastic band from her hair, she strolled back through the city, feeling a little lighter in some respects and a little guilty in others. Her mother really did have her best interests at heart but couldn't bear to think that she had her own opinions – and her own tastes in men.

Although it was beginning to rain, she didn't mind that much. Her slip-on shoes were getting wet because she was purposely walking through puddles, but she really didn't mind.

Hard it might be, but running her own business, her own hotel in one of the most beautiful cities in the world, was very satisfying. OK, she wasn't making big bucks, but that didn't matter. She was independent and that *did* matter.

The sound of a car horn made her jump. A car was sliding into the kerb beside her. She was quite used to people she knew pulling up and offering her a lift.

With a ready smile, she turned round to see who it was. She didn't recognize the car. Neither did she register the passenger or the driver.

The passenger window slid silently open.

'Would you like a lift?'

His teeth sizzled with whiteness, his features finely chiselled. She tried to think whether she had seen either him or the car before. It just didn't register. The car was a blue Bentley. She definitely did not know that many people with a Bentley. Only Casper, she thought. I'm sure he's got one.

The man behind the wheel leaned across. 'I'm sure I'm going your way.'

She knew him! She definitely knew him. But from where? It occurred to her that this might be the man her mother had been trying to fix her up with. She should be safe enough if that was the case and might have got in if a pink Cadillac coupé hadn't driven in behind the Bentley.

Mary Jane was waving to her.

The rain got heavier.

She straightened. 'My friend's here,' she said to the man in the Bentley. Before he could make comment she was sliding on to the white leather passenger seat of Mary Jane's car.

The first thing she did after fastening the seat belt was to say a silent prayer to the god of road traffic accidents. Mary Jane was a kind friend but had to be the lousiest driver in Bath.

'Who was that guy?' asked Mary Jane.

'He might be a suitor for my hand in marriage.'

'Really? He looked a dish!'

Mary Jane was all feverish interest, her old eyes shining, perhaps with a few memories of her own.

'Did he?'

'He did too. My instincts tell me he was Italian.'

Honey viewed her with surprise. 'My, I didn't know psychics could pinpoint nationality.'

'Oh, nothing to do with that. It was the plates. They were Italian. Sicilian more likely. Syracuse, I think.'

Honey slid down into the seat, her eyes shifting nervously from side to side. The Bentley hadn't come along by chance. It had probably followed her to her mother's house, stopped outside, and waited for her to come out.

'Did he offer you a lift?'

'Yes.'

'It could have been fun.'

'I don't think so, Mary Jane. I think it was one of the guys who want to cut off Clint's assets.'

The car swerved. 'Oh, dear. Do you think he might have hurt you?'

Honey swallowed and closed her eyes. She could have answered yes, he might have hurt her. On the other hand a worrying answer might make Mary Jane swerve again – which could be just as dangerous and far more immediate.

141

Chapter Twenty-three

'So, David Carpenter was not David Carpenter. He was this guy Mandril.'

'Yes.' Doherty was curt. He wasn't looking at her, he wasn't being forthcoming. The obvious conclusion was that he had no wish to be reminded of work. 'The wine looks good.'

They were at the Assembly Rooms, attending the wine tasting for which Casper had borrowed the Victorian table centrepiece.

Hoteliers and restaurateurs had travelled into the city from miles around, lured by the promise of free booze and an evening away from grumbling guests and bolshie staff.

The company doing the honours this evening represented the very best South Australia's wine growers had to offer. Realizing they were catering to the professionals, the people behind the bar were pouring generous measures which were quaffed, tasted, and swallowed. Nobody suggested they spit out between each measure, besides which no receptacles had been provided in which to spit. Obviously the merchants and wine growers knew their market well. The professionals of the hospitality trade could handle their drink.

Honey definitely detected a holiday atmosphere, or at least that of a good night out. She'd dressed accordingly and thought she looked particularly fetching in a little black dress. Doherty was unchanged in fashion savvy, sticking firmly to smart casual. He didn't do tux and ties. 'Not good for my street cred,

Hon,' he'd said sagely.

Tarts and toffs had frequented the Assembly Rooms from the moment it was built, back when men wore britches and women swooned at the thought of their assets.

Overhead the chandeliers sparkled from high ceilings of elaborate plasterwork. The room was bright with light and hummed with conversation.

A circlet of tables had been set up in the centre of the room, surrounding a brace of barmen. Glasses and glossy bottles of amber and blood-red wine sat on silver trays, which in turn sat on sparkling white cloths.

Forming a backdrop to the barmen was a kind of tiered wedding cake arrangement formed by placing one small round table on top of a larger one. Both were covered in crisp white linen. At the very summit, instead of a bride and groom, perched Honey's very own gleaming glass epergne, a large affair that she'd bought from the local auction room.

Perched was a worrying word. It certainly worried her.

'I paid five hundred pounds for that. I hope Casper's got it insured,' she murmured.

Doherty didn't appear to hear what she said. He was too busy getting into the spirit of the occasion.

'Was that a Shiraz I had just now? Can I have another?'

Honey nodded at the waiter. 'Give him another of whatever it was he had just now.'

The waiter was sniffy. 'It's only one tasting per person from each vintage.'

She asked the obvious question. 'Will it make a difference if I buy a case?'

The obvious answer came back. 'OK.'

The waiter poured. Doherty swirled, sniffed, and finally sipped his second glass of Shiraz.

'Very nice.'

Honey cradled her glass while fixing her eyes on him. She

144

detected some reluctance to discuss the subject of David Carpenter further and she didn't really know why – which made her all the more determined.

'So why was Mandril at my place?'

'This is very nice,' he said, slurping before swilling the wine around his mouth.

'You're being evasive.'

He laughed, sipped, and shook his head all at the same time.

Honey wasn't fooled. There was something he didn't want to tell her. A sudden flash of worst-case scenario caused her to take a pot shot at what it might be.

'He was there to kill me? My God! That's what he was there for!'

'No.'

He said it in a way that she didn't quite believe. Doherty was a policeman, man being the optimum word. He knew how to lie.

He didn't meet her eyes but appeared to be surveying the gathered throng, smiling stupidly at people he didn't even know.

'They'll think you're a gatecrasher.'

'What?'

'Grinning at people like that.'

'Just being friendly.'

'Was Mandril just being friendly? Had he come round to say, "Howdy, I'm a dangerous man and I want to know you better"?'

'Don't be silly. Mandril isn't – wasn't – the sort to do something for no reason – or for nothing.'

'Do you want to elaborate on that?'

Tipping his head back, Doherty studied the big bright chandeliers with one eye closed.

Honey knew that look. She might get the truth or there again she might not. Doherty always took on that kind of look

145

when he was weighing up the odds. It was up to her to push it.

'OK,' she said, jumping in at the deep end. 'Let me put my psychic hat on.'

Glass clutched in one hand, she fanned her fingers around the sides of her head and closed her eyes.

He looked at her with a mix of surprise and wry amusement. 'Come on, Honey. You're joking. Right?'

She made a funny humming noise that seemed appropriate to what she was doing.

Doherty was taken in. 'Can you really do psychic?'

He sounded sceptical. Well, she could go along with that. Everyone had a right to their own beliefs.

'Silence. I'm going into mind-reading mode. I need to bring all my faculties to bear.'

'Honey, you're freaking me out. I don't believe you can do this. And since when?'

'Mary Jane taught me. She reckons I'm a natural sensitive.'

That clinched it. He snorted with laughter.

'You?'

'Why not me?'

The laughter continued to rumble. 'Look, I've had enough psychics march into the station offering me their services to know the score. They all say that it's a gift – you've either got it or you haven't. And I don't think you have,' he said, kissing her on the forehead while tickling her ear with his pinky.

He was being evasive about Mandril and it was winding her up.

'The mind can be trained,' she stated firmly.

He smirked. 'Go on then. Tell me what I'm thinking.'

'OK.'

She made a serious face, her eyes still closed.

'Right. The spirits are coming through. I'm getting messages here, but I really don't need them. I'm so in tune with the vibes I'm getting a reading all by myself.'

146

'Go on then. Tell me.'

'Right. Right! It's coming through now. You, Steve Doherty, are thinking that we might round off the evening with a nice meal at your place and be safely tucked up in bed by the witching hour.'

'Am I that predictable?'

'Yep.'

'I'll make everything up to you. I promise.'

Honey's eyes flashed open. 'Aha! So you've done something for which you need to make amends.'

He eyed her quizzically, that 'I think I've just been rumbled' look on his face.

She fixed him with a piercing glare. 'You are now going to tell me something that I won't like. True?'

'Ah!'

She snatched his wine glass away. 'Cough up, buster. Was Mandril at my place looking for Clint or not?'

He sniffed. 'I can get another glass. I'll try the white.'

Honey formed a barrier, which basically meant nuzzling tight up against him. Even a glass of Chardonnay wouldn't tempt him to forego that experience.

'Look into my eyes.'

He looked.

She saw the wavering before he finally broke.

'Mandril does – sorry – did private detective work and he wasn't looking for Clint. We've been through his case notes. He was working for the beauty clinic.'

'The Beauty Spot?'

'That's who was paying him. I think he was there asking questions about you because you had been asking questions at the clinic and they were suspicious.'

'My! How badly did I rattle their cage?''

She was shocked. Her impression had been that she hadn't found out very much at all, now it appeared as though she

147

might have. But what? Surely not the fact that Dr Dexter and Serena Sarabande were having an affair? No. Something else had been going on there and she'd stumbled on it without knowing she had. But what?

She asked Doherty if he suspected something really serious was going down there.

'Could be. We're not sure. Not yet, but we're reopening the case of the woman with the lesions – Miss Pansy Porter. The fire department record makes interesting reading. Flour is combustible. Did you know that? That was how the Great Fire of London started in Pudding Lane.'

'So I hear.'

Her eyes were wide open now. She saw the guilty look on Doherty's face. In her mind she was seeing her hotel going up in flames. If Mandril – the man booked in as David Carpenter – hadn't died, would her place have gone up in flames?

Doherty caught the worried look on her face. He ran his fingers down her cheek.

'Honestly, Honey, if I'd thought sending you there was going to be dangerous …'

'Did he have a box of matches in his luggage?'

Doherty shrugged. 'I'm not sure …'

'I think I'm about to resign my post as Crime Liaison Officer. Casper will be here tonight. I think I'll suggest he finds someone else.'

'He might not have been there to burn the place down. He might just have been checking things out …'

'Prior to throwing a match in …'

'You're being melodramatic.'

'No,' she said shaking her finger, her whole body feeling as wobbly as jelly. 'My mother is melodramatic. I am *never* melodramatic. Just scared.'

The shivers resulting from thoughts of what might have happened ran like iced water down her spine. None of the crimes she'd dealt with so far had ever come home to roost. Crime and murder had stayed firmly outside the door – until now.

The body inside the little black dress kept shivering. She wished she was wearing a fleece rather than the low-cut number with the string straps.

'I'm covered in goose pimples. I can't believe he was in the Green River – basically in my home and asking questions of my family.'

Doherty snaked his arm around her. 'I wouldn't have asked you to go there if I'd known. Please forgive me.' He paused. 'You do forgive me, don't you?'

She nodded. 'I went willingly.'

'And did a good job. You obviously hit the right buttons.'

She shrugged. 'The damage is done. Strange though. I didn't go overboard. Mostly I asked Karen Perfect.'

'Who?'

'Karen Pinker.'

'That would do it.'

'It certainly must have done. They fired her.'

Honey frowned. She noticed Steve Doherty was frowning too and guessed they were thinking the same thing.

She voiced her conclusion. 'They must have something very big and bad to hide. Something a bit dodgier than colonic irrigation.'

'What's that when it's at home?'

'Bottom in the air and long plastic tube. Get the picture?'

'I wish I hadn't asked.'

She was suddenly distracted by a figure she thought vaguely familiar. The man was tall with sleek dark hair. If he wasn't an actor of some sort then he should be. He had presence, a strong jaw, and was wearing a white dinner jacket.

He glanced in her direction, looked away, then back again. A slight smile twitched at his lips.

149

Honey felt her face burning. She'd been wearing a small towel and a black rubbish bag when she'd last seen him – only a brief glance but enough to take in the details.

Doherty noticed.

'Anyone I should know?'

'The doctor at the clinic. I only glimpsed him …'

'Was that when you were wearing … correction … not wearing the teeny weeny towel?'

She nodded.

'He remembered your face. I suppose that's something.'

'Thanks.'

Doherty was not bashful about the predicament she'd described to him. He wasn't jealous either. He suggested it might be a good idea if she were to re-enact the scene in private. The thought was tempting. She declined for now but promised she might indulge his fantasy at a later date.

It wasn't easy, but she set her mind back on track. 'I take it you interviewed him after the murder?'

'Of course I did. His alibi checked out.'

Honey flung back her head and closed her eyes. 'Don't tell me! Serena Sarabande said he was with her.'

'How did you guess?'

She suddenly had a thought. 'Was she with him tonight?'

'Tonight? It was a woman. Not Ms Sarabande though. A dark-haired woman. Quite pretty.'

'Hmm,' Honey grumbled. 'She has to be a hotelier or from the tourist board or something.'

Although the wine tasting was ostensibly for those that purchased wine, some others were invited along as a matter of course. Councillors rubbed shoulders with bank managers, accountants, and solicitors. Anyone deemed to be worthy of the upper-crust social scene in fact.

'What colour dress was she wearing?'

Doherty looked vague. 'A dress. Right.'

Probably black, thought Honey, which means we're on a hiding to nothing. Doherty was still searching his memory banks. Why was it men didn't notice what colour dress a woman was wearing but would notice the colour of her underwear?

'Pink,' he said suddenly.

'Are you sure?'

'Sure. It could have been his wife.'

'I didn't know he was married.'

'If what you say is true, then Dr Dexter is definitely playing away from home – if what you say is true.'

She fixed him with a knowing look. 'Believe me, it's true. I'm experienced enough to know an orgasmic note when I hear one.'

'It takes one to know one.'

Ignoring the wicked twinkle, Honey slugged back some wine. 'This makes me feel a little paranoid. Do you think they'll send someone else to spy on me?'

He shook his head. His eyes were everywhere as he spoke. He couldn't help it. Observing people was second nature.

'I doubt it.'

'Good. I'm paranoid enough as it is. I thought it might be him who tried to pick me up the other day in a blue Bentley, but it wasn't.'

'Is that so?'

Doherty wasn't prone to jealousy – or so he'd told her – but she felt his look.

'Whoops!'

'What have you done?'

She batted her eyes innocently. 'Nothing. What do you mean?'

'You always say "whoops" when something suddenly comes to you that might involve trouble. Do you have something to tell me?'

151

'We … ll … I was just thinking that I might have been followed here tonight.'

'By him?'

Doherty's eyes searched the venue even though he'd seen Dexter leave.

'Nothing to do with the doctor. It's about Clint. He's being threatened.'

'What's he done?'

Doherty showed no sign of surprise at Clint being in trouble, but then, he wouldn't. Clint was as well known at Manvers Street Police Station as he was at the Sunday market in the nearby city of Bristol where he ran a beads, seeds, and incense stall.

Honey told him about Clint falling in love with the nude model at his life drawing class.

'It turns out that she was Luigi Benici's wife.'

'Bloody hell!'

It wasn't very often that Doherty expressed surprise at any of Honey's acquaintances or adventures. She fancied his brain was compiling a police record sheet listing things he knew about Luigi Benici.

'Mr Benici threatened to deal with Clint in such a way that he'd never seduce anybody else's wife – well – anybody else at all come to that. Do you get what that means?'

Doherty nodded. 'Knowing Benici he's threatening castration without an anaesthetic. Is Clint really that stupid?'

She nodded. 'Possibly. Apparently her husband didn't know about the posing for the art class. He's the old-fashioned type and she wanted her own piece of independence.'

'Sounds as though she ended up getting more than she bargained for.'

'It gets worse. She's pregnant.'

Doherty threw his head back and blurted out a whole string of expletives. Basically they meant that Clint could end up as the main ingredient of a bolognaise sauce.

'I take it he's skipped his responsibilities.'

'It seemed a good idea for the girl – Gabriella – to tell her old man that the kid was his. But he has his doubts, hence they're still out looking for Clint in order to extract confirmation – as well as revenge. And yes, you're right. He did skip his responsibilities and I – correction – we helped him to get out of town.'

'How?'

He looked pensive. Doherty always got a bit concerned about the legalities of some of Honey's actions. She put him straight.

'Nothing to worry about. Mary Jane sneaked him out of town in her car.'

'A death-defying event in itself,' mused Doherty, hardly able to control his amusement.

She liked the way one side of his mouth curled up into a smile while the other side tried to stay serious. It wasn't easy, but she forced herself to keep her mind on the job.

'So the blue Bentley could be tailing me with a view to discovering Clint's whereabouts.'

'I'll put a tail on the tail.'

He fixed it up there and then.

'I'm grateful,' she said to him. 'I'll prove how much later.'

'Good idea. And afterwards we can make plans. A day out. We can start with a visit to Ms Pansy Porter's partner.'

Chapter Twenty-four

Built in the days before the railways, the Kennet and Avon Canal had been the M4 motorway of its day as far as heavy goods traffic was concerned.

At one time it had wound alongside the river through the Avon Valley like a strip of silver silk. The railway chose the same route later. Now all three wound through together.

So far the proposed road link connecting the city of Bath to the docks at Southampton had not further blighted the valley. If it ever did come the road would go underground.

Jocelyn Trinder, cohabiting partner of the deceased Pansy Porter, lived on a narrowboat. Along with many other live-aboards, the vessel was moored on the Kennet and Avon Canal.

Doherty informed Honey that the vessel was called *Gypsy*.

The weather was cold but the sky was clear. The grass lining the towpath was wet, the taller plants decorated with spiders' webs that sparkled in the weak winter sun.

A pair of ducks dashed for the water at their approach, making a soft plopping sound as they hit the surface before paddling away.

Gypsy was long and green. A ginger cat stretched languorously around a metal chimney. A finger of what looked like steam or smoke stretched upwards.

The narrowboats used to carry massive loads in the days before the railways. The boatmen (never to be called bargees) and their families had lived at one end of the boat, a tiny area barely measuring eight feet by eight. Nowadays the whole boat was given over to living accommodation, fitted out with space saving in mind.

People were attracted to living on them because not only were they cheap to run, they were often moored in attractive places within walking distance of a town or city centre.

Doherty leaned over and knocked on the roof.

'There's a door,' Honey observed and made as if to go aboard.

Doherty stopped her.

'It's not done to go aboard a vessel without the skipper's permission,' he told her.

She jutted her chin in a nod. 'OK. So you knock on the roof.'

She'd expected someone living on a narrowboat to be of a hippy persuasion, complete with dreadlocks, nose piercing, and a haphazard look to his eyes. Jocelyn Trinder was far from that. He looked like a retired businessman. His hair was white, his skull was pink, and a black cigarillo jiggled from one corner of his mouth.

'You all right?' he asked in a northern accent which Honey presumed was Yorkshire, though it could just as easily have been Lancashire. Her ears weren't that well tuned to northern dialects – especially people who came from Tyne and Wear, whom she couldn't understand at all.

'Thank you for agreeing to see us. Sorry it's so early.'

Doherty had checked the file for Jocelyn's mobile phone number to ask if they could come. He'd thought it might be too early, but Jocelyn had been up and about. Apparently he always was.

'Don't sleep much when you're older,' he said with a grin. His eyes strayed to Honey and suddenly twinkled. 'Don't sleep much when you're younger either – but for different reasons.'

Her cheeks were already pink from the morning chill, so a

little blushing wouldn't be noticed.

'Come aboard,' said Jocelyn, with a wave of his hand. 'Coffee's on the job. Do you fancy breakfast?'

The smell of grilled bacon wafted out into the morning air.

Honey's stomach rumbled. 'Well, actually …'

'We could murder a bacon butty – if you can spare it that is.'

Despite running on nothing more than a sip of fruit juice and half a slice of cold toast, Honey had been about to refuse. Doherty hadn't given her the chance, so it was all his fault if she put on a few excess pounds. At least that's what she told herself. After all this fresh air, grilled bacon and fresh coffee wouldn't go amiss.

Inside the boat was warm and welcoming, a place of light oak fitments, comfortable seating, and all mod cons. A plasma screen was fitted on to one wall opposite white leather seating. The interior had nothing in common with the boats of old except that it was still narrow.

A laptop computer winked from a fitted desk behind which were fitted bookshelves.

He led them through to the kitchen, inviting them to sit around a wall-mounted kitchen table that folded easily away when not in use. The chairs were of chrome and stylish light oak.

'Take the weight off your feet and I'll be mother.' With a nod of his head he indicated the table and chairs.

Doherty and Honey sat down, Honey undoing the zip of her jacket. The interior warmth was in total contrast to the chill outside.

'Mr Trinder,' Doherty began.

'Call me Joss,' said Jocelyn, while slicing fresh bread which he proceeded to layer with rashers of crisp, hot bacon. 'Here you are.'

He placed a round of bacon sandwiches before each of

them, plus mugs of steaming hot coffee.

Seeing as it was difficult to speak while munching and drinking, no questions got asked until they were done.

'More coffee?' asked Joss.

Doherty nodded.

Honey held up her hand. 'I'd love one, but then I'd need to use the bathroom.'

'It's along there when you're ready,' Joss told her. 'Pansy used to be like that. When we travelled anywhere the first thing she had to know was the whereabouts of the lavatory.'

'It's psychological,' replied Honey, feeling immediate empathy with the burned-to-a-crisp Pansy Porter.

'That's what Pansy used to say.'

He poured her a second cup.

Bacon butties duly consumed, they were about to get down to serious business. Honey could tell that Doherty was considering his words carefully. He'd had another look at the report from the fire brigade. There was no outright proof that arson may have caused the blaze, but it couldn't be entirely discounted. Unproven, as he'd said to Honey. Nothing was definite.

'You know the fire brigade were not entirely sure about the blaze.'

Joss nodded and although earlier he'd been cheeky to her, Honey noticed his eyes turn from twinkling to sad at mention of the fire and his partner's death.

'I still can't believe it.' He shook his head mournfully. 'Me and Pansy had plans. We'd been going to sell the flat, buy ourselves a boat, and sail away into the sunset.'

'Wow,' said Honey. 'Not many women would give up their home to do that.'

Doherty looked surprised. 'Why?'

'Women are natural nest builders. Nests get built on land, not on the sea.'

He didn't look convinced. He didn't get the difference.

'To some extent you're right, petal,' said Joss. 'Funnily enough it was my Pansy that wanted to sell up and sail away. I was keener to buy one of these.' He gestured at their comfortable surroundings. 'I kept telling her that I was getting older and chuffing up and down a canal suited me better than hoisting up sails and such like.'

'It must have cost a pretty penny,' said Doherty, his eyes sweeping over their smart surroundings.

'Thanks to the insurance money,' sighed Joss. 'I wasn't keen on rebuilding, so I took the money and placed the property at auction. Only thing you can do with a burned-out shell. So I bought the *Gypsy*. Had her built from new. She wouldn't suit everyone but she suits me.'

'So as regards Pansy. What was the point of her going to The Beauty Spot?'

'She wanted to look twenty years younger like them programmes on television. I told her she didn't need anything like that, but she was dead set on doing it. We had a row about it. I don't like mucking about with nature, me. Be satisfied with what you got. That's my motto.'

The bacon sandwich was lying a bit heavy. Honey was afraid that if she opened her mouth she'd burp, so she left the questioning to Doherty.

He was frowning policeman-style, his hands clasped tightly together on the table between his body and the empty plate.

'You said you hadn't realized that she'd be at the clinic for so long. How long was it?'

'About four weeks.'

'Four weeks?'

Honey couldn't help it. She burped. 'Pardon me.'

'Granted. Now let me see,' said Joss as he lit up a second cigarillo. 'She said she'd be there for at least two weeks, which I thought was a pretty long time for all that stuff. I didn't

159

realize it would stretch to four.'

Doherty had a way of freezing when he thought he was on to something. Honey thought she knew what it was; according to Jocelyn Trinder's original statement he'd said she was away for two weeks and hadn't expected it to be that long. Now he was saying she'd been away for four weeks.

He pointed it out to him.

Honey waited for a look of unease to appear on Jocelyn's face. It didn't. He pulled the cigarillo from the side of his mouth, slid back the window, and discarded both the smoke from his mouth and the ash from the end of the cigarillo.

'I was away for two weeks just before the two weeks she said she'd be away. It's only recently I found out from one of her mates that she'd been away for a whole month.'

Honey chanced another burp. She was that intrigued. 'A month? But no one stays at a beauty clinic for a month?'

Doherty interjected. 'Do you know for sure that she was at the clinic all that time?'

'They said she was.'

Recalling Serena's information on plastic surgery and Venezuela, Honey's brain was going into overdrive. 'What did she look like when you came back from being away?'

Joss flicked more ash and blew more smoke out of the window. 'Fantastic! I'd never seen her looking so good and took back all I'd said to her about beauty treatments.'

'Do you know whether she had any other treatment at the clinic and what it comprised of?'

He shrugged. 'I couldn't tell you. How would I know? I'm only a man.'

'Point taken. Do you mind if I use the bathroom now?'

His earlier twinkle-eyed interest in her body returned. 'Be my guest.'

He escorted her along the narrow passage leading past a bedroom to the bathroom at the end.

160

'Cosy,' she said as his big arm squeezed past her shoulder to open the bathroom door.

He breathed an innuendo into her ear. 'If you need a hand, just give me a yell.'

Although affable enough, she'd decided she didn't like Jocelyn Trinder. Granted, he and Pansy Porter had been an item, but he hadn't thought twice about buying this boat following her demise. She wondered how long he'd waited before the purchase. She also wondered whether any new 'shipmate' was on the horizon.

The bathroom was small but perfectly formed. There was no bath but the shower was big enough for one. Two showering at the same time and they were likely to be stuck in there for eternity.

As she was washing her hands in the basin, she looked at her reflection in the mirrored bathroom cabinet. Then she looked at the cabinet. It was amazing what people kept in their bathroom cabinets; toothbrushes, headache tablets, a spare bar of soap and some aftershave …

Yep, that was all she was likely to find, so why did she want to open it?

There was no way she was going to find anything appertaining to the case inside this cabinet. All the same, when curiosity called who was she to ignore it?

A key was hanging from the lock. Now if Joss Trinder had anything to hide, he wouldn't leave the key in the lock – would he?

Of course not.

The key, she decided, was an open invitation. Carefully and very slowly she turned it and opened the cabinet.

The usual accoutrements of a hygienic lifestyle were all there as suspected. However, there were one or two additions. Number one was a can of deodorant – *Sea Petals*. For women. No self-respecting male would use a deodorant named that.

Nestled next to it were a packet of tampons, a nail file, and a tube of manicure adhesive. Joss Trinder was in his sixties – and male. He wouldn't have a use for any of these, would he? OK, she'd give in on the nail file. But not the manicure adhesive, and certainly not the tampons – unless he had a daughter!

Back in the kitchen, Doherty was getting ready to leave and thanking Joss for the bacon sandwiches and coffee.

'If you come up with anything else, give me a call.'

'I will.'

Honey purposely left her bag behind, then suddenly remembered it when her head was out in the fresh air and the rest of her body was still inside the boat.

'My bag,' she said suddenly, stopped and shot back towards the kitchen.

Joss had been coming up behind her, but stepped back to let her pass.

He caught her arm. 'Do you get out much?' he asked.

She managed a smile. 'Sometimes.'

'Do you ever wear a uniform?'

She was about to say that she was not in fact a policewoman, but held back.

'Sometimes.'

His breath was hot against her ear, his thigh pressed against hers.

'A woman wearing a uniform does wonders for my sexual performance.'

Having been in the hotel game for some time, she'd been propositioned by experts. Jocelyn Trinder's approach didn't faze her.

'I need to get my bag.'

'Of course.'

He let her go but followed.

'My daughter bought it for me,' she said once the strap of

162

the big brown bag was firmly over her shoulder. 'Mustn't lose it. She'd never forgive me. You know how it is with kids.'

'I'm afraid not,' he said as he escorted her back to the way out. 'Never had any kids myself. Neither did Pansy.'

'Were you both happy about that?'

He shrugged. 'I suppose it must be nice as you get older, but then, what you've never had you don't miss.'

His palm brushed her bottom as she climbed the steps. Obviously there were certain things Joss Trinder was missing – or was he?

The question was answered more quickly than she'd hoped. The moment they were out on the cockpit, Joss Trinder's demeanour changed somewhat.

At first Honey didn't see what – or rather who – he was seeing. A figure was coming towards them along the towpath. No big deal. The odd jogger had trotted past along with the odd cyclist and people walking their dogs. Another figure wouldn't have made any difference, except for the wave.

Joss Trinder didn't wave back. The affable expression became flustered.

'Do excuse me. I have to get on.'

'If there's anything you come across –' Doherty began.

'Of course. I'll be in touch.'

With that he ducked down out of sight.

'He's got a visitor,' Honey murmured, nodding in the direction of the figure coming towards them. 'One he doesn't want to admit to.'

The woman was perhaps approaching forty, give or take two or three years, though it was hard to tell with any real accuracy. So many women were into beauty treatments and gym membership in a bid to defeat Father Time.

The woman had a sporty look about her: fresh-faced, bobbed hair, and gleaming white teeth. She uttered a bright good morning as she passed.

163

Honey and Doherty stopped and turned round. Blissfully unaware of their interest, she bounced on the balls of her feet in the general direction of Jocelyn Trinder's boat. Placing one hand on the railing running along the back she vaulted over the side.

'How old was Pansy Porter?' Honey asked.

'About fifty-six, I think.'

'That figures. There were things in Mr Trinder's medicine chest that might not have been of much use to an older woman.'

Doherty had an intuition about the tone of Honey's voice. He knew when she was talking women's stuff and he never asked questions about women's stuff – their personal things – bodily functions and all that. He just nodded as though he understood – because he did.

Chapter Twenty-five

When Steve Doherty told Honey she was being taken on a day out and he wasn't wearing anything special, she knew they were off 'making further enquiries'.

Lady Macrottie, the woman who had suffocated on a mudpack and/or drowned in the mud bath, had lived in a grand mansion to the south of the city. Entrance was through a wide gateway bounded by high stone pillars.

The steps to the front door were straight out of *Pride and Prejudice* in that they went off at either side, meeting in the middle at the front door.

Honey took the right set. Doherty took the left.

Outside the door, Doherty raised his hand to knock.

'If you wants 'is lordship, you'd be finding 'im in the veg patch.'

They looked down over the parapet to where a ruddy-faced man wearing a flippy-floppy hat looked up at them.

'Worzel Gummidge,' muttered Honey.

'Too fat to be a scarecrow,' Doherty whispered back. 'Where is the veg patch?' he asked the man.

The man pointed. 'Thur!'

'Thur,' mimicked Honey quietly.

The old guy walked off, his pace slow, possibly by virtue of the fact that his legs were bowed with age. His clothes looked as though he might have mugged a scarecrow. Top drawer they were not.

Though it had been vague, they followed where the finger had pointed. The sound of a cultivator motor helped with direction.

The vegetable patch was something of a surprise. It was large and consisted of one-third lawn, the size of which was diminishing with each pass of the cultivator.

The man pushing the machine was tall and middle aged, his face hidden by a large sombrero. His clothes were better than the ruddy-faced guy's out front, though tired and obviously way past their best.

He did not acknowledge them until their shadows fell across where he was turning over the earth.

Something bordering on elation swept over his expression. The machine was switched off.

'Are you from English Heritage?'

'No.'

Doherty presented his warrant card. He introduced Honey as his assistant.

Lord Macrottie's face visibly dropped.

'That's a shame. I was expecting English Heritage.'

He sounded terribly put out – as though they were only pretending not to be from English Heritage.

'Sorry,' said Doherty putting his card away.

'What do you want?'

'I wanted to ask a few more questions about your wife. Is there somewhere we can talk?'

'Oh. Her.'

Judging by the look on Macrottie's face, the last thing he wanted to do was talk about his wife. Begrudgingly, he pulled off the oversized gardening gloves he wore and gestured to a hut. The door of the hut hung open, swaying and squeaking on its hinges. Inside it smelled of compost and creosote and wasn't that big. The three of them huddled close around the door as a few drops of drizzle began to come down.

'I don't mind living alone. It's very soothing.'

Lord Macrottie's face was upturned as he said it, almost as though her ladyship was in heaven and he was talking directly to her.

'It must have been something of a shock, your wife going to the beauty clinic and dying. I mean, it's not what you expect.'

'No.'

His voice sounded hollow and impassive.

'Had she had similar treatment before?' asked Honey.

'I believe so.'

'Did she complain about it itching?'

Doherty shot her a warning look. They were not here to compare notes about allergic reactions.

'Of course not,' snapped his lordship. 'If she wanted to plaster her face with mud that was up to her. I prefer to grow vegetables in mine.'

Doherty was as uninterested as Lord Macrottie with regard to the mud. He was here to go over a few things, not that he felt it likely he'd find out anything new. It was just to clarify a few things in his mind.

'Your wife had no enemies?'

Lord Macrottie threw him a disdainful look. 'Everyone has enemies! Even you, Mr Policeman! Come along. I think the rain has stopped.'

'This is a lovely building,' said Honey, looking up admiringly at the Elizabethan brickwork and the lead-paned windows through the pouring rain. 'Has it been in your family for long?'

Lord Macrottie inhaled deeply, his chest expanding with pride, his eyes moist with affection as he too admired the elegant façade.

'It's been in my family for four hundred years, or perhaps I should say that my family has been in this house for four hundred years. After so many years it becomes that the house owns you. Its history is my history. There is nothing I would not do to keep this house in the family.'

'So who might want to see your wife dead?'

'A few people, I suppose.'

His gaze stayed fixed on the house.

'Can you give me any names?'

'Not really. My wife upset a lot of people – including that harpy Serena Sarabande and that shit, Dexter.'

Doherty's ears visibly pricked up. 'You didn't mention that before. Any particular reason?'

'Any particular reason they didn't get on, or any particular reason that I didn't mention it before?'

'Both,' Doherty replied curtly.

Honey stepped away from the hut. Even the possibility of getting caught in another downpour was preferable to witnessing two men squaring up to each other.

Nobody told her not to go wandering, so off she wandered. Luckily she'd worn flat shoes and hadn't strayed on to the mud, though there had been a few blobs here and there. At the edge of the path she scraped off the blobs that had managed to stick to her soles.

Retracing their steps, she followed the paths back round to the front of the house, stopped, and took a look.

The façade was imposing, the tiny squares that made up the lead-paned windows glittering like diamonds. One or two windows seemed to have lost their glitter, plywood covering the gaps where glass had once been.

Funny, she hadn't noticed that before. Even the balustrade bordering the parapet in front of the canopied entrance seemed a little worse for wear.

Not having noticed things annoyed her. 'Shoddy observation, Hannah,' she muttered to herself.

A second look wouldn't hurt. A second look she would have.

168

Chapter Twenty-six

This time she chose the steps on the left side. She stumbled half way up as a piece of stone edging flaked off as easily as a biscuit crumbles.

Bath stone was notoriously soft, though a beautiful buttermilk colour. While wiping one grit-encrusted hand against the other, she noticed that more than one stone step was the victim of corrosion. She proceeded more carefully.

It struck her forcibly that they hadn't been replaced in years, perhaps since the place was built. Some of the brickwork was also in need of repair.

The hugely imposing front door they'd stood in front of earlier was of solid oak that was whitened and dried with age. The door knocker needed painting. A white plastic bell push had been crudely inserted into the door surround, offensive against the ancient wood. Where was the bell pull, normally an ornate Victorian item of cast iron and ringing tone? Where was the butler come to that?

Overcome by a flash of pure mischief, something she was often prone to, she pressed the plastic bell.

The electric ring seemed to resonate inside and out.

'No good pressing that.'

She looked over the parapet. The same ruddy-faced old guy they'd seen earlier had reappeared pushing a wheelbarrow.

'Is it the butler's day off?' she asked politely.

'Too bloody right it is. He's 'elping 'is lordship. We need to plant some spuds shortly. Can't be wasting time doing butlering.'

As the old guy wandered off Honey regarded the garden and sweeping driveway. Judged from its gardens and a cursory view of the outside, Hamthorpe Hall looked the part. On closer inspection the building was a little tired and servants seemed more than a little thin on the ground. No one had come to answer her ring on the door bell and the guy with the ruddy cheeks doubled up as butler and gardener.

An obvious conclusion bobbed into her head like an apple floating on water; his lordship was strapped for cash.

Looking sidelong at the windows made her curious about the interior; would it be neglected, the furniture shabby, and the old oak panelling suffering from woodworm? Very likely, though the woodworm wouldn't notice much, of course

There was only one way to find out. She had to have a look through a window. Better still, she needed to get inside.

The Elizabethans had been very keen on building their houses in the shape of an E in honour of their queen. The middle of the letter was formed by the entrance and the bigger end bits were formed by brick-built wings embellished with huge oriel windows with stone mullions and tiny leaded panes. Her first intention was to take a peek through one of these.

Balancing on the steps gave her something of a view, but stretching one leg out and placing one foot on the window ledge gave her an even better one.

Despite the big window the room was sombre, the light swallowed up by the dark woods of the floor and walls. On the whole it looked tidy enough, furnished as it was with period furniture which, although not exactly in the first flush of youth, suited the room.

After retrieving her leg from the window ledge on one side of the house, she repeated the action on the other. This time her leg didn't seem anywhere near long enough. Some analysing was called for. Either one of her legs was shorter than the other or some old-time builder had used an extra brick, because the gap seemed wider.

However, she determined not to be beaten by an old-time brickie being slack on the job. A big breath, a leap of faith and … her foot was on the window ledge.

But it wasn't easy. Another inch and her legs would snap off, at least that's what it felt like.

And that wasn't the only problem. The foot left behind was balanced on the very edge of the step. The old masonry was beginning to separate into flaky layers and one flaky layer was moving on top of the other.

She caught only a glimpse of the other room before the flaky stone crumbled. First things first, she could either fall or leap with both legs onto the window ledge. She chose the latter.

Fingernails that she'd been determined to grow (yet again) snapped off as she grabbed the soft stone mullions, digging her fingers in as best she could.

The window ledge was narrow, the stone mullion difficult to hold on to. She was going to fall.

Ordinarily it might not have been far to fall, but the steps swept down and away from the building. There was a fair drop to the ground, not enough to break her neck perhaps, but a broken leg wasn't beyond the bounds of possibility.

She was very likely to fall. There wasn't enough grip in the mullion.

Frantically she searched for a finger hold. There wasn't much to choose from: a lump of metal that formed the outside of the window catch; the hanging frond of a wisteria, not yet in full bloom, scratching the window with each breath of wind.

She was going to fall! That was all there was to it.

Then she spotted a third option. A portion of glass was missing. A piece of plywood had been nailed over the gap on the inside of the window.

Feeling like a vandal, she punched at the plywood. It gave. There was just enough room for her fingers. She could cling on. In the meantime she called for help.

Then it started to rain – heavily. The sound was astounding. Driven by a rising wind, it was hammering against the building, clattering against the windows. Puddles were already forming in the flower bed below – when she happened to glance that way. After all, if she'd been climbing Everest or even the face of the Empire State Building, someone would be telling her not to look down. And she wasn't going to. No way!

Her voice was getting lost on the wind. It was also getting weaker, the loud yell reduced to something like a croak.

Chapter Twenty-seven

Doherty was thoughtful as he made his way back along the path to the front of the house and his waiting car. Just as Honey had done, he stopped and admired his surroundings.

'Very nice,' he murmured.

And it was.

Lord Macrottie was a stickler for keeping the greenery in order and was very keen on growing his own vegetables. Doherty had commented on his green fingers and expressed his admiration that his lordship was helping the environment.

He'd thought his comment would have been welcomed with some graciousness but it hadn't happened. Either his lordship was consistently ungracious or the comment was irrelevant.

The gravel crunched beneath his feet as he made for his car, opened the door and slid in.

It was something of a surprise to see the empty passenger seat. He stared at it for a split second as though he might be mistaken and Honey had merely flipped off into another dimension and would reappear at any minute.

But Honey was no character from a fourth dimension, he told himself – though it sometimes felt that way.

Although the rain was beating a samba on the roof he had to go and find her; it was the gentlemanly thing to do.

Luckily he'd brought an umbrella, a snazzy telescopic one that leapt fully open at the touch of a button.

He headed away from the car and towards the house. He

called her just the once. Calling for a second time seemed a waste of effort, the way the rain was hammering down.

'Honey?'

Puddles were forming fast on the driveway, which made him think the gravel had been applied only thinly, just enough to hide the grit and mud beneath.

One puddle was beginning to run into another and another and another, each one nearer the house. The sight of it filled him with boyish nostalgia. He could remember damming up puddles with bits of brick, stone, and mud when he was a kid, or digging his own version of the Panama Canal and channelling the water from one puddle to another.

Happy days, he thought, but then reminded himself that the present wasn't so bad either, especially since he'd met Honey. Not that he'd told her that. But he would soon. And that wasn't all he had to tell her. He had to mention Cheryl. He knew she'd noticed his furtiveness when answering phone calls from his ex-wife. She'd looked at him questioningly. He'd avoided admitting anything, but it couldn't last. He'd get caught out sooner or later.

His eyes stayed fixed on the puddles while the rain continued to hammer on his umbrella.

His cell phone suddenly chirped into life. It was her. Cheryl.

'She's not home yet!'

'Well she isn't with me.'

'How do I know you're not lying?'

Doherty sighed. How the hell had he and Cheryl got together in the first place? He came to the conclusion it must have been sheer lust. It certainly couldn't have been compatibility and certainly not love. They loathed each other. His daughter was the only good thing to come out of the marriage – though she was only good sometimes.

'Look, Cheryl, I can't talk now. I'm busy.'

'You always were.'

She cut the connection before he had chance to say anything else, like pointing out to her that she was always spending money – more than he earned.

He stared at the phone wondering whether she could read his thoughts. No, he decided. Technology hadn't gone that far just yet.

The trouble with Cheryl was that she continually fretted when Rachel was out of her sight – more specifically when she thought she was with her father.

The girl was old enough to be out and about on her own, for God's sake!

The phone chirped for a second time. Sensing it was Cheryl again he considered ignoring it. Still, he couldn't count on that.

The number shown on the readout was not instantly recognizable. It wasn't Cheryl.

'Hello.'

'Dad?'

Rachel!

'Where are you?'

'I'm still in Bath. I'm looking for a flat. I'm not going home. I don't care what you say, I'm not going home.'

'So you want to be independent.'

Cheryl wouldn't believe that, of course. He sensed a storm brewing and it had nothing to do with the rain coming down in sheets.

'Will you help me get somewhere to stay?'

'Where are you at present?'

'In the park.'

'Christ!' He threw back his head. 'You're not sleeping there?'

'No. I got offered this place by some guy who was going away for a while, but it's only temporary.'

'OK,' he said, nodding slowly. 'I'll get you somewhere to stay.'

They arranged to meet.

What with the rain and the phone, he didn't hear Honey trying to attract his attention – not even when he'd terminated the connection.

Water was dripping from the building. Some droplets were bigger than others and the noise on his umbrella was deafening.

Honey saw him from out of the corner of her eye.

'Hey!'

He was on the phone. He didn't hear.

She turned as far as she dared without losing her grip. She couldn't see his face and couldn't really hear what was being said.

Anyway, curiosity about who might be phoning him was of secondary concern.

The soft lead of the window frame was getting softer beneath the heat and the pressure of her fingertips. The small square of lead was beginning to bow outwards.

'Oh, help,' she said to herself in a wee voice. Then louder. 'Steve! Help me!'

The rain was furious, the wind whipping it on to Steve's umbrella with hurricane force.

He was right beneath her now, oblivious to her shouts and seemingly mesmerized by the sight of the puddles and a small duck that had decided to take up residence.

Her fingers were going numb. Her hair was soaking wet and plastered against her head. The lead framing of that particular section of window frame was like putty beneath her touch. It was ballooning outwards, more and more, and more …

Suddenly it went.

It was hard to make out who was the most surprised; Honey, Steve Doherty, or the duck that had perhaps been looking for a quiet life, isolation from its extended family. The duck went screeching into the air. Steve fell solidly on to his back.

He'd tipped both his head and his umbrella back at the right moment. She'd caught him squarely amidships so that he ended up spread-eagled in the puddles he'd been admiring, the umbrella spinning off like a top.

'What the hell were you doing up there?'

He sounded angry. He looked angry. It wasn't often he lost patience with her, but this was certainly one of those times.

'Nothing broken,' she exclaimed with relief.

'There wouldn't be,' he said between wheezing breaths. 'I can't say the same for myself.'

He was holding his arm protectively across his midriff. The breath had been knocked out of him.

Apologizing profusely, she helped him to his feet. He leaned forward, hands on knees and trying to catch his breath.

'Phew! Fooo,' he said, which Honey roughly translated as 'I think you've punctured my lungs, but don't worry, I'll get over it.'

A few coughs followed before he straightened and asked the question he'd asked previously – though this time more vehemently, and with a lot more bad language.

Honey winced at each word, not daring to interrupt. At last it appeared he'd either run out of words or run out of breath; possibly both.

He fixed her with those deep blue eyes of his. Another time, another place, she might have leapt on him again, though less violently. But not today. The grass was too wet and the weather inclement. All the same, she couldn't help making some kind of affectionate gesture.

'Steve, sweetie. Let me kiss it better.'

She threw her arms around his neck and hugged him close.

He yelped with pain. 'Ouch!' One hand went to the small of his back, another to his ribs as he rocked on his heels.

'Sorry! Sorry! Sorry!'

Honey reached for him again, but didn't dare touch.

'Does it hurt that much?'

'You're no lightweight.'

'Ouch! That hurt. I did call out to you, but you didn't hear me.'

He immediately regretted what he'd said. 'OK. So what the hell were you doing up there anyway?'

She cosied up to him like Guy Fawkes admitting he had a barrel of gunpowder in his back pocket. 'Haven't you noticed?'

Detective Inspector Steve Doherty prided himself on being a pretty observant copper, but what he might have observed and what Honey might have observed were two different things.

Honey went ahead and enlightened him.

'Look at it.'

She pointed at the window where she'd been clinging like a sparrowhawk just a few minutes earlier. 'That window isn't complete. It's got bits of glass missing – luckily for me as it turned out. And these steps,' she said, pulling on his sleeve, dragging him to the steps and pointing at the crumbling stone. 'The brickwork is crumbling too.'

Doherty took it all in and agreed that some aspects of the old building needed a bit of TLC.

'Isn't that why he's been in contact with English Heritage? Don't they fund renovations and all that?'

She agreed that they did. 'But they haven't got bottomless pockets. Inside as well as out, this place needs more than tender loving care. That's what I was doing up there; I wanted to see whether the inside is as rough as the outside. The room on the left seems OK, but the one on this side needs serious attention. Most of the ceiling is on the floor, there are gaps in the floorboards, and the windows are falling out.'

'You learned all that being perched on a windowsill?'

'I had a lot of time to study the subject due to a lack of knights in shining armour.'

Doherty looked thoughtful. 'Well, we can't hold letting an

historic house fall to rack and ruin against him.'

Honey stared at him, shaking her head in disbelief.

'Don't you see? He has to plant vegetables in order to survive. He's strapped for cash, Steve. Stony broke, in fact!'

'And your point is?'

She shrugged. What was her point? The fact was that she was so carried away with all this she'd forgotten that Lord Macrottie was not a suspect. And why should he be? His wife had been staying at the beauty clinic while he'd held the fort at home here, planting his veggie patch and such like.

'He could have sneaked in and done her in for the insurance money.'

Doherty shook his head.

'He's got a cast-iron alibi. He was playing skittles at the local pub. There were witnesses.'

'Oh!'

She thought again of the sighting of the scruffy character in the grounds of The Beauty Spot. 'He was wearing the right clothes,' she pointed out.

Doherty sighed. 'And before you mention the gardener and the fact that his clothes are scruffy, don't go there. You're clutching at straws.'

Honey exhaled a lungful of air which helped blow wet fronds of hair away from her face.

'It was a thought. Shall we make tracks?'

His phone rang. It surprised her when he walked off hugging it to his ear, one hand cuffed around his mouth.

This was new.

'Was it something I said?'

He didn't hear her. She hadn't said it loud enough for him to hear.

He'd checked the caller on the screen before heading off, so he knew who it was and he didn't want her to hear the conversation.

She'd never had him do that before. Even if the Chief Constable was on the end of the phone, he'd still stay close to her. There had never been any secrets between them and definitely no subterfuge. Having him make it so obvious he didn't want her to hear shouldn't hurt her, but it did.

Ever since they'd got together they'd been open with each other. A small incident, she said to herself. Take no notice.

But she couldn't help it and when she thought about it, she realized he had been a little offhand lately. Usually he'd invited her along to interview just about everyone connected with the case. Initially he'd had her stay at The Beauty Spot. Something had happened just after that to change things and she didn't know what.

Yes, just lately he'd definitely been a little offhand. Not in a nasty way, it had to be said, but furtively, bluntly, as if he was half way to telling her his problem but couldn't quite make it.

But what problem?

What secret?

Another woman?

It was the obvious solution. Her insides crawled around at the thought of it. She tried swallowing and telling herself she was letting her imagination run away with her. It didn't work. There was an empty feeling in her stomach as though she hadn't eaten for days.

He nodded silently and looked away from her. Something was on his mind. She could tell. He hadn't said anything saucy. Doherty always said something saucy to her, especially when he was about to get her alone. OK, his car was small, but it was cosy. Thighs and shoulders rubbed nicely together as they drove along.

Usually he would kiss her once they were seated and belted up. But he didn't.

'Is something wrong?'

He switched on the engine. 'I've got something to tell you.

Something I should have told you before.'

The houses around the old mansion that housed The Beauty Spot were recently built and although two-thirds of the project was complete, the final third was still in the construction stage.

The truck delivering yet another load of cement which would form the foundations of another detached house had backed into position. The huge drum was turning, keeping the cement at the right consistency. The chute that would deliver the cement was in place.

Everything was set to go until the driver spotted something he didn't like. Usually there were at least two construction workers working the chute so that the cement was laid evenly. Today there was only one.

The driver shouted. 'Are you all there is this morning?'

Nodding, the man shouted over the din. ''Fraid so. Me mate's gone for the tea.'

The driver rolled his eyes and swore under his breath.

He glanced at the clock in the dashboard of the truck. He didn't like delivering part of the load with only one bloke keeping his eyes on things. Normally he might have hung about until someone else arrived, but he had another drop to do after this. There was no way he could hang about.

'I'll chance it,' he muttered to himself and pressed the button.

Kevin, the guy who was overseeing the operation, was feeling pleased with himself. He was young and inexperienced but loved to feel important. He'd almost whooped with joy when old Charlie had pronounced he needed a cup of tea and the bathroom.

'Give me a shout when the cement arrives,' he'd said.

Kevin had said that he would do that, though in reality he had it in mind to prove to all and sundry how efficient he could be – given the chance. And here was the chance! He could do this by himself. All he had to do was to make sure the cement went in evenly. If it didn't then it was in with shovels to even it out, and nobody wanted to do that.

The pump kicked in and Kevin was there, positioning the chute so that the mix coming out went to where it was wanted.

Like a thick grey pudding mix, it spewed out of the chute into the waiting trench.

Unfortunately for Kevin, he hadn't considered that the force of the ejection gave the chute an energy all of its own.

Like a huge serpent, it writhed away from him, promptly filling then overfilling a portion of trench while Kevin tried frantically to bring it back under control.

Horrified, he gazed at the mountain of cement building up in one place.

'Shut it off! Shut it off,' he shouted.

Out of the corner of his eye he saw old Charlie staggering towards him as fast as his old legs could go.

He could see the old guy's mouth opening wide and imagined what he was saying.

'Shit,' he muttered as the chute came to a juddering halt. 'Shit!'

He saw old Charlie looking into the trench. It was difficult to read the look on his face, but it certainly wasn't pretty, in fact it was the worst look he'd ever seen on anyone's face.

In his mind he was already collecting his cards and wages due plus a warning never to darken the site again. Perhaps if he apologized and begged profusely enough …?

The driver leapt down from his cab, fists clenched and face red with anger.

At first sight he'd looked as though he was going to use his fists, but there must have been something about the look of horror on old Charlie's face.

His expression a mix of anger and puzzlement, the driver gave Kevin a push as he strode by.

Old Charlie was pointing now, his mouth open but no sound

coming out.

The driver stood next to Charlie. His jaw dropped too.

Kevin, feeling pale and wobbly, looked down to where they were looking.

The painted fingernails and the fine white hand looked incongruous among all that cement.

Kevin balked and shook his head. 'I didn't see her. Honest I didn't.'

The driver, his eyes still on the woman's hand, got out his cell phone and called the police.

Chapter Twenty-eight

Honey opened her eyes and briefly wondered whether she really was at home in bed or was only dreaming that she was here. Closing her eyes again, then opening them swiftly, brought her to the same conclusion; last night she had slept in her own bed. It came as something of a shock, mainly because she'd got so used to sleeping in Steve Doherty's bed. She slept well in Doherty's bed, even though it was slightly lumpy and in need of replacing. She presumed it was his closeness and the smell of him that had something to do with it; that and the sexual Olympics they usually indulged in before dropping off to sleep.

She was here for a reason and as her brain began to adjust to the fact that she had to get out of bed and get on with things, the reason for her sleeping here got clearer. Even if it hadn't, Lindsey suddenly appeared to put her straight.

'Just as well you're here. Dumpy Doris has phoned in to say she's got stuck in a stairwell.'

Honey frowned. Dumpy Doris, her breakfast cook, lived in a modern townhouse of standard proportions. The fact that Doris was of non-standard proportions had never caused a problem before.

'I've seen the stairs at her house. They can't be a problem. Even for Doris.'

'Not at her house. A neighbour drives one of the sightseeing buses – a double decker with an open top. Doris fancied a bit of fresh air and decided to squeeze herself on to the upper deck. Unfortunately she failed to squeeze herself back down again.'

If she hadn't been preoccupied she would have at least smiled. Doherty had told her about his daughter, Rachel. He'd also told her about his wife.

OK, she shouldn't get so uptight. Steve Doherty had made no secret of the fact that he was divorced. She couldn't quite understand why he hadn't told her about Rachel. What was worse, it kind of deflated her view of him. She'd thought there were no secrets between them. Now it appeared there were.

Lindsey came and sat on the side of the bed. She was fresh out of the shower, a white towel wound around her head, a bigger one around her body.

'So what's the problem?'

Somehow Honey didn't want to confide in her daughter that her affair with Doherty, that had seemed to be going so well, had hit the buffers.

She shrugged at the same time as swinging her legs out of bed, her toes curling over as her feet hit the floor. The furry rug had slid away some time during the night – or when she'd flung herself into bed. Why the hell had she insisted on having the bare boards of the floor sanded and polished? Why hadn't she just carpeted the place throughout? Individuality, she told herself. You wanted to be different.

'Just one of those things,' she said to Lindsey.

She felt her daughter's eyes following her to the wardrobe, the chest of drawers, and the bathroom door.

'Did he ask you to marry him?'

Honey laughed. 'Of course not. Whatever made you think that?'

'I didn't. Not really. Gran did. She wasn't pleased.'

Honey grimaced. 'She wouldn't be. But never fear. He hasn't asked me to marry him so there's no problem.'

'I see.'

It was the way that Lindsey said 'I see' that caught her attention.

'That's a cryptic tone.'

Lindsey pulled the towel from her head. Her hair fell in wet tendrils like polished seaweed. The colour of the month for March was chocolate brown – with a blonde stripe rising from her forehead and sweeping over her crown. The style reminded Honey of Cruella de Vil from *One Hundred and One Dalmatians*, or Mrs Munster.

'You're giving me cryptic responses.'

Bland expressions weren't Honey's thing but she did her best – that and lying.

'Steve had to work last night. There was no point me staying there by myself.'

Fresh flowers adorned Reception. 'I put them straight into water,' said Anna.

The bouquet was obviously meant as a personal gift, but Anna was on some kind of efficiency drive and was being extraordinarily willing of late.

A dozen red roses! They had to be from Steve Doherty.

'Was there a card?'

'Yes.'

The card was as upmarket as the bouquet; gold lettering and edging plus a personal message.

'*I'm in town. Would love to reacquaint.*'

It was signed John Rees.

John Rees had been on the scene a while back when she'd first landed the job of Crime Liaison Officer with the Hotels Association. He'd vied for her affections with Doherty. Doherty had won through, possibly because they ended up spending a lot of time together, plus the fact that John had disappeared from Bath, his bookshop run by someone else in his absence.

187

There was a telephone number.

Now, she asked herself, looking up at the ceiling as if for clarification. If this was a romance novel my heart would be skipping a beat. Is it doing that?

She knew quite a bit about romance novels, mainly because her mother kept a whole library of them. Her mother was an out-and-out romantic, the sort who thrilled at the sight of men drinking from her slipper.

Honey viewed herself as more pragmatic; she liked men to act like men, smell like men, but give her a bit of leeway for feminine expression.

John fitted the description. So did Steve Doherty for that matter, but not telling her about his daughter had nailed her. What was that all about?

'Lovely,' said Lindsey, burying her nose in a bright red rose. 'Dear Steve is obviously sorry for whatever he did.'

'No he isn't.'

Flicking the card between her first two fingers, Honey headed for her office.

John Rees had sent her flowers, Steve Doherty had not. He'd missed his chance. She picked up the phone and dialled John's number.

Chapter Twenty-nine

There were many bad traits Steve Doherty remembered about his wife and one of them was that she had no patience. If she wanted something done, she wanted it done pronto. Never mind about work. What she wanted came first. Time had not mellowed her.

'When are you going to talk to Rachel?'

'Not now. I'm busy.'

'Your daughter should come first.'

'I'll get there when I can.'

His wife didn't understand him, or at least she didn't understand that his job ruled his life. She never had.

He cut the connection fast before she could make any more demands. He had a driver this morning; Christine Palmer, the same one who served him coffee on the dot every morning.

He knew she fancied him and she was a very likeable girl, but much as he disliked admitting it, Honey was the one who kept him on his toes. It was just this business about his daughter. His own fault, he reckoned. Why hadn't he told her?

He'd scrolled through a few reasons for his reluctance. Honey had a daughter. Lindsey was well-adjusted and old beyond her years, whereas his daughter was wilful, undoubtedly taking after her mother. Could it be that he'd felt she'd consider him a failed father? Only a psychiatrist could answer that one.

The day was grey and the prevailing westerly was doing its

utmost to keep the rain at bay.

'Right down the end,' he said to Christine, pointing to where the crime scene tape was fluttering like bunting and a group of official vehicles had gathered.

The medical examiner had done his thing. 'She's dead,' he said on spotting Doherty. 'But then,' he added with the kind of grin that acts as a shield against emotion, 'she was up to her elbows in cement. Very alkaline, you know. Burns the skin in minutes.'

A uniformed officer helped the medical examiner off with the heavy-duty Wellington boots he'd been obliged to wear.

Doherty nodded, then turned to watch as the body was retrieved from the trench, the sticky morass making a gulping sound as it was pulled free and placed on a plastic sheet.

'Not very old is she, sir?'

Christine smelled of fabric softener. It was a fresh smell, not unattractive.

Doherty nodded. 'It looks that way.'

'Nice legs,' she said. 'Nice shape too.'

It was about all that could be said about the corpse at this stage, seeing as it was still covered in grey sludge.

Her comments made him feel uncomfortable. He moved away, addressing a scene of crime officer he knew pretty well – Boyd, his name was.

'Do we know who she is?'

Boyd shook his head. 'Not yet. There's no handbag or purse or anything.'

The medical examiner had overheard. 'She's wearing an identity card under her jacket. I didn't notice the name.'

Doherty's eyes met those of the scene of crime officer, who immediately leaned over the mucky bundle lying on the ground. Being careful not to disturb evidence – in this case a thick layer of cement that was already drying – he gingerly fingered the identity card. It was the sort of card conference delegates are given – plastic bagged and pinned to the chest.

He looked almost triumphant, like a warrior home from the war rather than a copper up to his knees in muck, when he declared who it was.

'Karen Pinker. Do we know who she is?'

Doherty nodded. 'Yes. We do.'

Careful to keep his shoes clean, he went to take a look. Dead people were never pretty no matter how they'd died.

The medical examiner was still hanging around. 'She didn't drown in it. The cement truck had only just arrived.'

Doherty nodded in response. He was in no doubt that this was the girl Honey had described as Miss Perfect. She'd been referring to Karen Pinker's appearance. The girl was the sort who had always been well turned-out, the sort who'd never left the house without full make-up and immaculate presentation. A bit like his ex-wife really. Some girls like her grew up, got over their angst, and sniffed the roses. Some, like his ex-wife, never changed.

'Get the report to me on cause of death asap.'

'I can tell you that now. She was skewered on a piece of railing. Old railing with a sharp point on top. Just one piece fixed upright in the ground, almost as though it had been done purposely. As though it was waiting for someone to fall on it.'

Doherty heard Christine retch before running off and spewing her breakfast away from the crime scene.

She looked embarrassed when she got back, wiping her lips with a crisp white handkerchief.

'When you're ready.'

He headed for the car. He had reports to make out. No time for dealing with a wayward daughter.

Christine Palmer kept close on his heels.

'Poor girl. Do you think whoever did it lured her here, to this specific place?'

He nodded. 'Certainly. The site was prepared.'

He stopped in his tracks realizing what he'd just said.

'It was prepared in advance.'

But why a railing? Why a mudpack, come to that?

The answer came later that day when he was still ploughing through paperwork, avoiding his wife, and planning to get hold of Honey. He'd barely had chance to get her on the phone and when he did he got no response. Normally he might have phoned the hotel on the landline, but he wanted to speak to Honey directly, not be passed on to her. It was a personal matter and he wanted to keep it private.

The site was prepared!

Christine had just brought in yet another cup of coffee. He was beginning to think she did that just to see more of him. Somehow he had to let her down gently that he wasn't interested.

When the thought hit him Doherty put the cup down so that the coffee slopped from cup to saucer.

Dear God! Was it usual for a woman to have a mudpack at the same time as bathing in the bloody stuff?

He rang Serena Sarabande and asked her the self-same question.

'Not usually, unless by special request.'

He followed that call with one to the pathologist. He spoke to an assistant.

'Was there any difference in the mud on her face and in her throat to that in the bath?'

'Now there's a question.'

'I know,' Doherty growled. He thought he knew the assistant, a young chap too cocky at times for his own good. 'Can you answer it?'

'It'll have to go for analysis, but bear with me. I'll get it done pronto.'

He sounded full of confidence, but then why shouldn't he? He was young, Doherty reminded himself.

Steepling his fingers in front of his face he thought things through. Lady Macrottie hadn't drowned *in* her bath. Someone had applied a mudpack to her face – all of her face. Nose, mouth, eyes; and they'd held her jaw shut. That would explain the broken tooth noted on the post mortem.

His wife phoned him again half way through the afternoon. He rolled his eyes and turned his gaze heavenward.

'I can't see her just yet. I've got a fresh murder case …'

'You always did have! You always had something more important to deal with than your wife and daughter!'

The phone slammed down at her end. Sighing, he brought his mind back to the job in hand. He was reading the printout from Karen Pinker's phone. The last call received had been from a call box in Bath. Checking back through the report he found that it wasn't the first time she'd received a call from a public payphone number. She'd received one on the very day Lady Macrottie had been murdered. But from a different phone box – one much nearer the scene of the crime.

By eight o'clock that night he was absolutely shattered but smugly satisfied. There had been a difference between the mud in Lady Macrottie's bath and that in her throat. The stuff in her bath and on her face might have been volcanic and sourced in Hawaii. The mud in her throat was common clay and probably sourced from a particularly muddy patch on the building site.

He made it to his daughter's digs. She was sharing a detached house with three other girls. The house was modern and situated just off Brassmill Lane. The roof was chalet style, the blockwork it was built of making some effort to look like Bath stone.

A bicycle leaned against the window at the side of the door. The front garden was covered in wood shavings; grass cutting wasn't a high priority for tenants, especially four young women with other things on their mind. Like men, he thought worriedly to himself.

The door bell seemed to work. He heard it ring. He pressed it three times before seeing a figure wax and wane on the other side of the glass-panelled door.

A girl with tired-looking eyes and ruffled hair answered. She was sniffing and dabbing her nose with a paper tissue.

'I'm looking for Rachel Doherty,' he said.

'She's not here.'

'I'm her father.'

Sniff, sniff.

'She's still not here.'

'Do you know where she is?'

She shrugged. 'Out clubbing. Somewhere.'

'Will you tell her I called?'

She said that she would.

Today had been heavy. Searching for an errant daughter helped drain his energy. He needed light relief. Honey fell into that category. She had a bubbling enthusiasm for whatever she did even when things went wrong, turning her hand to anything if she had to. She bounced back. That was the thing with Honey. She *kept* bouncing back and that's what he wanted to do. He wanted to bounce back.

Because he couldn't get her on the phone he swung into the hotel. Mary Jane was sitting in the reception area lying on a couch with her feet up and reading a magazine – something about things going bump in the night.

She looked up and saw him. 'Hi there, Steve.'

There was something hesitant about the look on her face.

'She's not here, you know.'

He was disappointed.

'She's gone to some gala evening up at the Assembly Rooms.'

He hid his disappointment. 'Do you know when it finishes?'

She shrugged. 'I'm not sure.'

There was something about her demeanour that made him

194

think that she did know but for some reason was holding back.

'Never mind. I'll take a chance.'

'You shouldn't really …'

She was half up from the couch, but didn't reach him.

'I get it,' he called over her shoulder. 'She's got company.'

'Whoops,' said Mary Jane.

The double doors swung back together.

'Problem?' asked Lindsey, who had only just come out of the office.

'Could be,' said Mary Jane. 'I've just told your mother's boyfriend where to find her. Unfortunately I didn't mention that she was with someone.'

'Whoops.'

Chapter Thirty

'Bath is becoming very untidy,' said Casper St John Gervais.

'I quite agree. I think the fast food containers are the worst, that and the discarded alcopop cans,' said Honey, nodding in agreement. She was clear-headed due to the fact that she was alternating taking a sip of wine with taking a sip of water.

She had on her best little black dress, which was complemented with a shiny red belt. She'd read somewhere that a belt took inches off a middle-aged waistline. To help things along she held her stomach muscles in. She couldn't keep it up all night so kept it for when she was standing up. At present she was sitting down, relaxed muscles hidden by the tabletop.

They were attending a gala evening for tourism awards. Casper was up for one of the top awards: Small Independent Hotel of the Year. If he won it again it would be his fourth time.

Honey was there with John Rees. It had been lovely to see him again. Nothing much had changed in the kind eyes, the lean figure, and the warm smile that split his bearded face in two.

John was of an easy-going nature and his gentle voice had always made her go weak at the knees. For a bookshop owner he was not a wordy man. He chose his words carefully and his sentences were short, but boy, oh boy, were they straight to the point.

Casper fixed her with unblinking, dark grey eyes. 'I meant bodies, Honey. Dead bodies that have not achieved that estate by natural causes. I mean murder.'

Honey blinked and although she was loath to do it, she tore her gaze away from the door through which John Rees had disappeared.

Presuming he meant the murder at The Beauty Spot – as yet unsolved – she gave that wise nod of the head again.

'Ah yes. The murder.'

She hadn't heard anything from Steve Doherty. He'd told her that he had to find his daughter, make sure she was OK, and then report back to her mother.

Perhaps it was the 'report back to her mother' bit that had irritated her and inspired her to ask John to escort her to the gala evening. Whatever, she hadn't heard anything from him.

'I mean this latest murder.'

Honey took in the chiselled features, the sharp hooked nose, and the firm structure of the chin. Casper looked as though he'd been sculpted from stone – marble of course. Casper had impeccable taste – that's why his hotel, La Reine Rouge, kept winning the Small Independent Hotel of the Year award.

He obviously wasn't talking about the mudpack murder.

'I haven't heard from Doherty with the details yet.'

There was no way she was going to appear ignorant of events. She presumed a knifing event or something of that nature outside a nightclub in the wee hours of the morning, a skirmish that had gone wrong. Steve Doherty wouldn't contact her about something like that. He'd only get in touch if it was anything affecting the Hotels Association before Casper got on to him.

The chairman of Bath Hotels Association still had his beady eyes on her, looking hard and questioning, as though she'd just said something to slight his intelligence.

'You're not going to have one of your silly moments, are

you?'

She shook her head. 'I don't know what you mean.'

On catching a hint of movement, a door opening and closing again, her eyes returned to the door. John was on his way back.

She was aware of Casper leaning closer.

'I meant you're not going to leave me and this fair city in the lurch are you? You're not going to throw in the towel as our bastion between Bath and the barbarian hordes that would bring us low?' Casper spoke in a very eloquent, olde-worlde fashion at times, as though Noël Coward was still as fashionable as silk-lined smoking jackets and garters with little bells on.

He meant that he did not wish her to relinquish her position as Bath Hotels Association Crime Liaison Officer, a position she had accepted under duress. Do it and her room occupancy would benefit, not do it and she could answer to the name Bleak House.

'A young woman. On a building site, I believe. A beauty therapist.'

A bell jangled in Honey's brain. She instinctively knew that Doherty had been in touch with Casper. But he hadn't phoned her. It hurt. She didn't like it.

'Have I missed anything?' John asked.

'Nothing of note,' Casper responded. His look was glancing. He didn't know John Rees very well, although he did know he kept an independent bookshop in a small alley in the centre of Bath.

Impatient to receive his prize, his eyes went to his watch. 'Twenty more minutes,' he muttered. 'Excuse me.'

'Was it something I said?' asked John.

He smiled as he said it.

Honey shook her head. 'No. That's the way Casper is. He's here for one reason and one alone. To win that award – yet

199

again.'

'Nothing's cut and dried, is it?'

His hand covered hers as he said it. For a moment she considered there was a double meaning to his question. He might be asking her whether their friendship was likely to go further. She decided to take it that he was referring to Casper.

'Let me explain. La Reine Rouge is eclectic and perfectly presented. Chocolates wrapped in silk lie on your pillow at night. The sheets are washed in a rose-scented liquid. The tea of your choice is provided in your room. Slippers, dressing gown, you name it, La Reine Rouge has got it.'

'So it's not exactly warm and cosy family run.'

The smile persisted.

'Are you making fun?'

He shook his head. 'I would never do that.'

John was older than her. He'd come over from Kansas some years ago and never gone back. She'd never quite been sure why. In his far distant youth he'd served in Vietnam on a destroyer delivering arms to the Mekong Delta. He still had the physique of a fighting man, though the eyes of a peacemaker. His voice too. When he talked to her – mostly about pretty general things – she listened, to the exclusion of everything else.

She hardly noticed that Casper had come back and that the dessert crockery had been taken away and coffee had arrived.

The awards ceremony had started. She saw Casper tense, his eyes unblinking and staring at the compere as though he were willing him to get on with it and award the prize for the best small independent hotel.

Honey wasn't concentrating on what was being said. She was thinking about John Rees and his lovely voice but she was also thinking of Steve Doherty. There had been another murder. Doherty had informed Casper but had failed to inform her. The murder had occurred on a building site.

'The Beauty Spot,' she whispered, and got immediately to her feet.

John Rees looked up at her.

'John. I have to go,' she whispered.

He nodded affably.

It occurred to her that he thought she was off to the bathroom. There was no time to explain and although she badly wanted to plant a kiss on his upturned face, she resisted. Doherty had kept his distance and the truth was that she didn't want him to keep his distance.

Outside in the foyer she got out her phone and punched in his number. Nothing happened. She was about to repeat her action when she noted the 'batteries low' sign blinking blue at her.

The sound of loud applause came from the audience on the other side of the door. She guessed the prize had been announced. Casper would be striding up to the stage preparing himself to give a victory speech. If she were ever so lucky as to win something like that she'd just about be able to murmur 'Thanks to everyone for voting for me'. In Casper's case he'd have a prepared speech to hand which would go on for at least fifteen minutes.

'Not again,' she muttered to herself, heading for the cloakroom to get her coat. If she couldn't get to Doherty by phone then she'd get to him by taxi. She needed to know what was going on.

Chapter Thirty-one

The police station was a fair step away, though all downhill. Normally she might have walked there, but she was wearing killer heels and a lightweight evening dress. High heels were not meant to be walked on, only to be seen in.

It was nine o'clock and she needed a taxi. The trouble was that by the time she got to the nearest rank she'd be halfway to Manvers Street.

On top of that it began to rain. The elegant hairdo flopped like a soggy loaf of bread on top of her head. The more she blinked the more her mascara ran, trickling down her face and taking her foundation with it.

Not a single, solitary taxi went by and the rain was getting heavier.

Walking in high heels on ancient pavements and downhill threw her off balance. The rain blinding her eyes obscured elements of the uneven surface. A heel went one way and her ankle went another. The other heel wedged in a crack between two paving slabs. Her legs couldn't cope. Down she went.

'Aaghhh!'

Swear words stuck in her throat. One white knee poked through a shiny black stocking. Both shoes were still on her feet but the heel had parted from one, sticking up from the crack between paving slabs.

The brakes of a car squealed to a stop right opposite her. The doors closest to her sprang open and two men leapt out.

She found herself being lifted into the air, her toes not touching the ground.

'Put me down.'

'Give us one good reason why we should.'

'I know karate.' It was rubbish. She had gone to a karate class once but decided it took too much effort. It also seemed to depend too much on wearing loose white pyjamas and shouting as you attacked whoever might be attacking you.

Warning somebody you were about to attack them seemed silly.

The thugs who had hoisted her off her feet were obviously of the same mind.

'We're dead scared,' they said as they threw her into the front seat of the car.

Obviously they were not. Far from it.

'This is no way to treat a lady,' Honey protested.

Her skirt was clinging to her thighs, her stockings were laddered, and she felt like a sack of potatoes. Nothing seemed to be covering anything any more.

Her instinct told her that these guys meant business. One word and she could be in big trouble. But her mouth didn't know that. Her mouth went on motoring.

'Let me out of here. I'll have you know I have friends in the police force.'

'I'll have you know that I couldn't give a damn. Close the goddamned door!'

The same person speaking to her was giving the orders. She recognized Luigi Benici, big trouble with a capital B and T. If that door closed the car would be off to who knew where and she would be going too. And all for the sake of the latter-day punk who came in to wash her dishes. How crazy was that?

She fixed her eyes on that door and the fresh air blowing through it and up her skirt. If that door closed and they drove off, she was dead meat. Luigi Benici had lost face. She could lose a lot more than that if she didn't tell him what he wanted to know.

Before one of the brutes he had hired grabbed for the door, she swung her legs round. Her back was resting on the seat, her legs flailing furiously and her bottom was hanging between the edge of the seat and the dashboard.

'Get her legs in,' Benici shouted.

The men – probably family members, the similarity between them was quite apparent – did their best.

Honey prided herself on having strong legs. She could kick like a mule if need be. That's exactly what she was doing now. Every time one of the thugs reached for the door, she screamed and kicked and struggled so much that her remaining shoe came off. The shoe went flying, clocking a pedestrian in the back of the neck.

Last she saw, the pedestrian went down and a sympathetic crowd was gathering.

The situation had not altered by the time they made the lights at the bottom of Lansdown Hill. Her legs, up to and beyond her stocking tops, were waving from the front passenger seat, the door still wide open.

She'd prayed the lights were red and momentarily glimpsed them before the car took a violent right swerve, then a left into Lansdown Hill.

'You've run a light,' she screamed.

'Book me!'

One of the goons in the back was trying desperately to shut the car door. The other was trying just as desperately to drag Honey back into her seat.

She kept kicking, though she felt her strength flagging. *This is a hostage situation. Fighting is a definite option, but I can't keep it up. What else can I do?*

Reason with the man. That's the ticket, she decided.

'Look, Mr Benici. What Clint did was wrong, but that

doesn't mean he's a bad man or that your wife isn't the woman she was before. I mean, think about this carefully. Ask yourself what you're going to gain from pulverizing poor old Clint into mush.'

'Satisfaction. I'm going to mix him with my garden compost and spread it on my roses. They'll smell sweeter for all that.'

Honey gulped. It wasn't for the want of trying, she told herself. Poor Clint. She'd done her best, but what about her? What had he got lined up for the woman who'd spirited Mrs Benici's lover out of Mr Benici's reach?

She gulped. The world the likes of Luigi Benici inhabited bore little resemblance to hers. OK, he was like her in that he was involved in the hospitality and catering trade, for he owned restaurants. But there the similarity ended. She'd heard rumours that Mr Benici had fingers in other pies, ones that didn't necessarily get cooked in ovens – though there had been whispers. People who'd upset Mr Benici seemed to disappear pretty frequently. The more naïve took the view that they'd got out of town. The more pragmatic suggested that Mr Benici's Parma ham was not all that it should be.

They shot up Lansdown Hill with the door swinging and two pairs of hands still trying to contain matters.

Mr Benici was not enthralled with their efforts. A torrent of swear words poured out from his sensual mouth – some appeared to be in Italian.

My, she thought, the citizens of Bath are an education in themselves!

Swinging around in a car with a door wide open and a pair of legs sticking out was obviously not in Benici's game plan. He was going blue in the face, shouting at his driver, shouting at the two guys who were trying to rectify the situation.

Somehow or other, she didn't know how, she managed to wriggle right down into the well between the seat and the dash.

Fingers on big fat hands splayed out to grasp her. The time line between being grabbed and being free was fine. All it would take was a little inattention from the driver – and it happened!

The car swerved round a bollard to the right at the same time as it hit a bump in the road.

The speed stalled just long enough.

Curling into a ball – she'd at least been taught how to do that at her single karate class – Honey rolled and was out.

At school she'd taken part in amateur dramatics. Her most lauded part had been as a hedgehog in *The Wind in the Willows*, rolling up into a ball like frightened hedgehogs do.

That's exactly what she did now, keeping herself in a tight ball and rolling across the pavement until she hit a signboard outside the door of The Farmhouse, a large pub on the corner of Camden Crescent.

Lansdown Hill was never that busy during the day except for traffic and it certainly wasn't that busy this time of night. One or two pedestrians were strolling up or down; none was close enough to be of any assistance and nobody had come out of the pub.

Just as she'd feared, Benici's car came to an abrupt halt. They weren't going to let her off that easily.

The big bruisers that worked for him got out. She could see them looking around as they buttoned their jackets. It must have made their day to see that witnesses were thin on the ground.

Honey was trying to get up but it wasn't easy. Although her body had stopped doing cartwheels, her head was still coming to terms with being upright.

She shook her head. 'I feel sick.'

She couldn't look up at them but kept her eyes fixed on their feet. They were coming to get her; those big size twelves were plodding across the pavement.

Swinging one arm to one side, she attempted to get up, but her head was still spinning.

The feet stopped half way to her.

She heard a voice.

'OK, guys. I'll take care of things from here.'

'Get the hell –'

'He's a cop,' somebody said.

The feet receded. The car doors shut and she was vaguely aware of it driving off.

Then there were another pair of feet and someone in jeans was bent down. Placing his fingers beneath her chin, he raised her face so she had to look at him. She couldn't help smiling. Being a cop's girlfriend certainly had its advantages.

His look was relieved but also reproachful.

'How come I can't leave you alone for five minutes and you're off with other men?'

'Fatal attraction,' she said with a grin.

Steve Doherty had caught up with her.

Chapter Thirty-two

Karen Pinker was dead. Doherty filled her in on the details, not least the bit about the calls from public phone boxes.

'Including during the time you were there.'

Honey gulped down half her drink. Steaks were sizzling and the usual blue smoke was whirling in the meagre lights piercing the darkness of the Zodiac Club.

The news about Karen was unwelcome. The smoke was otherwise, seeing as it was helping to dry out her rats'-tail hairstyle and the little black dress that was clinging in all the wrong places.

Doherty had offered to help her off with her ragged stockings. His face had dropped when she'd refused his offer on account of the fact that she had no shoes on her feet, so her stockings had to stay. He'd probably have to carry her home.

At least she was warm. It was now twelve midnight and the club was filling up with warm bodies jostling for space at the bar. Her bedraggled appearance wasn't likely to be noticed. The patrons were here to eat, drink, and escape the rigours of being part of the hospitality profession. Most were hoteliers, guest house owners, and pub landlords. Twelve midnight was their time to have fun.

The drink helped soften the blow of Karen Pinker's death. So did the touch of Doherty's fingers brushing wet strands of hair away from her eyes.

However, she couldn't help feeling guilty about Karen's

209

death and questioned whether it was her fault. She'd urged Karen to talk about The Beauty Spot and as a result of that Karen had lost her job. The question was, had she also lost her life for the same reason?

Twirling her glass like some kind of crystal ball did nothing to allay her guilt. But she had to keep focused.

'Penny for them?'

Doherty was doing that thing with his fingers again. Normally his touch would send tingles to places no one else's touch could reach. Tonight it was encountering blockages; enjoying things like that seemed somehow obscene when someone you knew – however briefly – had been murdered.

'I was thinking …'

'That Karen opening her mouth to you had contributed to her death.'

'Spot on.'

'You can't know that.'

'Don't you think so?'

He took hold of her chin. There was something powerful about him doing that. It made her feel vulnerable – which she was – and yet bathed in his protection – which she was.

'Look. Nothing is for sure. It could have been a jealous boyfriend. I mean, what the hell was she doing on a building site?'

Somehow Honey couldn't imagine a girl like Karen with a builder boyfriend – not in the guy's workplace anyway. She recalled the phone ringing and Karen disappearing. Could the same thing have happened on the day Lady Macrottie was killed? Highly possible.

She put it to Doherty and he took it on board. 'Pity we don't know who it was.'

Doherty cleared his throat and grasped his drink, fixing it with a jaundiced eye. 'Talking of boyfriends, I do think Luigi Benici is a little out of your league. Other guys play hard to get. Benici plays hard. Period. What the hell were you doing in his car?'

'He offered me a lift, even though I didn't want one. Well, not from him anyway.'

He nodded sagely. 'Well, that puts my mind at rest. It did seem as though he'd swept you off your feet, seeing as your legs were hanging out of the front passenger door.'

'Thanks for coming to my rescue. Lucky that you were around.'

'That's me. Steve Doherty. Knight in shining armour.'

Honey sighed. His fingers had travelled to the nape of her neck. She was finally beginning to relax.

'I wasn't exactly there by chance. I went to the Assembly Rooms first. Casper told me you'd disappeared just as the award was about to be announced.'

She was suddenly smitten with a thought of the utterly impossible.

'I didn't win it, did I?'

He shrugged. 'I wouldn't know. I didn't ask.' He frowned. 'That bookshop guy was there too.'

'Ahh. Well. You get a lot of people at gala evenings.'

He nodded slowly. She could tell by the look in his eyes that he wasn't buying it. Never mind. She wasn't giving forth either. John Rees had been around and he hadn't. She couldn't put her life on hold for a good-looking police officer who worked odd shifts, could she? The jury was out on the answer to that one.

Doherty was no fool.

'Two men in one night. Didn't your mother ever tell you not to get in strange cars?'

If her glass hadn't been empty she might have thrown her drink over him. That's what she told herself. Then again, perhaps not. He was trying to be funny. He was trying to cheer her up and helped things along by getting her another drink.

211

'Tell me the details,' she said as she watched the ice, the lemon, and the vodka and tonic being poured into her glass.

Doherty obliged.

Honey took a sip of her drink before making comment. 'Mud and a wrought-iron railing. Strange weapons. Are the two murders really connected?'

When Doherty shrugged, his leather jacket made a squeaky noise.

'Is that new?'

She touched it, suddenly noticing that it certainly smelled new.

'I gave the other one away.'

He sounded embarrassed about it. Odd, she thought. It was no big deal to give something away.

'I gave it to my daughter. She wanted it.'

She half-turned so that she was facing the bar full on rather than him. This daughter thing was odd. She asked herself why she felt so uncomfortable about it, but couldn't come up with an answer.

'Is she moving in with you?'

'Hell no! And those are her words.'

Honey smiled at that. Lindsey would have said pretty much the same thing at that age.

'Benici is a tryer. You need to know that.'

Honey's face froze.

'Great. That's all I need, some mad Italian to go with my mad chef and my mad – correction, – sex mad – washer up.'

'I'll pay him a visit. A little hint that I've got my eye on him should help. I don't like that scared expression on your face.'

'It shows that bad?'

'Fear has a habit of doing that.'

Honey shivered. 'I wouldn't like to end up in a bed of cement.'

'You're thinking of the murdered Miss Pinker again. Care

212

to go for a ride tomorrow?'

She eyed him silently, unwilling to say anything that might stop his fingers easing the tension from her neck.

'First The Beauty Spot and then Karen's friend …'

'And then Clint.'

Doherty looked baffled. 'Why Eastwood?'

'My motherly protective instinct is only part of this. Clint knows some pretty scruffy guys that sleep rough hereabouts. If there really was somebody like that hanging around the clinic, then he might know who it was. He does voluntary work now and again, a lot of it for the homeless,' she explained in response to his look of surprise.

Rodney 'Clint' Eastwood was full of surprises. He lived on the shady side of life and had part-time jobs all over the place that made him a reasonable living. Whether he ever got round to paying any of it over to the taxman was neither here nor there. The probability was that he did not. But he had a good heart and fitted his voluntary work in with his paid jobs. The man wasn't all bad. He was just giving something back to society, though not – it had to be said – money.

'Worth a visit?'

Doherty nodded. 'OK.'

He was thinking that he needed a break on this case. He also needed time to sort out his commitments. Honey was one of them.

Chapter Thirty-three

'So where are you going?'

It was just so typical. Here she was, all set to sneak off for the day with Steve Doherty – primarily on police business, but there was no doubt a little personal recreation might sneak in – when her mother phoned.

'We're off interviewing witnesses.'

'People who actually saw what happened? Will they tell you all the details?'

For somebody who preferred Mills and Boon to murder and mayhem, her mother had a bloodthirsty streak.

'Not exactly. These people just might have some bearing on the case. They're not suspects.'

'You don't know that for sure.'

Her mother sounded like a voiceover for *Tales of the Unexpected*. For somebody who dressed in Dior and wore kitten-heeled shoes, Gloria Cross had a chiller-thriller side.

Honey played at being Mrs Level-Headed. 'We'll ask questions. They'll answer. That's all there is to it. To put it professionally, they are helping police with their enquiries.'

'Let me know if there's any juicy bits. The girls will want to know *everything*!'

The 'girls' were Gloria's friends and none of them were less than seventy-five. Most of them had lived through the Second World War and still blushed at the memory.

As one of them had once said to her, 'You youngsters think

you invented sex. Well, you didn't. We did. We had to have something to do in the blackout!'

The girls liked gossip; especially juicy gossip, anything to do with bloodlust or lust by itself. They were up for it.

'Mother, I've got to go.'

'Not yet!'

Why was it she obeyed her mother's voice as swiftly as a dog might obey its handler?

Tone of voice. Yep! That was the one!

'I suppose you shared his bed last night.'

Honey glanced over at Doherty. Guessing who was on the other end of the phone, he'd hidden beneath the bedclothes.

'I'm over twenty-one, Mother. In fact I'm over forty-one.'

'There's no fool like an old fool!'

Honey almost choked. This was the pot calling the kettle black! Who was her mother to talk, she who still welcomed compliments and sometimes wore a lacy suspender belt – depending on the virility of the guy she was dating.

Honey found her voice. This time she spoke through clenched teeth.

'Mother. I have to go.'

'Can you find some time in your busy schedule to drop in? I want your opinion on a wedding outfit.'

'Not yours?'

'Of course not. I haven't met Mr Right yet.'

'Of course not.'

'Enid Bevan is getting married. She's marrying a guy she met on a Saga cruise.'

Saga organized cruises for older folk. Older folk loved cruises. Her mother loved cruises. It was one of the few times when she got to dance with someone who wasn't wearing high-heeled shoes. Women over a certain age got sick and tired of dancing with other women. Male dancing partners was much more exciting. The crew provided 'escorts', members of crew required to dance with guests as part of their contract.

Obviously Enid had found a boon partner, someone of her own age. Enid Bevan was close to seventy-five years of age and had been determined to remarry following the death of her husband. She certainly hadn't taken long about it. Her former husband had only been dead six months or so. But Honey understood Enid. She'd met her a few times and the conversation had always been about romance. Honey had come to the conclusion that Enid was the sort who couldn't function without a man. Any man.

Thinking that it wouldn't be any real bother to go through her mother's wardrobe and advice, Honey agreed to her request.

Hearing the conversation come to an end, the top half of Doherty's face reappeared from beneath the bedclothes.

'Any problems?'

'None!' Honey said brightly. 'Except that I promised to call into my mother's on the way back.'

'Shit!'

Doherty disappeared beneath the bedclothes.

Chapter Thirty-four

The midnight blue BMW driven by Serena Sarabande glided into the reserved parking place. Just like her car, Serena did not so much move getting her bag and other things together, she glided. Every movement was smooth, just like her appearance and her swept-back hairstyle.

Before getting out she brought down the vanity mirror on her side of the car, examining her skin just in case a tiny speck of something alien had dared sully her satin-smooth complexion.

Satisfied that all seemed well, she heaved a deep sigh.

As usual she would have taken her keys from the dashboard and gathered up her things, but something stopped her.

Flipping the mirror back into place, her eyes happened to catch a glimpse of movement.

He was standing half-hidden by the bushes on the lawned area that separated the grounds of The Beauty Spot from the building site beyond.

She quickly reached for her mobile and dialled a number. Dexter answered.

'He's here again! What shall I do?'

Dr Dexter paused. 'Call the police.'

'He'll cause trouble.'

'He's *in* trouble, so let's stir it a little more.'

'When will you be here? I'll feel safer when you're here.'

'I'll be there soon.'

'What about Karen? The police are bound to call. What shall I tell them?'

He laughed. 'All the more reason to point them in the direction of our shadowy friend.'

The connection was severed.

Her lips were dry and her heart was galloping. She fumbled for her phone. Before dialling she checked the bushes. There was nobody there. If he was gone, there was no point in calling the police.

Breathing deeply she lay her head back and closed her eyes. Her heart was still hammering. The phone was still in her hand. Her mind began to drift to sunlit beaches and a turquoise sea. That's what Roger Dexter had promised her when all this was over.

A sudden tapping at the car window brought her upright. She'd thought to see the vagrant. Instead she looked out to see someone she vaguely recognized. It suddenly came to her that he was the police officer she'd seen at the time of Lady Macrottie's murder.

She made a big show of gathering her things. Obligingly, he opened the car door for her.

She kept her cool. 'Don't I know you?' Her tone was imperious. Never show fear. Never show nerves.

'I thought I recognized you, Ms Sarabande,' he said. 'Detective Inspector Steve Doherty.'

She decided she quite liked his smile. She'd thought the same on his previous visit. Not that she'd show any sign that she did. It wasn't her way.

'You're not wrong there. Can I help you with anything?'

She gripped her briefcase and her handbag more firmly.

'No thank you.' She shook her head as though she were a dizzy blonde rather than an iceberg. Sometimes it paid to pretend to be helpless. 'It's nothing much. Is there something I can help you with, Detective Inspector?'

'Call me Doherty.'

'Doherty.'

'And I'm Honey Driver.'

Serena Sarabande's head twisted round at the sound of a woman's voice. She did a swift double take. Honey was recognized. Serena's face visibly soured.

'I didn't know you were with the police.'

Her voice was as chill as ice and her face was pale and rigid. Nobody liked having their space infiltrated and Serena Sarabande certainly didn't.

'Mrs Driver is an associate consultant,' Doherty explained. The charm was gone. Serena had to know that he meant business. 'Can we go inside and talk or do you want to wash your dirty linen out here?' he added, his smile more incisive – less warm.

They ended up in her office. She didn't offer them any refreshment. They didn't want anything except for some answers. Doherty was determined to get to the bottom of things and Honey was keen to exonerate herself from causing Karen Pinker's death.

'I take it you're aware of the murder of your former employee, Karen Pinker?'

She lowered herself into the big black leather chair behind her desk. There was a rustling sound as she slowly and gracefully folded one graceful leg over the other. She held Doherty's gaze as she did it, purposely seeming to avoid looking at Honey.

'I did hear, though I really can't see how I can help you.'

'You don't know of any reason why she was on the building site?'

She shook her head. 'Absolutely not.'

'You don't know whether she knew someone there? Whether she was maybe having a relationship with someone working there?'

The smile that came to her face was cold and contemptuous. 'I wouldn't be at all surprised. Karen had a penchant for rough diamonds.'

Chapter Thirty-five

Honey wasn't convinced that she'd seen the last of Luigi Benici, which made it all the more important that she get to see Clint. She didn't like being linked with his transgression. Being stalked and taken for an unscheduled ride was a big no-no.

She had some crazy idea of convincing Clint to come clean and apologize profusely to Mr Luigi Benici – failing that, perhaps he'd like to consider emigrating to Australia, or even Alaska.

Clint's ex-girlfriend, who was sheltering him, lived in a residential caravan, courtesy of the landowner who grew organic produce and lived in a log cabin.

The whole plot was surrounded by forest, long grass, and a profusion of wildlife. The place was situated in the Forest of Dean, an area of outstanding natural beauty where the descendants of archers at the Battle of Agincourt enjoyed the rights to graze their sheep freely on forestry land. The killing of French archers had repercussions down the ages.

Glades of oak trees nestled among modern fir trees and the rough scrub beneath was criss-crossed by rough forest tracks.

'This is not good for my suspension,' Doherty remarked as his sports car hit another pothole. The Toyota MR2 was low-slung and cosy for two but was not made for bumpy forest tracks. Doherty was proud of his car. Only two hundred of this type had been manufactured and each had its own number engraved in the upholstery leather. His was number 192.

However, a four-wheel drive would have been a better bet.

Yet another bump sent Honey headbutting the car roof.

'It's not good for me either,' she mumbled as she rubbed her head.

It was a surprise to see a pink Cadillac parked alongside the caravan in a leafy glade. Honey immediately felt a twinge of apprehension. Spending two or three nights a week with Doherty meant not being around much, interacting with guests as she'd always done. Time spent back at the Green River Hotel was usually taken up with a mountain of paperwork to catch up on. Socializing with guests was something she had to fit in when she could.

'Cooeee!'

Cheeks flushed pink, Mary Jane was hanging out the door of the caravan, waving frantically. She looked totally at home in her greenwood surroundings. As tall and as spindly as a young birch tree, she was dressed in a lime-green tracksuit that would have sent Robin Hood heading for cover.

'I didn't expect to see you here,' said Honey. She pulled herself out of the car, rubbing her head with one hand and her rear end with the other.

'I get such good vibrations here,' Mary Jane explained. 'Clint's friend Anthea tells me it's to do with the oxygen levels and it being unpolluted here by light and civilization. Personally I think it's more to do with the spirits of the trees. They float around here without being interrupted by anything except deer and latter-day naiads.'

Honey looked at her blankly. All she could think of saying was that the bumpy ride up the lane was vibration enough.

Doherty looked at the gangly Californian the same way he always did; as though she was slightly dotty. Honey wouldn't disagree with that; it was just that she never showed it.

'Anthea knows what she's talking about. Her and the girls are a coven of wood nymphs,' explained Clint. 'You could call them white witches, but they prefer being called naiads. There's one of them now. Morning, Violet.'

They all turned to see a naked and very plump lady with purple-veined legs stroll by. Describing her as a 'girl' was pushing it a bit.

Violet was carrying a loaf of bread and a truckle of cheese on a tray. The tray also seemed to be supporting her large breasts, which competed with the other items for room, sitting on the tray like uncooked dough.

Mary Jane glanced as though naked fat ladies walking by were an everyday occurrence. Perhaps they were in California, mused Honey.

'My. She's quite an earth mother,' exclaimed Mary Jane. 'I've seen loads like her in ancient temples all over the world. Ancient peoples worshipped women of her shape, you know.'

Honey was dumbstruck. 'Nowadays they go to Weight Watchers.'

Clint waved at the woman. 'A bit fresh today don't you think, Violet?'

'At least it's dry,' the naked lady called back. 'No matter the weather I must make obeisance to the trees.' She indicated the tray. 'Any day and in any weather is good for an offering.'

'She must be freezing.' Doherty was alarmed.

'Of course she's not,' said Clint. 'She's a wood nymph.'

There was no answer to that and no real explanation as to why being a wood nymph made you impervious to the cold. It was only spring – an English spring. Summer was two months off and there was no guarantee the sun was going to shine and the temperature reach the seasonal average. Even June could be a bit nippy around the extremities.

Herbal tea was offered in heavy mugs that seemed, judging by the names printed on the sides, mostly to be souvenirs from seaside resorts. Brighton. Blackpool. St Ives.

The steaming brew gave off a perfumed odour vaguely

reminiscent of dusty nettles and crushed rosehips.

Seeing as they'd had nothing since this morning, they accepted, though Doherty did look a bit doubtful.

'Not bad,' said Honey after taking a sip. Healthy brews were not really her thing.

Doherty took one sip and looked as though he were about to throw up. 'Christ! What's this made from?'

Clint was his usual exuberant self. 'I made it myself from fresh dandelions,' he said proudly.

'Not nettles?' Honey knew nothing of natural brews but nettles seemed the usual ingredient of most of them.

'No. Dandelions. It's a diuretic.'

Doherty flashed Honey a questioning look.

She smiled wickedly. 'It makes you pass water a lot.'

Doherty tipped the contents of his mug on to the grass. 'I'll pass. I've got to drive back to Bath.'

Honey had expected to see Clint not exactly cowering in a corner, but not far from one. He seemed totally unfazed by the fact that he was number one on a Mafia hit list. She had no evidence to confirm that Luigi was Mafia, but at mention of Benici and Mafia in the same breath, Doherty had adopted an odd, noncommittal expression.

First things first. Ask him about inebriates likely to be dossing round and about The Beauty Spot.

Clint frowned when she asked the question. 'I don't know everybody who lives in Cardboard County,' he said. He sounded offended.

Honey apologized. 'I should have known better.'

'It's a long time since I was of no fixed abode,' Clint stated. 'I have an address.'

She could have said, *one you dare not be seen in at present.* But she didn't. There was still a glimmer of hope.

'So who do you suggest I ask? Is there anyone who might know?'

He jerked his chin. 'Could be.'

Honey waited. Clint eyed her, looked at Doherty with narrowed eyes and then looked back at her.

'I'll write it down for you. He don't like coppers.'

Doherty threw Honey one of his long-suffering looks.

Clint fetched a supermarket receipt out of one pocket and a pencil from another. Honey took the scribbled note once Clint had folded it in four, still harbouring a squinty-eyed look every time his eyes travelled Doherty's way.

Honey thanked him. One job was out of the way, but there was still one to go.

The time was ripe to suggest Clint might want to try and make peace with Luigi, or at least come back to Bath and keep low.

He shook his head vehemently at the suggestion.

'Man, are you kidding?'

'Mr Benici might see sense. After all, he hasn't thrown his wife out or killed her. She's still the woman he married. A woman's a woman for all that,' stated Mary Jane as though she were repeating some sacred mantra.

'Except that she's pregnant.' Doherty grinned.

Clint grimaced.

Unfazed, Doherty continued. 'And bearing in mind that she's another man's wife, your days as a fully-fledged male are numbered.'

The four of them fell to silence, all staring at the ground as though an answer might pop up at any minute.

Honey was in thought mode. She needed her washer-up and basically, deep down, he was a good sort who had been born out of his time. He should have been adult – or almost adult – around the Summer of Love. He believed in free love. He expected everyone else to feel the same.

'What we need is confirmation that the baby is not Clint's – without resorting to DNA evidence,' said Honey.

'Too bloody right!' Clint looked shifty about ending up on the police DNA database. He didn't like being on police databases full stop. The DNA one was way beyond full stop.

'It's all about rumour and reputation,' Honey stated, sure of her ground, sure she knew men and their egos that well.

Doherty shook his head. 'I don't get it.'

Honey clarified. 'What I'm saying is that we need to provide evidence that Clint can't possibly be the father.'

Doherty looked unconvinced. 'Isn't that the same thing?'

'You're not listening to what I'm saying.' Honey folded her arms and shook her head. What she intended saying next wasn't going to go down too well; Clint was a man and men were proud of their fertility almost as much as their virility.

'We need to prove that it's impossible for Clint to be the father.'

Doherty still wasn't getting it. 'Sorry to have to say this, Clint, old buddy, but you were caught with your pants down – literally!'

Clint gave his version of the soft shoe shuffle – his head tipping from side to side as though his neck had suddenly rubberized. To his credit he didn't blush.

'Yeah. You're right there. I'd put my pants over a chair but got into them damned quick when Benici came hammering at the door. Flew out of the bloody window, in fact!' He shook his head. 'The guy should be more cool. He'll give himself a heart attack going on like that.'

'That's nothing to what he's likely to give you,' muttered Doherty.

Honey understood Clint. His view of the world was that you should be free to do anything you wanted to do providing it didn't hurt anyone else. Regardless of the fact that he'd been born too late, he had a Summer of Love view of the world. Unfortunately for him, Luigi Benici didn't share his view.

'Do you have any children, Clint?'

He shook his head. 'Not that I know of.' He grinned suddenly. 'And I ain't married. I'm gonna stay single and bring all me kids up the same way.'

At any other time the joke might have raised a smile. But Clint's physical health could be at risk here and it wasn't funny. Honey pointed it out to him, plus the very hurtful comment, 'So you might be firing blanks.'

Clint looked as though she'd landed him a physical punch rather than a verbal one.

'What? I'm not sure that I like that.'

'If we could prove that you are not the father … merely by saying that despite the fact you've had numerous liaisons, you have never fathered a child … Benici might listen. Italians are notoriously macho; they all have to be stallions. How long have the Benicis been married?'

Clint shrugged. 'A few years.'

Doherty groaned and rubbed his hand over his face. 'How are you going to do this?'

'Luigi Benici is bound to try and pick me up again. This time I'll make sure he knows that Clint fires duds. OK?'

Clint looked horrified. 'Hey, just a minute! What about my reputation?'

Doherty shook his head and grinned. 'Ah, yes. Your reputation. Comments about big weapons and firing blanks are going to come pretty thick and fast.'

Clint glared. He'd never been buddies with the police and wasn't about to start now.

Doherty had got over the shock of the fat woman and her having a close relationship with trees. Clint's virility being brought into question was good for a laugh. Any time he bumped into him in future he'd grin wryly; the joke was on Clint.

Mary Jane's eyes were turned heavenward. A long thin finger was poised on her cheek.

'Do you know that eunuchs were much prized in the harems of the Sultan of Constantinople? By the women I mean. Because there were so many of them they didn't see the Sultan's bed too often – perhaps once a year. So the eunuchs came in handy. Now how did they put it? "*They enjoyed the flower of passion but not the fruit.*" Yeah! That's what they said.'

Clint blinked, his tight expression loosening as the implications of what she'd said hit him hard between the eyes – and in his pants.

'Bloody hell! I could have a field day.'

Honey rolled her eyes. Obviously she hadn't known men well enough. She'd forgotten the cardinal rule. Go for the positive aspect. She could almost imagine him putting the word around the city of Bath.

Want sex without risk? Rodney (Clint) Eastwood's your man!

Chapter Thirty-six

A call came through on Doherty's cell phone just as they were about to leave.

He rendered Honey his apologies.

'Sorry, doll. Duty calls.'

'Anywhere interesting?'

'The morgue.'

'Oh!'

Honey didn't like morgues – or at least the thought of them, since she'd never entered one. However, she'd weighed up the alternatives: drive to the morgue with Doherty or home with Mary Jane. The morgue was likely to make her feel queasy, but then so was Mary Jane's driving.

Doherty cupped her elbow and put some distance between the two of them and Mary Jane and Clint. Clint was showing Mary Jane some seedlings that were just sprouting.

Doherty slipped his hand up the front of Honey's T-shirt, hooked his fingers into the waistband of her jeans, and tugged her close.

She pretended to be offended. 'You're taking liberties!'

'I'm making up for lost time.'

'Since when?'

'Since tonight. My bed will be empty. Personal matters.'

'Your daughter.' The fact that he hadn't told her he had a daughter still rankled, but she'd put it to one side. He must have had his reasons.

He sighed. 'I promised her mother I'd pick her up and take her home.'

'To your wife.'

'My ex-wife.'

He said it vehemently, as though the reference left a bitter taste on his tongue. She hoped it did. To leave a sweet taste would mean he was still sweet on her. Wouldn't it?

'OK. So I take my life in my hands and drive home with Mary Jane.'

'You've drawn the short straw, babe.'

Once he'd removed his hand from her waistband, he chucked her under her chin.

'Keep it warm for me, babe.'

Nothing could make her enthusiastic about driving home with Mary Jane. She had no choice.

'It's such a long time since we had a really good chat,' Mary Jane was saying while guiding Honey gently but firmly towards the pink Cadillac coupé that she'd had specially shipped over from the States. 'You and I have been passing like ships in the night, as they say. Of course I can understand it, what with you having a love affair with that rascally policeman, so let's take this as an opportunity to catch up on things, shall we?'

While Mary Jane was doing her all-girls-together thing, Doherty had gone, his car bouncing off down the drive looking more like a child's toy car than a real sporty sort with all the gizmos.

Men liked gizmos, Honey thought to herself as Mary Jane guided her into the front passenger seat.

Honey belted up.

'No need to put the safety belt on just yet,' said Mary Jane in her usual blasé manner.

'Better to be safe than sorry.'

You bet it was. Mary Jane was far from being the world's

best driver. She'd learned to drive on the right hand side of the road in the United States and no amount of time would ever entirely erase that notion. The British Isles drove on the left. Mary Jane seemed to have it in her head that it was time they changed to the *right* way – the right hand side.

Mary Jane wittered on about Sir Cedric most of the way home. Sir Cedric was the resident ghost who had haunted the old hotel for centuries. Supposedly her long-dead ancestor, he lived in the corner closet in Mary Jane's room – if lived was quite the right word.

It wasn't until they'd crossed one of the two bridges spanning the Severn that Honey managed to get a word in.

'My mother's going to a wedding.'

'That's right. Have you seen her costume?'

'No. Have you?' The word 'costume' was a little off-key. Outfit, thought Honey. The word should be outfit.

'Yes, indeedy! It's brilliant. I told Sir Cedric about it. He remembers that kind of thing well, of course ...'

'Does he?'

Honey was getting a bad case of the jitters. The word costume was dancing around in her head.

'She went for the empire line. It was either that or the drapes of a Roman lady. Your mother thought it would make her look too matronly.'

Honey frowned. 'Is this a fancy dress party or a wedding?'

'A themed wedding,' Mary Jane announced at the same time as cutting up an articulated truck with Polish numberplates. 'Regency and Roman. Choose which you like.'

Honey didn't exactly feel guilty that she hadn't been privy to this information, merely surprised. Her mother had asked her to come round and run her eye over her wedding outfit, but she hadn't got around to it. A vision of the wedding guests popped into her mind. Ancient Romans. Historical Regency.

Driving with Mary Jane meant that you were stiff most of

the time because your nerves were always on edge. You also squeezed your eyes closed a lot. Doing all this was very tiring.

'How about we take the next exit and pop into the services for a coffee?'

Drinking overpriced coffee from cardboard cups in plastic surroundings was hardly Honey's idea of epicurean delight, but Mary Jane appeared to be having a race with any eight-wheeler that got in her way. She just had to overtake even when they were keeping up a good speed. The trouble was she kept forgetting herself and overtaking on the left instead of the right. The left hand lane was actually the hard shoulder, the place where vehicles experiencing a sudden puncture or mechanical breakdown pulled over. So far they'd avoided two such vehicles and survived to tell the tale. The third, Honey decided, they might not be so lucky.

As predicted the coffee was grim. The ladies' cloakroom was welcome. So was a packet of aspirin from the on-site shop.

Mary Jane had gone on back to the car. Honey had purchased a bottle of water besides her aspirin. She was never tense while driving. She wasn't even tense while driving with Doherty or anyone else. It was just Mary Jane. There should be a health warning on Mary Jane's driving, she decided as she made her way out of the concourse.

A little fresh air would help the medicine go down. She took a right. An area of grass fringed the path dividing the building from a metal guardrail overlooking the river.

A salty breeze was blowing. Leaning on the guardrail, she took deep breaths.

It felt good – though not for long.

She was jerked off her feet and spun round. She found herself facing Luigi Benici. He didn't look pleased. He wasn't exactly handsome, though not ugly either. Just angry. The tension had been diminishing. Now it did a U-turn. Benici was having an adverse effect on it. The tension was coming back.

'I want a word with you.'

Honey tried humour. 'Have you been to Wales, Mr Benici? Thinking of joining a choir, are you?'

'No. I have not. Lucky I came in here to relieve myself. We can resume our little discussion. Now. Where is Eastwood?'

She was tempted to say in Hollywood. After all, that was where the movie idol – Rodney's namesake – lived, didn't he? Judging by Benici's expression it might not go down well, so she held it down.

Despite the big maulers holding her, she managed a casual shrug.

'How would I know?'

He pointed a finger. The tip of it jabbed between her eyes.

'Don't lie to me. I saw him go in your place, but I didn't see him come out. Now tell me – before I let Bruno here have some fun with you – where is Eastwood?'

It crossed her mind that Bruno's idea of fun wouldn't fall in line with her own. Whatever he enjoyed she would not.

Now was the time to put her plan into action – if she could. It was difficult when you were being held in a Boston Crab, a beefy arm heavy across the jugular.

She croaked what she had to say.

'I hope you've forgiven your wife, Mr Benici. Especially now you're about to be parents …'

It was difficult to breathe, let alone speak, but somehow she managed it despite the arm around her throat.

'It's his! She told me it's his!'

'Not … possible … Clint … has … had …' She paused. This was ridiculous. She hit the restraining arm and at the same time kicked at his shin.

'Let me breathe!' she shouted at the top of her lungs.

The guy holding her was taken off guard.

'So breathe,' said Benici. 'Now talk.'

He nodded at the guy holding her. His grip loosened.

'As I was saying, Clint – sorry, Rodney – has a bit of a reputation with the ladies. He's put it about something chronic. And that's all he's done. No offspring have ever resulted from one of his nights of passion. The baby your wife is expecting cannot be his. In which case, it can only be yours.'

Benici's cheeks moved in and out as he chewed at what she'd said.

Honey wondered at how his wife was faring. After all, he was hardly the forgiving type.

'Your wife's still the woman she was. Her affair is finished. She's still your wife and she's expecting *your* baby.'

She studied his face, hoping to see a softening of expression but not really seeing anything at all except a clenched jaw and small, narrowed eyes with dark brown centres.

'I'll kill him anyway.'

This was not going as she'd planned. She'd planned for him to be enlightened enough to see the sense of it. Luigi Benici was not that kind of man. What did it say in the wedding service? *Those who God have joined together, let no man put asunder.*

Clint was that man and judging by the response of Gabriella's husband, Clint was likely to be *pulled* asunder if he didn't watch himself.

'Sure, sure, sure. I'm going to let bygones be bygones and I'm going to invite him to my restaurant. We'll have a little pizza, a little Chianti. I'll even give him a guided tour around my establishment. And when we get to the kitchen I'll invite him to lie on a stainless steel table while I get my sharpest knife and chop off his balls!'

Honey saw her chance. It was sudden and speedy, but there was no point in staying. She didn't have any balls he could chop off, but you could never tell what alternatives his sort might come up with.

Taking both Benici and his henchman by surprise, Honey

236

was off running, taking off from the bend in the path and leaping down the grass bank.

It was quite a distance to fly through the air and attracted admiring looks – or at least curious looks – from people in the car park.

'Drive,' she snapped to a surprised Mary Jane.

Mary Jane looked in her rear view mirror, something she rarely did when driving. Up until now it had purely been there for decorative purposes.

'Are those gangsters?' she asked, her voice tinged with excitement.

'You bet!'

Honey looked over her shoulder. Benici and his colleague were piling into the dark blue Bentley.

'Let's burn rubber!' Mary Jane hit the gas.

The G-force pressed Honey back into her seat. The colour left her face. If she'd been scared of driving with Mary Jane before, she was petrified now. They didn't so much leave the motorway services car park, they flew low.

'Are they following us?'

Honey was staring at the road ahead. She was clinging to the seat with both hands. Looking behind was the last thing she wanted to do. She needed to keep her eyes on the road. Mary Jane might not!

Freeing one hand, she angled the rear view mirror.

'They're on our tail.'

Mary Jane laughed. 'Aha! Run, run as fast as you can, you can't catch me, I'm the gingerbread man!'

This had to be it! Mary Jane was finally flipping her lid.

They skirted the traffic island at the bottom of the incline for Severn Bridge Services and bombed up on to the motorway slip road.

'It's magic,' laughed Mary Jane, who was obviously enjoying flying out into the traffic lane rather than prissily filtering out like sane people.

The pink Caddy coupé flashed out into the nearside lane. At this juncture there were only two lanes. They swooped directly out into the fast lane as though there was nothing else on the road. There was; cars, trucks and road-racing motorcycles weaving in and out of the traffic.

Mary Jane shot out there with them. They could have been at Le Mans. They could have been at Silverstone. The blaring horns and screeches of brakes said otherwise. Mary Jane was in her element.

'Give them the finger!' she shouted. 'We're on a mission.'

Honey was terrified. Mary Jane was crouched over the wheel with a manic look in her eyes.

Never had Honey seen her look like this or heard certain words mixed with her determination that they wouldn't be caught.

The road ahead looked scary. They were weaving in and out from one lane to another, scaring the pants off foreign drivers and homegrown ones alike.

Honey was scared too, so scared that she chanced looking over her shoulder. Anything was better than seeing the hazards ahead.

The Bentley wasn't doing too badly considering it wasn't being driven by a maniac.

'They're right behind us.'

'Not for long.'

There was something about Mary Jane's low-pitched growl that chilled Honey to the bone. Difficult conditions jogged her brain. She'd heard that growl once before: from the evil demon from *The Exorcist*.

They shot out like a cork from a bottle from the M48 on to the M4, meeting three lanes and more traffic.

A young man with a boombox stared at them as they flew by. The sound of his dubious music thundered after them. So did the Bentley.

The M5 turnoff was packed with traffic tailing back. A sign overhead flashed that there had been an accident.

'We'll get off at the next junction,' shouted Mary Jane.

The next junction – Bristol – proved as packed as the M5 exit.

'Home then,' laughed Mary Jane.

Honey felt like Dorothy in *The Wizard of Oz*, being spirited away from normal surroundings.

Not that she was really being spirited away, and Mary Jane wasn't a bad person like the Wicked Witch of the West. It was all just so surreal.

They were racing along with only an intrigued young guy playing loud music between them and Luigi Benici's Bentley.

There were arrows marked on the road ahead. The idea was that you left two arrows between each vehicle as you travelled along.

Mary Jane did not appear to know this – either that or she was totally ignoring them.

As they sped along she gave a running commentary on the merits of a Cadillac coupé as opposed to a Bentley.

It was all going over Honey's head. Her knuckles were white; her head was spinning, except in those moments when she was planning her own funeral.

White flowers would be nice. And a cremation. She couldn't stand the thought of being eaten by maggots. As for the hymns, well she'd always liked 'The Battle Hymn of the Republic'. The hymn kind of suited Mary Jane's driving and the end of the road – both figuratively and literally.

Leaving the motorway with Mary Jane at the wheel bore some similarity to an Apollo moon shot; it was breathtaking.

Honey glanced behind.

The grinning guy with the boom box was still behind the wheel, smiling broadly. Being young he had no problem keeping up with them. The Bentley was right behind him – which was bad news of course.

'We haven't managed to shake him off,' Honey said.

'Trust me,' replied Mary Jane.

They flew up the slip road. At the top was a traffic island. It was turn right for Bath. The traffic lights changed to amber, then red.

Mary Jane shot through.

The cars behind might have followed except for one incy-wincy thing; excited and coming from a country where car chases were the most exciting part of a film, Mary Jane did a right turn – except that she didn't go *round* the island as she was supposed to. She forgot to keep to the left. She turned right into the oncoming traffic coming up from Bath.

Cars screeched to a standstill. The guy behind them with the boom box stopped at the lights. The Bentley overtook but got T-boned by White Van Man, who was getting through at all costs and was already fazed by the old girl steaming right at him.

Leaving cars, trucks, and vans all over the place and sounding their horns, the pink Caddy shot down the A46 towards Bath the wrong way around the island.

'My!' Mary Jane cried breathlessly, her eyes shining with a strange inner light. 'Wasn't that exciting!'

Honey still had her eyes closed and her hands held tightly across her face.

Chapter Thirty-seven

It was purely on a whim that Honey decided to call in on The Beauty Spot.

She'd been lying in bed (her own bed), staring at the ceiling and unable to shake off the guilt she felt at the death of Karen Pinker. The girl had been friendly and although she couldn't be entirely ruled out as embroiled in Lady Macrottie's death, it didn't seem likely.

The guilt persisted. Honey had asked questions and Karen had answered. Now Karen was dead, thrown in a trench and covered in cement.

It wasn't fair to such an impeccably presented young woman. It wasn't fair for anybody to be murdered, for that matter. Honey was angry and her anger was directed at The Beauty Spot.

'Can you cope?' she asked Lindsey.

Lindsey pushed the mouse across its home on the mouse mat and gave her mother a sidelong look.

'I was born to cope. It's in my genes.'

Her daughter, Lindsey, was pretty mature for her age. Sometimes it unnerved her. It made her feel immature – even irresponsible – as it did now.

'That's brilliant.'

It was brilliant and she was probably right about the genes. However, the look on her face was a bit disconcerting. She'd seen that look before. Sometimes on Lindsey's face, but also somewhere else.

It didn't come to her until she was backing the car out of her allotted space in the underground car park. She used the car park on a regular basis and had a season ticket. It was cheap but it wasn't that great a garage. The concrete pillars supporting the roof were too close together, leaving little room for backing out or turning. She nearly ran into one when *that* look she'd seen on Lindsey's face came to her. Her mother!

Never mind, she said to herself as she headed along the crowded streets and off along the A4. She might grow out of it. Having a doppelganger of her mother was too much.

There were a lot of cars parked outside The Beauty Spot, more than when she'd stayed there.

She wondered why, then reminded herself it was Friday. Women who worked all week booked in for the weekend – a little respite and rejuvenation in a busy life.

A top of the range BMW had followed her into the car park. She prided herself on taking what looked like the last available space. The BMW stood idling.

She hightailed it into the clinic.

Dr Roger Dexter ran his finger down one side of Serena Sarabande's V-shaped neckline. His finger dipped into her cleavage and dawdled there, at the same time pulling her towards him.

'Almost there,' he said. 'Once JDS have exchanged contracts, we make plans.'

'And make speed,' Serena purred. 'Just you and me.'

Serena Sarabande, usually cool and collected, was as flushed and excited as a teenage girl. Roger Dexter had promised her a life in the sun – just the two of them in a villa overlooking the Mediterranean Sea. They'd have a clinic, of course – staffed by qualified local staff. The clinic would cater for the rich and retired living on Spain's Costa del Sol. They would merely manage the place – no interaction with clients. They were going to enjoy themselves.

'JDS are keen. They'll knock this place down, of course.'

'Shame. It's been here a long time.'

Roger laughed. 'So what do we care? Let him do what he likes *and* deal with the consequences.'

'What do we care?'

Serena's smile was wide and girlish, her self-control thrown to the winds. The inner Serena was coming out. That was the effect Dr Dexter had on her. She couldn't resist him.

'But in the meantime ...' He kissed her on the forehead, swam his finger around a bit, then let her go.

Serena's whole body seemed to heave with regret at the removal of his digit from her cleavage. Resigned that pleasure was over and now it was down to business, she sighed and handed him the file.

'Our last case. I think she's good for the money. Good for her age, too. She's shortly attending a friend's wedding and wants a quick job for a fair price. I haven't mentioned Venezuela. I'll leave that to you.'

He nodded affably, his eyes on the contents of the file he held in his hands. His smile was calculating.

'A little more cash in the bank wouldn't come amiss.'

'You reckon she's a dead cert for this?'

Serena nodded. 'A bit older than usual, but as long as her heart's strong, there shouldn't be any problem.'

Dr Dexter glanced up at her. 'I hope not. We don't want any more problems.'

'She's the sort that takes care of herself. Impeccably turned out. A bit of a clothes horse in fact. And she has money. That much is obvious.'

'Right, Mrs Gloria Cross,' he said addressing the file. 'Let's see how you respond to the prospect of two weeks in Venezuela – at a very attractive fee.'

Honey's mother had enjoyed the facial massage, the pedicure, the manicure, and the Indian head massage.

Enid had recommended the clinic and Gloria had gone along there mainly because she couldn't get in at short notice at her usual place.

This will suffice, she'd said to herself. And it was fine – as far as it went. What she couldn't get to grips with was the comments they'd made about her face. She took great care of her face and yet they'd mentioned plastic surgery.

She was not amused that they considered she needed something like that, and very shortly they would get a piece of her mind.

Chapter Thirty-eight

There was a new receptionist. She was just as well turned out as Karen had been and just as attentive. The smile was immediate and as crisp as her snow white uniform.

'Welcome to The Beauty Spot. What can we do for you today?'

Honey was just about to state her business when she felt a slight draught and knew somebody else had entered.

He was tall and spoke over Honey's head, literally jumping the queue – such as it was.

'Sorry to push in, love,' he said to Honey. 'I'd like to speak to Dexter. Now.'

'I don't think –'

The man stretched one beefy arm across the dividing counter, picked up the telephone receiver, and handed it to her.

'Do us a favour, love. Tell him that John Sheer is here of JDS Developments. If he wants completion on time, he'll see me.'

Honey was all ears. Completion. Completion of what?

John Sheer looked at Honey. 'Sorry, love. Important business.'

While the receptionist did as directed, Honey studied the new arrival, surmising that he was the driver of the BMW that couldn't find a parking space.

He was big and beefy. At some time he must have done physical labour, judging by the size of his muscles. He now oozed success. Labourer turned developer was written all over him.

He was wearing smart casual; a lemon cashmere sweater, pale grey chinos, and loafers. A bit overweight and fast approaching fifty, he looked as though he were using clothes and being well turned out to camouflage his problem with gym membership.

'It wouldn't hurt to say "I take it you're not here for a mudpack or a little liposuction",' said Honey.

'No. Though I could do with the latter,' he said with a grin, his hand patting his belly which she sensed he was trying to hold in.

He looked her up and down. 'So what are you doing here? A little beauty treatment? Certainly not surgery. You don't need it.'

She found herself responding to his flattery, flushing a little while allowing her ego to blossom.

However, he'd said something about completion.

'So you're not a surgeon or a doctor?'

He guffawed. 'Not bloody likely. I used to be just a builder but now I'm a builder and developer. I built the houses around this place.' He leaned closer, whispering so the receptionist wouldn't hear. 'I'll let you into a little secret. I'm about to buy this place and turn it into flats. If you want one I'll do it at a knockdown price.'

'Is that so? Any idea what the price is likely to be?'

'Dinner?'

Well that was a foregone conclusion. She had to admire his cheek and couldn't help smiling. Beneath it all her mind was ticking like a clock. He was going to turn this lovely old place into flats. It was the first she'd heard of it. The fact that he'd built all the houses round about plus those still being built was also interesting.

'Finding the body must have come as a bit of a shock.'

His amiable smile fell from his face.

'The worst thing of the lot.'

Honey frowned.

'We've had problems on the site ever since the day we laid the first foundations. Machinery vandalized, windows smashed. Somebody didn't want us to build and didn't want people to move in.'

'The girl that was murdered used to work here.'

He nodded and looked genuinely saddened. 'I didn't know Karen well, but well enough – you know – in passing. Not my type. Too perfect.' He frowned. 'I like natural women.'

Judging by the sudden way his eyes swept over her, loitering in the more intimate places, he meant what he said.

The receptionist interrupted to say that Dr Dexter was with a client but would be with Mr Sheer shortly.

Honey told her that she would see the doctor as soon as he was finished with Mr Sheer. In the meantime she'd grab a coffee from the refreshment station in the next room.

John Sheer said he would do the same and followed her through.

Things had gone exactly as planned. John Sheer had known Karen Pinker in passing. He was also responsible for developing the site. Instinct was gnawing at her insides. He had to know something interesting. In fact she *knew* he could tell her something interesting.

The bit about natural beauty had thrown her. Karen Pinker – or Karen Perfect, as Honey herself had termed her – had been just that. Too perfect.

'So Karen wasn't a natural beauty,' she said after taking a sip of coffee.

John Sheer did the same, shaking his head. 'Far from it. She was manufactured at the clinic's expense.'

Honey looked at him. His eyes twinkled as he returned her look and in that moment she had him worked out. He was sure of himself, still pulling the birds despite his advancing years and expanding waistline.

'How do you know that if Karen wasn't your type?'

'I had a little fling with a friend of hers. She told me that Karen had had a lot of work done at the clinic's expense. Dexter paid. He wanted someone up front as a kind of advert of what was achievable. Other women felt frumpy and inferior once they'd taken a look at Karen. It made them want to be what she was.'

Remembering she'd felt exactly like that, Honey chewed at her bottom lip before warning herself that it would get sore and unsightly.

'Anyway,' Sheer went on. 'I didn't think old Roger dug too deeply in his pockets. She had the work done in Venezuela. Apparently it's cheaper there.'

'Is that so?'

'Apparently.'

'Do you have the address of Karen's friend – the one you had the fling with? I'd like to talk to her about Karen. We got on well. I'd like to just – you know,' she said with a casual air. 'Just clarify things in my mind.'

'Like getting to know her better after the event?' he asked.

She nodded. 'Something like that.'

He looked around. 'I'm going to make this place look better than you're ever seen it before. A real luxury place offering top quality flats to well-heeled pensioners.'

'Did you think I was a pensioner?' She laid on the indignation big time.

'No! No! Of course not. I was just saying, if you fancy having one …'

She shook her head. 'No thanks. I'm already spoken for – I think. But best of luck. You'll probably need it'

He nodded. 'You could be right there, and thanks for not taking offence. The truth is it hasn't been that easy a project. I

248

couldn't get the finance the first time round for this as well as the grounds. That's how come the clinic bought it. I did try and persuade her ladyship – Carlotta Macrottie – to play ball, but she'd made her own plans. She was off to buy herself a nice little drum on the French Riviera.'

The conversation was getting more and more interesting by the minute.

'Lady Macrottie owned this?'

He nodded. 'All of it.'

And was about to fly south to warmer climes. Honey was taken by surprise by the revelation and regretted the receptionist interrupting to say that Dr Dexter would see Mr Sheer right away.

John Sheer didn't leave without giving Honey his card after he'd scribbled an address on the back. She took it gladly, even though she knew he was anticipating a closer encounter than she had in mind when they next met.

There was nothing to lose and a lot to gain. Sheer had told her plenty and with Doherty beside her might tell her a lot more.

Her instinct kicked in again. Karen's friend Magda came to mind, and when she checked the address on the back of the card she proved herself right. She wondered if she was acquiring psychic talents and felt quite pleased about it. It was possible, wasn't it? Without John Sheer mentioning her name, she'd guessed it was Magda he'd had his little fling with.

She made a snap decision. Magda first, then back here with Doherty. This was where it had all happened. She also made a mental note to check up on the vandalism that had occurred on the building site. There had to be police records. Perhaps someone had not wanted those houses built in the first place.

There was still a big question hanging over Serena Sarabande's evidence regarding the scruffy man. There was also the matter of the woman and the lesions; the promise that she would sue The Beauty Spot and her death in what appeared to be an accidental fire. But was it?

Recalling her promise to appraise her mother's wedding outfit, she took a detour to her apartment on her way back to the hotel. Her mother wasn't there. Neither was she contactable on her mobile.

No problem. She'd catch up with her later. At least she'd made the effort.

The Japanese couple were hauling yet more of their dubious purchases into the hotel. A taxi driver was puffing and panting as he assisted them with a marble tabletop. The supports consisted of two Egyptian-style sphinxes complete with claws and wings.

'Lindsey said we could put it in your garden. Our bedroom's getting a bit full,' Mrs Okinara confided.

'Fine.'

Honey nodded. Lindsey was in charge here. She was not going to interfere.

Everything would probably have gone to plan if the taxi driver hadn't keeled over, both hands grasping at his chest.

Luckily for the Okinaras the table top was leaning against the wall, so it remained intact.

'Sit him up,' Mrs Okinara ordered.

Honey phoned for the paramedics and an ambulance. In the meantime, the poor taxi driver, who had been sinking onto the pavement, was hauled up by the Japanese couple and perched on top of one of the sphinxes.

They took charge of the whole situation, one either side of the poor man, telling him to keep calm as he gasped for breath and winced with pain.

Hearing all the kerfuffle, Lindsey came out to see what it was all about, Mary Jane right behind her.

'He doesn't look good,' Mary Jane said, shaking her head.

The poor man heard her and groaned. If he'd looked like death before, he looked worse now thanks to Mary Jane.

The paramedics came whizzing to a stop, double parked on the other side of the taxi and a laundry van.

Honey left the taxi driver with the Okinaras.

'The professionals are here. Let's go inside,' she said to Mary Jane, taking hold of her arm.

'They won't save him,' sniffed Mary Jane.

Honey exchanged a forbearing look with Lindsey.

'I'll arrange coffee in the conservatory. There's something for you to look at out there,' she said to her mother. 'Gran brought it round. She wants your opinion.'

Honey headed in that direction, still holding grimly on to Mary Jane's arm. Mary Jane had a very laissez-faire attitude to 'crossing over'. If you had to go you had to go. Unfortunately the poor taxi driver didn't see things that way. Most people didn't. Mary Jane was a one-off.

The sight that met her in the conservatory was half expected. Gran had brought something round. There was only one thing it could be – her wedding outfit.

Honey braced herself for the viewing.

The outfit was hanging from a beam in the conservatory roof. The best thing about it was that it diverted Mary Jane's attention away from the man having a heart attack. The Jane Austen influence was obvious; it was high waisted and low necked with puffed sleeves.

Yuk to the puffed sleeves, but the colour was OK. The Jane Austen style she could leave well alone.

'Peach is my favourite,' drooled Mary Jane, her spidery hands passing the soft muslin between her fingers. 'Do you think she'd let me have it once she's finished with it?'

'You'd have to ask her.'

Honey didn't have a clue what use Mary Jane would have for the dress. Surely she wasn't thinking of wearing it? OK, her

251

mother and Mary Jane were both slim, but the similarity stopped there. Mary Jane was at least six inches taller.

'I could take the hem down or add some lace around it,' said Mary Jane, as though reading Honey's thoughts.

Asking where Mary Jane was likely to wear such an outfit was like a trip wire in front of her tongue. The answer was bound to be something to do with Sir Cedric. She talked about him as though ghosts came for tea every day of the week. Honey had never shown her disbelief because she wasn't sure that she disbelieved. Being neutral about guests' beliefs and aspirations was part of an hotelier's stock in trade. Same thing applied to shared secrets. Funny that people told the person behind the bar things they wouldn't tell their best friend, their spouse, or their parents. As though they were inanimate or incapable of passing it on.

Lindsey brought in coffee.

'Smudger's giving the Okinaras a hand.'

'How's the taxi driver?'

'Dead.'

'Sad.'

'Told you so,' said Mary Jane with a toss of her head. 'I could virtually see his spirit crossing over.'

Mary Jane and her premonitions made Honey nervous. An unknown future suited her fine. She turned the conversation back to the Regency-style dress and the matching bonnet. Regency and Romans. Nobody paid much attention to the settlement that had existed before Caesar and his cohorts tramped down into the valley, the first foreigners to visit the place. Before then the locals had painted themselves blue and worshipped at the hot springs. Not much was paid to the bit between the Roman and the Regency period. Not that there was much to report.

But the wedding should be quite a spectacle.

'I might see if I can wangle an invite,' mused Mary Jane.

252

Honey was thinking about Clint and his plans regarding a career in psychic development.

'Mary Jane, do you mind telling me what happened at the psychic evening you took Clint to?'

Mary Jane's sharp blue eyes flashed with an odd otherworldliness. She was being asked a question relating to her favourite subject.

'Ah, that's because of Lionel and his waterworks.'

'Yes.' Honey nodded like one of those nodding donkeys in a Texas oilfield; not because she had any understanding of Lionel – she had no knowledge of him and his waterworks – but purely to signify that she'd like Mary Jane to continue.

'Well, Lionel was about to give Clint a reading – Clint who was in disguise of course – when he had to dash to the bathroom. Lionel is having one hell of a problem with his bladder. The poor man can't travel more than fifty feet from the nearest convenience – and even then that's cutting it fine. He's got an appointment with a specialist, but you know what men are – nervous of having their private bits investigated.'

Honey had to agree with that. When a man catches a cold it's flu, and when it's flu he reckons it's pneumonia. Men are not just natural hypochondriacs; they don't like the thought of their private bits being subjected to medical examination. Just in case it's serious and they have to have something lopped off.

'So what happened?'

'Well!' exclaimed Mary Jane. 'A queue had begun to form and someone sat down in the chair opposite Clint. They thought Clint was the one doing the reading. So that's what he did. He went down swell. Can you believe that?'

'Amazing.'

So that explained Clint's newfound enthusiasm for becoming a psychic.

'The man he did the reading for was very pleased.'

'Great. So Clint's palm was crossed with silver – he earned

a big fee?'

'Better than that. He got invited out on a date.'

Mary Jane noticed Honey's look of alarm.

'No problem,' she said with an exuberant wave of her hand. 'I got him out of there before he could do too much damage.'

Chapter Thirty-nine

Best to get Doherty on board. That was Honey's decision with regard to Magda Church, Karen Pinker's friend and house-share companion. Scruffy, the down-and-out Clint had mentioned, would be a different matter, having no real place that he could call home except for the one Clint had mentioned.

He'd pointed her in the direction of a disused cellar beneath the railway arches. It was all that remained of a ruined house pulled down when the Victorians had gone railway mad and disposed of everything that might stand in the way of their new technology.

The viaduct proceeded at a great height, parallel to the A4. The deep cellar and its entrance was still there, a refuge for those of no fixed abode.

This, Clint had assured her, was the entrance to Scruffy's home.

'Don't take him there,' he'd warned her. She'd known he meant Doherty. His reasoning was understandable; abiding by the law of the land, Doherty would take note of the cellar's location and bear it in mind as a possible bolthole for those of no fixed abode and questionable income.

Magda would be far easier to locate. She had shared a mews house just off the main A4 with Karen Pinker.

Following her phone call Doherty arrived at the hotel complete with a bouquet of red roses, dark orange dahlias, and fragile white gypsophila. He'd bought her flowers before in their relationship – her birthday, Christmas, and Valentine's Day. Today was not special, so the bouquet was a total surprise.

'Steve, you shouldn't have. It's not my birthday.'

'Does there have to be a reason?'

Funnily enough she couldn't help thinking there was a reason. John Rees might very well be it.

Don't look a gift horse in the mouth, she said to herself. It's the thought that counts.

But what was the thought?

Giving herself a good inner talking to helped a little. It was the instinct thing again. She couldn't help thinking there was a reason.

After leaving the bouquet with Lindsey to put in water, they were off towards the mews house Karen Pinker had shared with Magda Church.

Doherty had phoned first to make sure she was there. She was. She had a cold and had cancelled what modelling engagements she'd had.

She sat wrapped up in a blanket. The heating was going full blast and a host of cold remedies sat on a small table beside her.

'I'm always getting colds. My mother says that I don't eat enough.'

Honey barely stopped herself from grimacing and reporting that her mother reckoned she ate too much.

'I appreciate you taking the time to see us,' said Doherty.

She didn't seem to recall Honey from the supermarket so Honey didn't enlighten her.

'So what do you want to know?' Magda asked. 'Stuff about Karen, or stuff about the clinic?'

'Both,' said Doherty. 'I understand that Karen Pinker had plastic surgery done in Venezuela.'

Magda nodded. 'She did.'

Honey noticed the girl pull the blanket more tightly around her. There were two interpretations for that. Either she was experiencing chilly shivers or it was a kind of protective reflex; the blanket as a safety barrier between her and the questions.

'I met her at the clinic. I thought she was truly sensational. In fact I christened her Miss Perfect,' said Honey. She tried to sound cheerful. The girl needed putting at ease.

Magda turned to look at her. A small frown line creased her head.

'You were in the supermarket. She remembered you. She said you were polite. Not all her clients are polite.'

'What a shame.'

Doherty interrupted. 'I understand that the plastic surgery was paid for by the clinic. Why was that?'

Magda's face was open, eyes wide and seemingly honest. 'She was the up-front face of the clinic. Dr Dexter wanted someone working the reception desk who women could aspire to – especially older women aching to recapture their youth.'

It was barely perceptible, but Honey noticed Magda glancing in her direction.

'I am what I am,' she blurted defensively.

'Good for you. But the fact is that the advertising industry use young women – some no more than girls – to sell anti-ageing cream. I know of one cosmetic company who used a girl of thirteen shown in a television commercial rubbing anti-cellulite cream on her thighs.'

The statement made Honey bristle. 'So they think we're stupid.'

Magda gave a curt nod of her head. 'Basically, yes.'

'I'm never, *ever* going to buy that stuff again.'

Magda laughed. 'Stick to fat pants. You know it makes sense!'

Honey detected sarcasm. She gritted her teeth. Along with a gradual dislike for the girl she couldn't help thinking that she was not so nice beneath the surface.

Doherty was making a face. The questioning was hardly going where he wanted it to go.

'Ladies, unless anti-ageing creams were involved in either of these murders, can we stick to the facts?'

Magda nodded and said yes.

'Absolutely,' echoed Honey.

'Lady Macrottie. How did Karen feel about her murder?'

She shrugged. 'Shocked. Just like the rest of us.'

Doherty kept his eyes fixed on this girl. There was something she wasn't telling them.

'It was Karen who administered the mudpack but you who found the body. Where was Karen?'

Magda stiffened. 'She had a call on her phone.'

'Did she answer it then and there or did she go off to answer it?' Honey asked, remembering that was what Karen had done when it was her having a mud treatment.

'We weren't allowed to have our phones with us when we were with clients. We had to leave our phones on the desk in the office. But we could hear them from the treatment rooms.'

'She was gone for quite a long time. Any reason for that?' asked Doherty.

Magda shrugged. 'Who knows?'

Honey frowned. 'Do you recall anything about the woman who was suing the clinic after suffering from skin lesions?'

That shrug again. 'Not really.'

'She went to Venezuela too.'

She shrugged again. 'Sorry.'

'Did Karen have a boyfriend?' Honey asked.

'Not recently, at least, not as far as I'm aware.'

Doherty kept his eyes open for reaction. Strange how a woman's questions could beat a different path to a man's. Honey was doing well.

'How long since she had a boyfriend?'

She shrugged again. 'I couldn't really say ...'

'Oh come on, Ms Church. Two women sharing the same house and you don't know whether she had a boyfriend or not? You're lying! Now come on. The truth please.'

Doherty's sudden outburst almost made Magda jump out of her blanket.

'She was obsessed with Dr Dexter. I told her she was a fool, but she carried on anyway.'

'She was seeing him?'

'Not so much recently. He phoned and made arrangements – and they fooled around a bit at work too.'

'Did he fool around with everybody?'

Honey's sudden question made Magda jerk her head round fast.

'He's an alpha male. Women flock to him. She was one of many.'

'How about you? Are you one of many?'

The question resulted in an angry scowl. 'No. No, I am not!'

'She was a little shivery,' Honey remarked. 'My gut instinct tells me it wasn't just because she had a cold.'

'I'd stake a dinner for two and a bottle of chateau wine that it was phone calls from Dr Dexter taking Ms Pinker from her work.'

'I'm not taking your bet – not as a bet anyway. But dinner for two seems like a good idea.'

'Right. I'll see if I can get off ...'

'Not tonight. I've got something on tonight.'

He eyed her questioningly.

She met his gaze. 'You should know by now that running a hotel is never straightforward.'

'For a minute there I thought you might have a date.'

'No. Of course not.'

The subject of John Rees had come up in conversation.

Honey had explained that she'd needed an escort for the gala evening she'd attended and John Rees had been willing.

'You were sorting your daughter out.'

The girl had gone back to her mother. Doherty hadn't said as much, but she was pretty convinced that he'd picked up the tab.

As for tonight ... well, tonight she had another fish to fry – or rather a bloke named Scruffy to see. And she had to go alone.

The sound of the car leaving brought Magda springing from her chair, throwing the blanket behind her. She phoned Dexter.

'The police have just left. Don't worry. I haven't told them anything – not much anyway. Have you sorted everything out?'

He told her that most things were in place and that Sheer had come today to finalize the sale of the clinic.

'And the bitch – have you told the bitch?'

He was hesitant.

'We may have to circumvent that problem,' he told her.

She believed him. He loved her. She was not one of many – she was the special one.

Chapter Forty

It was twilight and the sky in the west was lighter than that in the old alleyways and narrower streets of the city.

The odd cat scooted among the shadows and overhead a brace of starlings twittered good-naturedly as they cuddled up together on a brand new stone parapet, part of the rank of new shops.

Honey was walking with her head down, concentrating hard on the scrap of paper that passed as a map.

The developers of the new shopping mall had been forced by the local authority to respect the bushes, birch and willow trees growing between the site and the river. They wanted the building softened with greenery and seeing as there was still so much here, the cost of planting was knocked sideways. They had greenery so why cut it down?

The leaves of an overgrown buddleia tinkled overhead as she came to the place described in Clint's note. A variety of bushes grew like a protective wall around its base.

'*You have to push your way through, and a bit of wildlife will disperse at your arrival. But don't worry. They won't bite.*'

Rats! You mean rats?

Push my way through, she thought, telling herself what Clint had told her; rats were frightened of human beings. There was nothing to worry about.

Determined to overcome her fear, she switched her thoughts to other things. What would anybody watching her think she was doing? Relieving herself? Waiting in ambush?

Get on with it!

A quick glance around confirmed that there were people in the vicinity but none were looking in her direction. I mean, why should they be looking? Was what she was doing that unusual?

Unusual, yes, and sneaky.

'Shut up,' she muttered. Her mind could sometimes go off on a tangent. And it was Mary Jane's fault. She was sure of it.

However, back to the job in hand. Using both hands, she pushed and divided the bushes. The dark green leaves were shiny – definitely light reflective. She'd brought a torch just in case, plus a bottle of Bell's whisky and a pastrami, mustard, and tomato salad baguette, warm from the oven. Scruffy would gratefully accept both and tell her all he knew. That was the plan anyway, and she'd run it past Clint. He'd shrugged. 'If that's what you want to do. But beware,' he said raising a warning finger. 'Don't go there poshed up. Have you got a pair of wellies and a waxed Barbour jacket?'

'Lindsey has.'

Lindsey did own a pair of green wellies and a waxed Barbour jacket. They were residual apparatus from her horse-riding days. Life and being grown up had intervened.

'They're a bit grubby ...'

'Clean them. You wouldn't wear grubby things to visit your mother, would you?'

She wasn't quite getting this, though of course to go looking for Scruffy in evening gown and drop-dead heels had never, ever been on the menu.

On the other hand she hadn't expected to be warned to go clean. After all, living where he did hardly justified getup, did it? Dressing down had to be the thing. The torch she'd brought with her was the sort with a headband. It fitted neatly. She'd be able to see her way.

Thanks to the closeness of the building site, the bushes were thick with dust. Just as Clint had promised, she found a narrow opening.

Her shoulders brushed against the stones forming the entrance. Bits of it plink-plonked off, leaving marks on her nice warm coat.

The steps leading down were narrow and dark. She pressed the switch on the head torch. Its clear white beam lit the way ahead of her.

Leaves from last October scrunched beneath her feet. So did a few crisp packets and discarded chocolate wrappings.

A supermarket trolley was wedged half way down. By the light of her torch she could see a second one at the bottom of the steps. They'd been put there purposely, the inhabitants obviously being security conscious.

The steps ended opposite a blank wall on which was written, 'No Trespassers. Keep Out Or Else!' A run from the exclamation mark was finished with a dagger and drips made to look like blood. The whole of it looked to be written in red paint – at least she hoped it was red paint.

She paused, balancing on the heels of her feet. Toes and soles swept from side to side as if they were being sensible and were going to run up the stairs by themselves. Her heels acted as anchors. She was made to go on. What if the sign really had been painted in blood?

'Can't you bloody read?'

She spun round at the sound of the voice, jerked back to normality – or as close to normality as things ever were in the world of a middle-market hotelier.

The cellar went off to her right. The light from her torch picked out a grubby figure.

'I'm looking for someone.'

'Well you won't find 'em 'ere! Now shove off!'

'Are you Scruffy?'

'Is that a question or an observation, love?'

Somebody else had said that. The same somebody giggled.

'I was told that someone named Scruffy might be able to help me find a murderer. Clint sent me.'

'Clint?'

'Rodney Eastwood.'

For a moment there was no movement and then there was.

'Well if Clint sent you, you'd better come in.'

He pressed himself against the wall so she could squeeze past.

'Be right with you, love. Got to put the door back in place first. Don't want any bloody Tom, Dick, or 'Arry finding their way in 'ere.'

She looked around, surprised at what she was seeing. There was an electric cooker, an electric fire, and an electric table lamp. The latter was standing on a bedside table with glass shelves and chrome legs. It looked to be of sixties vintage.

There was also an old sofa covered in dark green velvet plus one other chair.

The centre of the room was lit by the table lamp. The rest of the room was gloomy, the shadows shifting towards the black mouth of what seemed to be some kind of tunnel.

The stench had to be smelt to believed; she didn't need a guided tour to know that there was no bathroom. Thankfully she hadn't eaten since breakfast time. Her stomach was empty.

This is controllable, she told herself. Of course it was – as long as she didn't stay down here too long.

'So my mate Clint sent you.' The person asking the question had tangled shoulder-length hair and was dressed in an old army overcoat. His legs were bare, his feet encased in a pair of boots that didn't appear to have any laces.

She did her best to avert her gaze from the bare legs between boots and coat and tried not to wonder about the state of his underwear.

'We knows Clint well, don't we, Poxy?'

The person he addressed as Poxy grinned a toothless grin. She couldn't see any blemishes on his face caused either by smallpox or acne. Politeness had nothing to do with not asking how he'd got his name. It was best, she decided, that she lived on in ignorance.

'That's right.'

'Sit yer bum down,' he said, indicating the only chair in the room.

A cursory glance reassured her that the seat was made of hardwood and there was no chance of something crawling out and biting her.

Focusing her mind on the job in hand helped obliterate everything else – though one question did vex her. Where was the electricity coming from to power the cooker, the light, and the fire?

Her curiosity must have shown.

'The city council,' said Scruffy. 'A mate of mine used to be an electrician. He wired us into the council mains. They're only along the road and the amount they use, they weren't going to notice the little bit that we use, now were they?'

She agreed with that. Local authorities often had money to burn. If they ran out they'd just approach the taxpayer for a little bit more to balance their budget.

Scruffy sprawled himself full length on the sofa, head supported on fist. The other guy, Poxy, sprawled himself out on the floor. She fidgeted at the thought that the chair she was sitting on was mostly used by him.

This is no time to be squeamish. She had to press on.

'There was a murder out at The Old Manor House – the place that's now being run as a beauty clinic. A scruffy man was seen running away from there. Clint suggested that the people you know have their favourite spots. He thought you might be able to pinpoint who it might be.'

'That was that woman who got drowned in her mudpack!' Poxy exclaimed. 'I never could see the point of that, you know – washing in mud.'

Scruffy guffawed. 'You could never see the point of washing in anything, Poxy. Neither could I fer that matter. I mean, you only gets dirty agin, don't you?'

Above ground their logic would seem odd. Down here, looking at the two of them, it was strangely philosophical in that it suited them; it suited their world.

'But 'e weren't one of us. No sir. He might 'ave looked like one of us, but 'e weren't. I guarantee it.'

Honey told herself that it was only natural that they should defend their own situation.

Not us, guv'nor. It weren't us.

This was going to get her nowhere. She shrugged. 'Shame you didn't see him, then you would know for sure if he wasn't one of you.'

'I did see 'im,' said Scruffy. 'We was out there scrapping. You know – looking roundabouts for a bit of scrap metal. When there's building going on, there's always a bit of rubbish left over for taking down the scrap yard and getting money for it. It's our job of work, you know – clearing up after other people.'

'Like the Wombles.'

'Yeah,' said Scruffy. Like her, he seemed to remember the children's programme about furry creatures tidying up Wimbledon Common.

'The first environmentalists,' laughed Poxy.

Honey could feel the rictus grin on her face. This was all so surreal, being down here with a couple of down-and-outs who really did go round cleaning up after people – in a manner of speaking.

'So you reckon you saw the scruffy man.'

'Definitely. We did consider going to police but then, you

266

know how it is. They'd want to know what we were doing there. They wouldn't understand about the scrap. They'd say we nicked it.'

What they said was very likely, so she wasn't going to push it.

'OK,' she said nodding slowly. 'So this man. You seem pretty sure that he wasn't one of your scene.'

A shower of dandruff came out as Scruffy shook his head. Honey tried not to breathe.

'Definitely not one of us. No sir. He was just an untidy bugger trespassing on our territory – though we don't do murders. Only scrap metal.'

Concentrating was becoming more difficult. Honey couldn't help her eyes wandering to the black tunnel and she could hear scuttling in the shadows. She wanted to ask whether they kept pets down here, but figured she wouldn't like the answer.

Swallowing her nerves, she felt glad that as an honoured guest – a friend of Clint's no less – she'd been given the only chair in the place. The old sofa looked comfy, but she suspected that it too might be home to other living organisms that couldn't be regarded as pets – unless you kept a flea circus. Just the thought of it made her want to scratch.

'Can you describe him?'

'Scruffy,' said Scruffy – which was definitely a case of the pot calling the kettle black. 'And tall. A six-footer, I should think.'

She opened her mouth to question the degree to which a person who was scruffy could describe a person as scruffy – it was pretty confusing. Scruffy and his mates were all, – well – scruffy.

'So what else?' she asked.

'His voice. He spoke posh but looked down on 'is uppers – if you knows what I mean.'

Chapter Forty-one

The following morning Smudger the chef was purchasing organic vegetables when Honey wandered into the kitchen. She'd been planning to go through the month's menu with her head chef, but he was presently busy so she lingered, waiting her turn. Chefs were famous – or more accurately infamous – for prioritizing in their own sweet way. She was only the hotel owner. The man delivering fresh produce had priority.

'Best there is,' Smudger was saying to the delivery man.

Honey did a double-take. She'd seen that man before.

He recognized her too. 'Howdy do.' He lifted his old-fashioned cap as he greeted her.

'You work at the Macrottie place.'

'I do indeed, ma'am. Have done all my life, right back when the place was really something to write 'ome about – if you get me drift. Course, the family had money back then – that's why they could afford to keep two places running.'

'Two?' Honey was intrigued, automatically pouring him a freshly brewed coffee.

Smudger looked intrigued, pulling up a chair, hooking his leg across and resting his hands and chin on the back of it.

Waiting for action, thought Honey. Well here goes.

'So they had two big houses.'

The old guy gratefully accepted a plateful of chocolate digestives, one of which he proceeded to dunk in his coffee. Crumbs scattered everywhere when he spoke.

'That place down in Lambton was her ladyship's. His lordship hated her selling it. He can't bear old parkland being built on and old buildings turned from houses into commercial places. Hated it he did! But ...' He shrugged. 'The old girl would have her way and seeing as it was hers by right – passed down through the family ...'

Dunk went another digestive, the chocolate slurped off; the soft biscuit left behind was sucked in after the chocolate. The old man had priorities.

Honey felt an odd tingling sensation. She'd been trying to get hold of Steve all morning. She'd failed to get hold of him last night but had left messages.

The old guy was adding fuel to the fire. Lord Macrottie, the last in a long line of the family that had owned Hamthorpe Hall, had crept into her mind last night at Scruffy's place and hadn't fully crept out again. Now, thanks to the old guy delivering vegetables, his presence was set in cement.

'How did his lordship take to his wife selling the place off for development?'

The old guy scowled and shook his head. 'Not well. But on the other hand the cash could be spent on the hall. Not that it's come to that – not yet anyway.'

Honey mused on what the reason might be. There were a few possibilities that all led to questions, but the delivery man had drained his cup and was about to depart.

'Oh well. Can't stand 'round 'ere gossiping.'

Honey tried phoning Doherty again.

'Steve. I've been trying to get hold of you. If you don't get back to me shortly, I'm going out to Hamthorpe Hall alone. I think the down-and-out Serena Sarabande saw was his lordship. I think he killed his wife because she was divorcing him. He wanted the money to do up the Hall. You saw what a state it was in.'

He'd go mad her going out there alone, but she was on a

roll.

'I should come with you.'

Lindsey was looking worried.

'Someone has to stay here and run things. How about Mary Jane?'

Honey frowned and shook her head. 'I don't think that's a very good idea.'

Mary Jane had inadvertently done damage to Benici's Bentley. She wasn't sure how things were in that area of her life – the abduction and possible murder area. The pink Cadillac was very noticeable. It made sense to go out in something less conspicuous.

'Hey! Did I hear tell that you're going out to Hamthorpe Hall?'

Smudger was still in his kitchen whites. His face was pink, he looked disgruntled, and he was brandishing a bunch of wilting asparagus. 'Look at the state of these! I paid good money for twenty-four bunches of fresh asparagus. It's May so they should be top notch and fresh as daisies, and fresh these ain't!'

A chef in need of fresh vegetables is a formidable force indeed. It seemed a good idea to take him with her – far better than taking Mary Jane.

'OK. Drat!'

She suddenly remembered her car was in for a service.

Smudger read her mind.

'We can take mine.'

'Mine' turned out to be a turbocharged BMW with big tyres and blue enhancement lights around the wheel arches. She couldn't help thinking it a bit of a pimpmobile but wouldn't dare say so. Chefs – especially Smudger – were notoriously sensitive.

First he loaded up the boot with the offending asparagus.

'I want exchange or our money back,' he declared on

271

slamming the driver's door shut. 'Otherwise, this means war!'

Smudger was passionate about asparagus. Figuring he was looking after her interests, Honey didn't mention that nobody in their right mind went to war over asparagus. Tulips, maybe. Asparagus? No!

Doherty took in the details of the pathology report. His eyes narrowed.

'Are you sure about this?'

Cranfield, the new boy on the block who hadn't long emigrated there from Australia, peeled off his latex gloves finger by finger.

'Absolutely. Leaf mould. The organic type chewed up and distributed to organic growers. Karen Pinker had traces of it on her clothes. We've done extra tests on the mud in Lady Macrottie's stomach and that checks out the same.'

'The mud contained it?'

Cranfield shook his head. 'No. The amounts were too small for that. Whoever pushed her under had leaf mould on their hands and clothes.'

Honey had left Lindsey with orders to check out the last will and testament of Lady Carlotta Macrottie. Just as John Sheer had said, her ladyship had owned a lot of property which she'd sold off. The dilapidated Hamthorpe Hall was the sole property of Justin Macrottie. Her ladyship had intended keeping all her money to herself, not spending it on her husband's property. On top of that she'd been seeking a divorce. Seeing as her mother had gone off somewhere, Lindsey had emailed everything to Doherty.

Head down and deep in thought, Doherty headed for his office with just one thought on his mind.

'Get a warrant for Macrottie.'

'What's his motive, do you think?' asked one of his detective sergeants. 'Insurance for the wife?'

'Something like that.'

'Is that going to be enough to arrest him on?' The sergeant sounded as doubtful as Doherty felt.

'It'll do for a start.'

Yes, of course he'd like more. His gut instinct told him there had to be more. Once he had Macrottie under lock and key he could fire off a few more questions that he felt sure would nail his man.

As for Karen Pinker … he hadn't quite got his head around that one just yet, but he was getting there. Once it was all over he'd phone the wife to make sure his daughter had got home OK. After that he'd invite Honey for dinner out followed by a dirty night in – all night.

The team were ready and raring to go, looking for him to lead the way.

Before he got moving he grabbed his phone, which had been playing up of late, running out of power at the worst moment. It had been on charge for a couple of hours. He checked the readout. It said 'fully charged'. It also listed several messages, all from the same number. There was no time to check them all, so he checked the last, staring at it in disbelief.

'Shit!'

Then he was off, a fleet of police cars dashing out towards the main A4 in the direction of Macrottie Hall.

Chapter Forty-two

Gloria Cross was not amused and the doctor and his assistant sitting across from her could see she was not amused.

'I got my friend Nancy to check what facelifts cost in Venezuela and they sure don't cost anything like what you're trying to charge me.'

The statuesque blonde shifted in her seat and tried a slinky smile.

'The establishments we use are very upmarket. Far superior to anything anyone else uses. We have many testimonials from satisfied clients.'

Gloria Cross, Honey's well turned-out, well switched-on mother, glared at her.

'Prove it!'

Serena Sarabande extracted a pale green binder from the desk. 'If you'd like to look at these …'

Gloria shook her head, one eye narrowed as though she were looking through a telescope.

'Let's face it, your reputation is in tatters. I wouldn't have come here if Enid hadn't recommended you. I should have known my daughter was here for a reason. She was working for the police, wasn't she? Looking into the death of that woman, poor soul! She only came in for a mudpack and went out in a coffin.'

If Gloria had given herself time to draw breath she would have seen their furtive looks, and the occasional secretive smiles that only lovers share. Now, Dr Dexter and Serena Sarabande exchanged looks of alarm.

'What exactly is it you want?' Serena asked her.

Gloria fixed her with an icy stare, the sort that could bring a shop assistant to tears and send her family running for cover.

'I want my money back.'

'Certainly. Here you are.'

Dr Dexter got out a cheque book.

Gloria eyed him speculatively.

'I'd prefer cash.'

The nib of his pen had only just touched the paper. He paused. She expected reluctance. Instead she got a slippery smile.

'Well of course, Mrs Cross. Shall I make it out to yourself?'

Gloria Cross had perfected different looks over the years and not just in dress style. She knew how to use her eyes, how to flutter them provocatively, how to give a sharp, piercing look that could skewer the strongest heart to the wall. 'You're not listening, buster. I just told you, I want cash.'

Both Dr Dexter and Serena Sarabande batted the same look backwards and forwards at each other. Gloria's eyesight was better than a rabbit on intravenous carrot juice. It wasn't so much about seeing in the dark. More about reading people like a book, and she could read these two all right!

Serena unfolded her arms. 'I'll get it,' she said softly.

Gloria noticed the way she touched the doctor's shoulder on the way out. She also sensed some understanding, some cross-referencing of emotions here. She hadn't lived over seventy years without picking up on the vibes; these two were having an affair. She was sure of it.

Dr Dexter cleared his throat as he shut the drawer. 'We are, of course, sorry to lose your custom.' His smile was practised.

'Have you ever been an actor?'

His smile wavered. 'No. Not really.'

276

'You should be. You'd make a good ham sandwich. Hammy through and through,' she said, turning away to admire what was left of the parkland outside the window. Three children rode past on scooters, another on a pair of roller skates.

Her eyes narrowed as she watched the kids outside. OK, she was vain but she wasn't stupid. These two were handing her back her money with little argument. They must have enough, she decided, and they're not worrying about repeat business. That could mean only one thing. They were leaving for pastures new and they were not coming back.

'That was close,' said Serena as Roger Dexter heaved her suitcase into the boot of her car.

Dr Dexter laughed. 'She was a shrewd old bird, that one. A damned good job the others weren't like her or the bank account would be a lot smaller than it is.'

Serena looked back at the mansion. 'I won't be sorry to leave it. I hope John Sheer knocks it down.'

'He can't. It's Grade Two listed.'

'But you told me that you had special dispensation to knock it down.'

He patted the car boot amiably, as though, she thought, he was patting a woman's backside. Any woman – not just her.

'I forged a document. Anyway, by the time he finds out I'll be long gone.'

'*We'll* be long gone,' she reminded him.

'Of course.'

His smile was as reassuring as ever. It was one of the things that had attracted her to him in the first place. That and the good sex. And an instinct for making money – in any way possible, and not necessarily legal – that matched her own.

She thrilled as he took hold of her shoulders, kissed her on the forehead, then on the tip of her nose. He was the only man

277

she had ever met who made her feel childlike and vulnerable. He was the only man who dared treat her that way.

He took hold of her chin between finger and thumb. 'I'm going to ask you something terribly important. Your answer may affect the rest of your life.'

Her heart leapt in her cast-iron chest. Deep down she was an old-fashioned girl. She wanted him to slip a ring on her finger and say that they would be together for ever.

She just looked at him, unable to move, unable to speak. She waited.

'Very simply, darling, it's this.' His voice was low and seductive. He kissed her again, this time lightly on the lips. 'Quite simply, do you have the tickets?'

If he noticed her crestfallen expression he made no comment. His own smiling countenance was unaltered. Brave bunny that she was, she nodded and smiled, though a knife was cutting her guts into garters.

'Of course I do. Rio here we come.'

'Indeed. Now. You know what to do. Get the luggage cleared and I'll catch up with you – and I'll bring the tickets with me.' He glanced at his watch. 'I've got enough time to clear out my desk at home. Don't go without me now.'

Again he treated her like a little girl, flicking at her nose with his pinky. Again she went all gooey inside, totally at odds with her crisp, cold exterior.

Glowing in what she interpreted as affection, Serena Sarabande did as she was told. Chivalrous to the last, Roger Dexter closed the car door after her and blew her a kiss through the glass.

Half an hour later he was on the other side of the city, his case packed and secure in the boot of his Aston Martin DBS. He saw her wave to him from the window. Before he'd got more than half way from car to house she'd opened the door.

'Magda, darling.'

Her arms were around his neck in no time. Her nubile young body was firm and held promises of unending vigour – just the sort of girl he adored.

'Have you got the tickets, darling?'

He patted his chest. 'Two one-way tickets to the Maldives where we pick up our yacht. From there the world is our oyster.'

Chapter Forty-Three

'I don't approve of what you did. It weren't right and you deserves to be punished. I'm going to the police.'

Lord Justin Macrottie took pleasure in the fact that he could mimic anyone and everyone if he had a mind too. Mimicking Jake Blunt, his Jack of all trades who had served him and his family for years, was no exception. Poor bloke. That was all over now.

The old sod hadn't seen it coming. He was now lying dead at his lordship's feet, a pool of blood spreading around his head like a liquid halo.

Justin Macrottie leaned on the shovel, his weapon of choice. Very fitting, he thought, that old Jake had been bludgeoned with a tool he'd used all his life for digging and planting.

'Now 'tis your turn to be planted,' drawled Justin, still mimicking the voice of the dead man.

Luckily for him, Jake was lighter in weight than he looked and of compact build. This meant he fitted quite well into the wheelbarrow.

Eyes glazed, arms dangling, old Jake was wheeled out of the potting shed and around to the vegetable garden.

Beds of newly planted vegetables sparkled green in the fresh clear air.

Justin paused for a minute to admire his and Jake's work. In future he would have to hire gardeners from outside to help him in his organic venture. While Carlotta was alive he hadn't been able to do that, but now he could – thanks to her wanting a divorce.

He hadn't been able to allow that of course. She'd dangled the money she'd made from selling the old manor house in front of his nose for years before finally deciding she would not spend it on Macrottie Hall but would divorce him and spend it on herself. Stupid cow!

Jake must have guessed but hadn't been unduly fazed by Carlotta's demise. They'd loathed each other. She'd wanted to get rid of him, but Justin wouldn't hear of it. 'Jake has been here for ever.'

The odd thing was that he would indeed now be here for ever, but Justin was sure he would be pleased that he was still aiding plants to grow.

The ground was muddy so it took a bit of effort to push the wheelbarrow off the path and on to the grass. He'd dug an oblong hole that once filled with earth would become an asparagus bed. It was all set with lovely, squashy compost that was rotting nicely. Old Jake would rot along with it, a fitting resting place for the old man. Jake would be caring for the plants in death just as he had in life.

'Heave ho!' Justin cried, sending a flock of crows from the beech tree.

A quick tip and old Jake fell like a broken puppet on to the mulch at the bottom of the hole.

Lord Justin Macrottie looked down at the sprawled body.

'There, old chap. Now look what you made me do. You've only yourself to blame,' he said wagging a warning finger. 'If you hadn't got so uptight about that Karen person this would never have happened.'

Taking hold of the shovel he'd placed beneath Jake's body, he began filling in the hole. As he did so he tried to piece together why Jake had reacted like that. The girl knew everything! Carlotta had told her of her intentions regarding the money she'd got for the development. That's why he'd followed her.

The fact that she was having an affair with the doctor from the clinic had been useful. He'd met him the once, heard his voice, and had it off pat.

His impersonation had totally fooled the girl. Karen Pinker had been besotted with the doctor. He'd heard it in her intake of breath when he'd phoned her. 'Karen, my precious ... I dreamt of you last night and of all the delicious things I would do to you when we next meet.'

He laughed. He just couldn't resist pretending to be somebody else. If he hadn't been born to grandeur – faded as it was – he would have become an impersonator. He had the talent. There was no doubt about it.

He would have continued filling in the hole but the sound of a car crunching its way up the gravel drive made him stop.

'Visitors,' he said to the corpse lying at the bottom of the hole. 'Won't be long, old chap. I'll be right back to cover you up.'

Stretching his legs and rubbing his back, Smudger took in the crumbling grandeur of Hamthorpe Hall and came out with a load of television mush.

'Viewers! Who lives in a house like this?'

Honey eyed him reprovingly. 'You know who lives here.'

Smudger eyed the old place with disdain. 'I know who *should* live here. The Addams Family. It's crumbling.'

'It's the Macrottie stately pile.'

'Yeah. And that's all it will be before very long. A pile of old stones and rubbish.'

Honey clicked her tongue in reproof. Smudger reached for his asparagus.

There was something worrying about a chef clutching bunches of asparagus like that. Any other vegetable might not

283

have been so bad; a cauliflower for instance. They were round and white, but asparagus had little spear-shaped heads. A chef looked as though he might do injury with a bunch of asparagus.

He accompanied Honey up to the front door, a step crumbling under his feet just as it had under hers.

He looked down at it. 'Crikey. This place ain't safe.' He waved his asparagus. 'I'll probably find Jake around the back. See you.'

Smudger disappeared out of sight.

'Here goes.'

Honey pressed the plastic doorbell and waited, listening for the sound of footfall from the other side of the door.

She was feeling nervous. Marching up to the front door had helped reinforce her courage.

She was nervous about what she had to do. Hopefully Doherty had checked his phone. On the journey here she'd checked her own phone. The batteries were down again. You need a new model, she thought to herself. Something with apps – whatever they might be.

Technology was not her scene. She left all that stuff to Lindsey.

Now what was she going to say to his lordship? She couldn't just barge in and accuse him of killing his wife. Mentioning Scruffy might help. If Scruffy knew his lordship then his lordship might know him. At the very least he would know he'd been noticed, so he couldn't lie – could he?

In a way she was hoping he might own up to killing his wife, just like they did in an Agatha Christie novel when the suspects all sat down at the end to learn who was guilty. While sipping tea of course, and munching on cucumber sandwiches or slices of Madeira cake.

The door creaked stiffly open and the smell of old dust and mouldy carpets furled outwards.

Justin Macrottie's face looked like a wax mask against the

interior gloom.

'Yes?'

Honey sneezed.

'I won't say anything stupid like bless you. Just tell me what you want and we can both be on our way.'

His lordship was obviously not in the mood for entertaining. Throwing caution to the wind she jettisoned any attempt to lie and say she was collecting information on behalf of some arcane organization. The truth came out.

'My name's Honey Driver. I'm with the police.'

'In what way?'

One of his eyebrows kept twitching. It was hard not to stare. His mouth was wide and his bottom lip drooped and was wet with saliva. He reminded her of a character from an old black and white movie; the 1930s version of a madman.

'I'm a consultant,' she blurted. It seemed a reasonably acceptable definition of what she did. Pity she didn't get paid the going rate for being a consultant. She'd shut the hotel down and spend one month every year in the Caribbean.

'So you're not a real policewoman?'

It was hard not to lie under his withering stare. 'Not exactly … I'm here by myself. Some questions arose …'

'Your questions or police questions?'

She hesitated. She was half way to being honest so she might as well go the whole hog.

'Well, mine, actually …'

Suddenly he smiled. On anybody else it might have made them look less mad. On him it did the opposite and gave Honey the creeps.

The door was opened wider. 'Come in.'

Her gut instinct was to dash back to Smudger's car and lock herself in.

Thinking of Smudger helped her feel less threatened. 'I have a friend with me,' she said.

'Yes. Me.'

He caught hold of her hand. 'I've just made some soup. Do you know I grow my own produce here? It's organic. Quite delicious. Do try some.'

She put her trust in him believing that she really did have someone with her. What difference would it make to try out his soup? He was obviously very proud of it.

He led her through the dusty passage and down an equally dusty staircase to the kitchen below.

Along one wall a series of pine shelves held everything from copper cooking pots to jelly moulds, huge china jugs, and vast meat platters.

The kitchen was heated by a vast cast-iron range set into the chimney piece. Free-standing pine units of cupboards and drawers ran all the way around the room and a brace of pheasants hung from the ceiling. The heat wasn't doing them any good. They were beginning to smell.

Luckily a more attractive smell was coming from the soup Macrottie was offering her. Her stomach rumbled. She'd had no breakfast. She'd had no lunch either.

'I grow my own mushrooms in the cellar. All naturally of course. No artificial fertilizers. All home-made and home grown. Mushroom soup,' he said, handing her a bowl.

The smell was enticing. He gave her a spoon. She was about to take in a spoonful but stopped. Was he going to have some too?

'Me too,' he said, licking his chops like a wolf about to take a bite out of Little Red Riding Hood.

He shovelled in two or three mouthfuls, evidence enough that it wasn't poisoned. He wouldn't poison himself, would he?

'Bread,' he said suddenly. 'I make my own.'

She could see that he did. There were loaves of every shape and size set out in neat rows on the dresser. He cut her off a piece, liberally spreading it with fresh, yellow butter.

Her mouth began to water. It was ridiculous, but her mouth was watering!

Now come on, she said to herself. Sort yourself out. You're here to ask questions.

Though not on an empty stomach.

She was sure that her stomach had its own message line to her brain and imagined it having a label on it. *Restricted traffic. Bread and butter pudding only.*

Still, she had to make the effort.

'You must miss your wife very much.'

He shook his head and there was an odd smile on his face. 'No.'

He turned to open the oven door, pulling out a tray of freshly baked bread, at the same time singing a snatch of 'The Wicked Witch Is Dead' from *The Wizard of Oz*.

The smell coming from the bread was wonderful. Things could have been better if she hadn't been feeling so hungry, so hungry in fact that she was beginning to feel dizzy.

A few more spoonfuls went down and a lot more soup was soaked up with the thickly buttered chunk of bread.

Half a dozen Lord Justin Macrotties were playing on a carousel that was going round and around her head. Up and down, round and round.

The spoon and bowl clattered to the floor.

Justin was smiling. 'Mushroom soup. Unsurpassable.'

'Magic,' she said, and put the two words together. 'Magic mushrooms.'

Gently, as though she were a maiden aunt in need of support – which quite frankly she was – he led her to the back door.

'You need some fresh air,' he told her.

The cold air hit her.

'Your carriage awaits you, Cinderella. I'll get you to the ball in no time. And no need to leave by twelve midnight. You can stay in there for ever.'

Her head was fuzzy, but she was convinced she really was hearing a female voice that really could be taken as that of the fairy godmother from the famous old story.

Honey couldn't quite work out what kind of contraption she was being lowered into. It was like a chair but not a chair.

It came to her in a flash. 'It's a barrow. A wheelbarrow,' she exclaimed. 'Get me out of here.'

'Get me out of here!'

It sounded just like her own voice! Was it an echo she'd heard?

And she hadn't been drinking. Bleary brained, it came to her that the soup – the mushroom soup – had a lot to do with it. Hot and heady. Too heady. And damn it all, she couldn't get out of this bloody wheelbarrow!

Justin Macrottie sang snatches of Rodgers and Hammerstein as he trundled her along. Her limbs flipped and flopped and her backside was bumped up and down. The path was bumpy. They went past the vegetable garden. She was vaguely aware of conifers and the scratching of gooseberry bushes, though it could just as easily have been brambles.

Her vision was blurry and her limbs had turned to jelly. Her brain was doing some kind of waltz inside her skull, interspersed with a few hip-hop moves. Quite bizarre. Quite crazy. Everything was spinning at varying speeds. Escaping the confines of the wheelbarrow of her own volition would have required gigantic will power. At present her will power was floating some way beyond her reach. She couldn't have stood up if she'd tried.

'Dum, dum, de dum, dum, de dum, dum, dum, dum, dum.'

His lordship's music of choice had changed. Rodgers and Hammerstein had been dumped in favour of what sounded like the funeral march – played ultra-slow but not without a little glee.

Suddenly the wheelbarrow came to a halt. Taking advantage to escape her captor and the wheelbarrow was a faint hope, but she tried anyway. Her limbs failed to respond to the electrical impulses from her brain. This was probably due to the fact that the impulses were having trouble getting through. The grey matter had turned to unbaked dough.

A thin hand patted her shoulder reassuringly. 'No need to worry, dear lady. It won't exactly be a Christian burial, but as near as I can get.' She heard him take a deep breath and could imagine him with hands clasped, eyes looking skywards. She wanted to say that she wasn't keen on *any* type of burial but the words were garbled and sounded like rubbish.

Her captor on the other hand seemed to be in his element. 'O Lord, we commit her body to the ground. Ashes to ashes, mulch to mulch ...'

Was it purely her imagination or did he really sound like the current Archbishop of Canterbury?

One flip and she was out of the wheelbarrow and over the side of the pit. She landed like a starfish; legs wide open, arms spread. The back of her hand touched something familiar. She managed to move her fingers, stretched them a little and found – a further set of fingers. They didn't belong to her!

Smudger had fully inspected the vegetable beds. Some plants, he noticed, were doing better than others.

A pile of mulch had been left at the side of the path. Taking a handful he got a whiff of it. Not pleasant, but not unpleasant either.

He wandered at will, fully expecting to come across Jake but never doing so. Purely out of professional interest he inspected the vegetables bed by bed, picking leaves, sniffing them, inspecting for size, blight and quality.

Eventually there were no more vegetables but a row of conifers that seemed to spell 'The End'. They were pretty tall and in need of trimming.

Jake had told him he'd planted a fruit garden and intended to grow asparagus among the fruit and shielded by conifers. He'd also boasted about his raspberries, a hardy variety and of exceptional taste.

Raspberries were one of Smudger's favourite fruits. If this place was growing seasonal raspberries then he was after some. He thought he could identify the canes if he saw them though he couldn't be that sure. Cooking veg and fruits was one thing – growing them was something else.

The gap in the hedge was staggered, one row of conifers set back four feet from the other so that the ends overlapped and the wind couldn't get through.

At the same time as Honey had found a set of dead man's fingers and Smudger had entered the fruit garden, Justin Macrottie was opening the front door to Steve Doherty. His quick eyes darted to the two cars waiting out front, their blue lights flashing. This was not a social call offering advice on security or chasing up an unpaid parking ticket.

By nature security conscious, he kept the chain on, asking his visitors what they wanted through a six-inch gap.

Doherty flashed his warrant card and stated his business.

'Justin Francis Macrottie. I have a warrant for your arrest. We are charging you with the murder of your wife, Lady Carlotta Chalmers-Macrottie, and also with that of Miss Karen Pinker.'

The door was slammed shut.

'Out the back,' shouted Doherty. 'You two stay here.'

Police ran off in all directions.

Doherty swore. The door had been slammed even before he'd gone into the niceties of reading the guy his rights.

Remembering the side gate he'd gone through on his last visit, Doherty swerved right.

Two of his officers were pushing against the green gate. Flakes of dried paint flaked off like snow on to their clothes.

'It's locked, guv.'

'Then unlock it.'

The order was sharp. They knew what he wanted.

Beefy shoulders slammed into the gate, disturbing more clouds of dusty paint.

'Use something! Climb over! Do bloody something!'

One of the younger officers began climbing the spindly trelliswork and rampant wisteria growing to one side of the gate.

There was no sign of Honey or of her car. Perhaps she'd changed her mind about facing Macrottie by herself. Only one car was parked here and it wasn't hers.

It was back to square one with the opening of the gate. The rotten trellis had snapped beneath the young officer's weight. He'd come crashing down, cursing and swearing about the state of his coat. It was nice; blue suede with leather-covered buttons. Doherty had admired it.

'There might be a key,' said some bright spark. 'You know. Under a plant pot. People do that; even posh people do that.'

The clouds in the sky had faces. Some were smiling and some looked glum. Staring at clouds was preferable to thinking about the corpse she was lying on. On a positive note she knew it wasn't Smudger because the body was cold. This was very reassuring because good chefs were hard to find, and what if he was a little touchy at times – all chefs were like that. It was part of their creed.

So who was the man she was lying on?

Her head was still swimming though she was willing it to stop. If only she hadn't been so hungry. If she ever got out of this she was never going to miss breakfast again. Wasn't that the wisdom – that breakfast was the one meal you should never go without?

First things first, she had to get out of here. Her willpower was coming back, though it was patchy. Her eyes kept doing cartwheels.

The green shoots of recovery were pushing through. In twenty or thirty minutes she'd be feeling a lot better than she was now. As long as Macrottie didn't come back that is. As long as he didn't resume burying her alive.

Just as she was studying a particularly pretty cloud that closely resembled the dent Doherty left in the mattress, a shadow fell over her. Dismay was too mild a word. Macrottie was back and he had a shovel in his hand.

'Sorry. Have to hurry.'

One shovelful of dirt after another showered down on her. She was spitting it out of her mouth, blinking it from her eyes. He was working furiously, determined to get her covered in double-quick time.

Suddenly she heard a voice.

'Hey mate. I'm looking for Jake. Is he down there?'

It had to be Smudger.

She saw the shovel silhouetted against the sky. Macrottie was aiming to strike a blow, but Smudger knew how to take care of himself.

The shovel flew sideways. Smudger was not a man to be trifled with. He had integrity. He also had big fists and a foul temper when roused.

Macrottie stood there as though spellbound while Smudger hit him across the face with something he was holding in his hands.

The assault seemed to take Macrottie off balance. Just as Honey managed to prop herself up on to her elbows, he toppled over straight into the hole.

Smudger was standing up above her, hands resting on his bent knees as he peered down.

'What the hell are you doing down there?'

Macrottie, his eyes wild, his hands like claws, was on his feet.

'I think I'm about to be murdered,' she managed to shout.

Macrottie's attention being fixed on her, he didn't see Smudger raising the shovel. The flat of the blade hit him squarely on the top of his head. His whole body wobbled and wavered and for a moment he seemed to hover there.

But seeing as he'd received a hefty bash on the head, she knew it couldn't last. What got bashed senseless with a spade was bound to fall over. And he did just that.

This was the moment when she found her voice.

'Don't fall on me!'

But he did.

Whoosh went the air from her lungs. His weight pinned her to the body beneath. Another man. Some women might dream of such a fantasy – though not quite this scenario, one dead and one out for the count.

Doherty's face appeared beside that of her chef.

'Honey, you've got no business being here.'

Smudger nodded in agreement. 'You're not kidding. Imagine the gossip. Well-known hotel owner found lying between two men.'

Honey screamed. 'Get me out of here!'

The big surprise was having Serena Sarabande turn police witness to Dr Dexter's malpractice regarding the referral of patients to a disreputable clinic in Venezuela.

The fact that he'd already flown away to pastures new with Magda Church was an undoubted hindrance to arresting him.

Lord Justin Macrottie was mad and didn't mind admitting it. He was also incredibly good at mimicking other people's voices. It was his voice Karen had heard on the other end of the phone inviting her to meet him. He'd sounded like Dr Dexter, so she'd left her client – Lady Carlotta Macrottie – alone long enough for Macrottie to sneak in and kill her.

Then he'd met her again on the site. He'd wanted negotiations for the sale of the manor house to be curtailed while he contested his wife's will. He'd thought a murder would hold things up.

'I'll miss his asparagus,' Smudger had stated. 'I'll have to buy foreign. By the bye, when's Clint coming back?'

'According to Doherty, pretty soon. It seems our Italian Jezebel jilted him for an older man, a millionaire with a motor yacht on the Costa del Sol, so Benici's forgotten all about Clint. Steve reckons he's a criminal, although like with the Benici family it's devilishly difficult proving it. Still, birds of a feather, as they say. Her family isn't likely to disapprove of the relationship. Hey,' she said suddenly on opening the post to retrieve a crisp white card from a strikingly white envelope. 'It's a wedding invitation from Jocelyn Trinder.'

Smudger was disinterested. If the post had no relevance to the smooth running of his kitchen, he wasn't interested.

Honey flicked the card against her smile. Despite his new relationship and the fact that he'd benefitted from the sale of the property, Joss Trinder had been genuinely saddened at his previous partner's death – and Steve had investigated and could find no link between Joss and the fire that had killed her. She couldn't help wishing him well – even though his hand had persistently sought out her bottom!

Chapter Forty-four

Bathing in bubbles while sipping a glassful of bubbles was bliss; it wasn't often she shared a bathtub with Doherty, but this was a special occasion. They had a lot to celebrate.

'This is so decadent,' said Honey, sipping at the glass of champagne.

Doherty, who'd drawn the short straw and was sitting at the plug-hole end of the bath, raised his glass.

'No. This is a celebration. Drinking champagne in the tub is the most civilized drinking you can do.'

'A little more room would be useful. Do you think you can move your toes? Your nails need cutting.'

'Sorry.'

It wasn't strictly true. The bathtub was the old-fashioned cast-iron type with ball and claw feet. It was absolutely enormous in length, very deep, and of quite outstanding width. A real stonker of a bath! Either the Edwardians had indulged in communal baths on a regular basis or they were built like boilers; big, round, and solid. There was bags of room.

The truth was that Doherty's toes were poking around in a very sensitive place and she didn't want any of that – not yet. This was the first opportunity they'd had of late for some time to themselves and she wanted it to last.

'I wouldn't mind bathing in champagne,' said Honey. She'd finished one glass and was busily filling up another. Doherty didn't say no when she held out the bottle.

'I suppose you could indulge yourself if you wanted.'

Doherty eyed the four cases of champagne that Honey had been given. Enid, her mother's friend, had jilted her fiancé and run off with a retired military type who had his name down for a place at Chelsea Hospital, the home for retired soldiers. Enid had obviously put a charge across the old guy's spark plugs and him across hers.

'Understandable for a girl's head to be turned when a guy has star status. Wouldn't you run off with a movie star if you had the chance?'

A few likely candidates had flashed through Honey's mind. It was worth considering, but the old adage about a bird in the hand won out. She'd stick with Doherty.

This was how come Honey had ended up with the champagne. In a surprisingly short time the attentions of the jilted bridegroom had swung to her mother.

'At our age you can't let the grass grow under your feet,' her mother explained. 'He's given me the champagne. Eight cases. You can have four. I don't like anything second-hand, so I'll probably give the rest away.'

Honey had wanted to point out that Cuthbert, the old guy in question, was more second-hand than the champagne. She'd decided not to look a gift horse in the mouth. She and Doherty had some catching up to do.

Honey eyed the freshly bubbling drink in her glass. 'I have a confession to make.'

Doherty slurped and grinned. 'Go on. It's been a day of confessions. Make my day.'

'I was biased against the folks at The Beauty Spot. I wanted them to be guilty of murder.'

Doherty eased himself down so that his bare shoulders were almost obliterated by bubbles.

'They were guilty of fraudulent practice. Not my department.'

His toes were back exploring intimate places again. She decided to be a martyr and put up with it.

'He also had a wandering dick,' commented Honey. 'Serena, Lady Macrottie, Karen and Magda – to name but a few.'

Doherty grinned. 'You could have been in the running yourself.'

'How do you make that out?'

His grin widened. 'Seeing you dressed only in a black plastic bin bag was bound to have an effect.'

'Down, Rover! By the way, now I've got my wedding dress, shall we fix a date?'

Their gazes wandered to the Regency style dress hanging behind the bathroom door. Her mother had insisted it should be used. Honey had insisted her mind was as yet divided on her choice of bridegroom. Still, it didn't hurt to cast around for a likely bite …

Doherty seemed to give it some thought for a minute.

'Ever thought about getting married at a naturist centre?'

'Do they allow black bin liners?'

'Sure to.'

'Definitely worth considering then.'

Another Honey Driver Mystery

Wicked Words

A sense of justice is felt amongst Bath hoteliers when an unpopular hotel reviewer is found dead stuffed inside a giant teddy at the bottom of an open grave. As the Hotels' Association police liaison officer, Honey Driver is expected to help solve his murder - even though she's something of a suspect herself. On top of that, she's lumbered with a distant friend's incontinent dog - and when it gets kidnapped, she hopes it doesn't come back .

ISBN 9781909520370

The Honey Driver Mysteries
by Jean G. Goodhind

Something in the Blood

A Taste to Die For

Walking with Ghosts

Killing Jane Austen

Deadly Lampshades

Murder by Mudpack

Wicked Words

The Ghost of Christmas Past

Death of a Diva

Blood and Broomsticks

For more information on **Jean G. Goodhind**
and **Accent Press**
please visit our website

www.accentpress.co.uk

**To find out more about Jean G. Goodhind
please visit**

www.jggoodhind.co.uk